STRICT AND PECULIAR

ANDREA FRAZER

Strict and Peculiar

ISBN 9781783751525

Other Novels by Andrea Frazer

The Falconer Files

Death of an Old Git
Choked Off
Inkier than the Sword
Pascal Passion
Murder at the Manse
Music to Die For
Strict and Peculiar
Christmas Mourning
Grave Stones
Death in High Circles
Glass House
Bells and Smells

Belchester Chronicles

Strangeways to Oldham
White Christmas with a Wobbly Knee
Snowballs and Scotch Mist
Old Moorhen's Shredded Sporran
Caribbean Sunset with a Yellow Parrot

Holmes and Garden

The Curse of the Black Swan Song

Author's Note

I know that there are still Strict and Particular *Baptist* chapels in existence, and I would like to state categorically that the chapel in this book, and those who followed its teachings either in the present or in the past, bear no similarity whatsoever with those who attend services in these buildings today. The beliefs and traditions of the chapel in this book are entirely fictitious, and a figment of my own (twisted!) imagination.

DRAMATIS PERSONAE

Residents of Steynham St Michael
Buckleigh, Bryony – a widow
Buttery, Noah and Patience – run the mobile library
Crawford, Craig – self-employed accountant and model train enthusiast
Kerr, Roma – runs ladies' fashion shop
Littlemore, Amy and Malcolm – run the village craft shop
Pryor, Dimity – spinster who helps out at the charity shop
Rainbird, Charles – antiques dealer
Raynor, Monica and Quentin – estate agents
Sinden, Elizabeth – reformed good-time girl
Warlock, Vernon – runs the local bookshop
Welland, Mike – landlord of the Ox and Plough

Workmen at the chapel site
Hillman, Dave
Stillman, Bob 'Sparks'
Warwick, Steve

From the College
Burrows, Daniel – student
Gray, Jocasta – tutor
Harrison, Amelia – student
Huntley, Jamie – student
Knightly, Antonia – student
Martin, Elspeth – student
Trussler, Aaron – student

Officials
Detective Inspector Harry Falconer
Detective Sergeant 'Davey' Carmichael
Detective Constable Chris Roberts
Sergeant Bob Bryant
Superintendent Derek 'Jelly' Chivers
Dr Philip Christmas

Prologue

Steynham St Michael was much as it had been when it had been touched by murder in the recent past. Its High Street still boasted a double row of individually owned and styled shops, and had retained the services of a dentist, doctor, bank, and estate agency.

The agricultural land surrounding it had remained undisturbed by the incursion of modern housing, or retail and industrial sites, due mainly to the fact that England, both urban and rural, was in a state of financial depression. New building was a thing of the past, no longer to be feared by village dwellers, who live where they did, simply because their community is not hemmed-in with executive four- and five-bedroomed houses, factories and vast out-of-town shopping 'opportunities'.

The only disturbances to the surrounding fields were the occasional crop circles, just before harvest, but the locals knew who was responsible for those, and were neither nonplussed nor worried by these apparitions.

That death had visited the village of Steynham St Michael in its most brutal form, was also absorbed and taken in their stride by those who lived there. The village had been in existence for hundreds of years, and a little thing like a death or two would not change its ways, nor mar its evolution.

That it was due for another disturbance of a similar sort was known by none of its inhabitants as our story opens ...

Chapter One

Friday 29th October

Η ΕΚΚΛΗΣΙΑ ΕΧΕΙ ΤΗ ΔΙΚΗ ΤΗΣ ΙΣΤΟΡΙΑ,
ΚΑΠΟΙΑ ΤΗΝ ΕΓΡΑΨΕ ΣΤΟΝ ΤΨΧΟ ΜΕ ΑΙΜΑΤΑ!

Detective Inspector Harry Falconer stood staring at the graffito on the internal wall of the Strict and Particular Chapel in Steynham St Michael, his lips moving silently as he read what had been daubed on the wall in red paint.

'Are we going to need a classicist, sir?' asked Detective Sergeant Davey Carmichael, utterly defeated by the strangeness of the letters used for the message, whatever that message may prove to be. It might as well have been written in Egyptian hieroglyphs, as far as he was concerned, for it didn't mean a thing to him.

'No need, Carmichael. This is Modern Greek and, if I'm not mistaken, it's an adaptation of the words of a popular song.' Here, he paused, and sang in a surprisingly tuneful light tenor voice, 'Ee ekklisia echei tee thikee tees istoria, Kapya teen egrapse ston teecho me aimata.'

'But what does it mean, sir?' Carmichael asked, not one jot wiser.

'The original goes roughly, "The road has its own story. Someone has written it in paint on the wall."'

'And?' Carmichael still knew no more.

'This has been adapted to give the message, "The church has its own story. Someone (female this time) has painted it in blood (plural) on the wall."'

'OK, I give up. What's it supposed to tell us?'

3

'That there's going to be trouble, Carmichael: trouble with a capital 'T'. We knew there had been some shenanigans up here, at least since the builders moved in to renovate the chapel, because the site manager has been in touch to complain of trespassers on the site and, can you believe it, small bunches of flowers left in various parts of the building.'

The chapel had long fallen into disuse, and Carmichael had visited it when they were in the village on another case. [1] The Strict and Particular Chapel had once housed the members of a splinter group who believed in punishment for the wicked, had the strictest of moral beliefs, and led exemplary lives, with the exception of the punishment they meted out on their own when they strayed from the path of righteousness.

Until recently, there had been a large wooden cross housed in the chapel, which its adherents had dragged out every Good Friday, taking it in turns to haul through the streets of the village, to emphasise that this was the day that Christ was crucified.

This cross, now an interesting artefact in itself, had been removed with the permission of those whose families had been members of the congregation to a more secure housing in St Cuthbert's (Church of England) Parish Church, in Castle Farthing, there being no Strict and Particular chapels still open and holding services.

The chapel was being renovated by funds collected by descendants of its original attendees, with a view to either re-opening, or using it as an historical exhibit of times gone by, and it was thought that the cross may be damaged, or even stolen, during said renovations. It would be restored to its rightful home when the work was finished and its future had been decided upon.

This latest act of intrusion, including vandalism this time, had been reported by the site manager first thing this morning, and Falconer and Carmichael had attended the scene, out of genuine interest rather than on their instincts as policemen.

---

[1] See *Inkier than the Sword*

Neither of them had been inside the chapel before, and both of them were 'gagging' to have a look and imagine what it must have felt like to be a member of such a tiny sect (or denomination, however you liked to refer to its members).

Falconer took a few photographs with his phone, and summoned a small SOCO team to the site, in the hope that whoever had done this would have left some trace of themselves, or themself, behind. As was drummed into all police officers now, a miscreant not only takes something away from the locus of a crime, be it fibres on their clothing, or something accidentally acquired on the soles of the shoes, but also leaves something behind. It may be a careless fingerprint, a drop or smear of blood, or it may just be fibres from clothing, but modern forensic methods had become so much more sophisticated than they were even twenty years ago, that a thorough search of any locus was a must these days.

Even in its nearly restored state, they could imagine how bleak the chapel must have been in its heyday. The walls were of whitewashed stone, the pews as unforgiving as the God of those who had sat in them, and the floor flag-stoned. The altar was a simple stone table with a wooden cross placed in its centre. It was so nearly finished that the desecration of it seemed much worse than it would have done if it had been committed earlier in the restoration.

After a couple of minutes of absorbing the atmosphere, both detectives shivered, almost simultaneously, and headed outside for some fresh air.

The weeds and long grass had been removed from the small graveyard, and some small effort had been made by locals to restore and make readable again the headstones, now all upright, rather than at the sagging angles that they had previously presented to the eye, like a set of teeth badly in need of orthodontic attention.

Once outside, they realised how cold it was for this time of year and did up their coats, pulling up collars over their ears to shield them from the biting wind. As they did so, they noticed Dimity Pryor, an elderly spinster who worked part-time in the village's charity shop, and Patience and Noah Buttery, all descended from fervent members of the chapel's now-deceased congregation.

Carmichael called out, 'Hi!' and loped over to meet them, while Falconer remained just outside the doors to pull on his gloves and get his scarf out of his pocket. He had not known it this cold at this time of the year since he was a child. There must be a severe winter on the way, if this was any indication of what was to come.

He joined the little group just after they had exchanged greetings and pleasantries. 'We noticed that the library was closed when we arrived,' said Falconer, addressing his remark to Patience and Noah, who had been librarians there when he had last visited the village.

'It went a few months ago,' explained Patience, letting her gaze fall to the ground as she remembered the event with sadness.

'We'd worked there together for a long time, and it was difficult to take in that it really wouldn't be opening its doors again,' added Noah.

'So what do you two do now?' Falconer asked, and immediately could have bitten his tongue off. What if they were existing on unemployment benefits, and living hand-to-mouth?

'We're on the wagon,' declared Patience, and gave him a little smile.

'Shouldn't that be the neighbours across the road?' asked Carmichael, remembering the trouble they had had before with the heavy-drinking Littlemores, Amy and Malcolm, who rather lackadaisically ran the craft shop in the High Street when sober enough so to do.

'Don't be silly! And 'that'll be the day' with those two. No, we're both working on the mobile library. A couple of people on the rota took early retirement during the cut-backs, and we were slotted in to take their places,' explained Noah.

'It's proved to be a great move for us.' Patience took over the story. 'Not only do we work less hours, but we meet so many people, going round all the villages and hamlets, it's like having a vast circle of new friends.'

'Usually, only people from Steynham St Michael came into the library here, with a few from other villages sometimes making the effort, but with the mobile, everyone's really pleased to see us, and it's like one long house party for us,' concluded Noah.

'And what about you, Dimity?' asked Falconer. 'Still working part-time at the charity shop?'

Dimity smiled at both detectives, and explained, 'Oh, no. I'm manager these days. The woman who used to run it decided she'd had enough, so they asked me to take over, and it was a good thing, because it filled in some of the time I would have expected to spend with Hermione. She left such a hole in my life.

'And are Mr Rainbird and Mr Warlock still in their old establishments?'

'Of course! How else would they occupy their time, except to bicker with each other?' she replied with a grin.

Charles Rainbird ran the antiques shop in the High Street, and Vernon Warlock the book and gift shop at the eastern extremity of the same street. Falconer and Carmichael had come to know them quite well, on a previous case they had investigated there.

'Would you like to come back to Spinning Wheel Cottage for a hot drink?' asked Dimity, always anxious about the welfare of others.

'That would be delightful,' agreed Falconer, 'but we'll join you in a few minutes, if that's all right. I just want a quick word with the site manager here, then we'll collect the car and be with you as soon as we can.'

Their chat with Dave Hillman, the site manager, didn't take long, and the time that had elapsed during their conversation with old acquaintances had been enough to allow the tiny SOCO team which had been assigned to this vandalism to arrive, so Falconer was happy that he was leaving the locus in safe hands.

It was cosy inside Spinning Wheel Cottage, and Dimity had already brewed both a pot of tea and a pot of coffee by the time they arrived, for Noah and Patience had also been included in the invitation even though they only lived next door in Pear Tree Cottage. Both homes were situated on the Market Darley Road, just down Tuppenny Lane, and a left turn from the chapel.

Although the sitting room of Dimity's home wasn't tiny, the presence of Carmichael in it made it look more like a room in a playhouse, so tall was he, and with a build to match. He had had to duck his head to go through the front door, and then again to enter the sitting room from the minute hall.

A path was immediately cleared so that they could warm their hands by the blazing log fire, and Patience went into the dining room to fetch a couple of extra chairs so that they could all sit down.

After Dimity had served them with the hot drink of their choice, goggling at the amount of sugar that Carmichael spooned into his cup, and handed round a plate of home-made biscuits, returned empty to her, in the hopes, of at least Carmichael, of a refill, she took her own cup and looked round at them all, sitting there enjoying the warmth of her home and her refreshments.

'Such a nice reunion,' she commented, then added, 'but also, so sad, that Hermione will never be able to join us again.' Hermione Grayling, a local author and long-time friend of not only Dimity, but of Charles Rainbird and Vernon Warlock as well, had been murdered back in January last, and Dimity still missed her regular company and their conversations about their shared history immensely.

The sergeant was squeezed into what had appeared to be a rather roomy Windsor chair, before he had decided to sit in it. Now he looked like an adult squeezed into a similarly styled chair but made for the proportions of a child. He had decided that now was the time for him to make a contribution to the general conversation.

'Anggy goffup?' asked Carmichael, through a mouthful of

oat- and chocolate-chip biscuit crumbs. This alien-sounding language was easily deciphered by those present as, 'Any gossip?', and Falconer suppressed a wince at his partner's intrusive question, then was surprised by the eagerness with which the others gave their answers.

'The Littlemores are still on the sauce, but I believe I mentioned that up at the chapel,' was Noah's contribution to the subject.

'And Elizabeth Sinden – you remember Buffy? – she's walking out with Craig Crawford,' added Patience.

'They're doing a real old-fashioned job of it, too,' interjected Dimity. 'They go out on proper dates, and hold hands like teenagers in the street. It lifts the heart to see two people getting on so well together, without throwing themselves into bed in the first five minutes of their relationship.'

Falconer was pleased to hear this, as he had considered Buffy Sinden a lovely person under all the heavy make-up and unsuitable clothes. She had determined, when he had last seen her, to turn over a new leaf, and it sounded like she was doing exactly what she had planned to do.

'Not much else is going on, though,' said Patience. 'Nothing much ever happens in Steynham St Michael.'

'Apart from our little contretemps at the beginning of the year, that is,' concluded Noah, then blushing as he saw Dimity's grimace, at having the subject raised again. 'Sorry, Dimity,' he apologised. 'Me and my big mouth!'

Abruptly pulling herself together, Dimity asked the two detectives, 'And what, may I ask, brings you back to these parts again? I assume it's something to do with the chapel? I was on my way there to see how they were getting on when we bumped into you.'

'It is indeed, Miss Pryor. There have been reports recently about someone trespassing on the site – leaving bunches of flowers, that sort of thing. The latest, however, is a case of vandalism. Some writing has been applied to one of the newly painted walls ... '

He was interrupted at this point by sharp intakes of breath

from Noah, Patience, and Dimity, and they all looked shocked. 'Whoever could have done that? What does it say?' asked Dimity, her eyes wide with shock. 'It's had so much work done on it; I don't see how anyone could have the heart to spoil it.'

'The writing, which incidentally was done in red paint, to simulate blood, I think, is in Greek – Modern, not New Testament or Classical. It says, and I quote,' he said, getting out his own notebook, '"The church has its own story. Someone has written it on the wall in blood." From the grammar used, it would indicate that the writer is a woman, and the word for blood is written in the plural,' he informed them.

'It's that bunch of crazies from the college,' Patience stated, with certainty in her voice.

'What bunch of crazies? What college? How do you know this?' Falconer's questions came along this time like London buses, in a trio.

'We've heard it from various people as we've gone round in the library van,' Noah informed them. 'Apparently they're from the Market Darley College of Further and Higher Education – that dump that's trying to get university status. They might as well confer that status on the baboon house at the zoo, for all it means these days.'

'Now, now, Noah, don't get on your high horse,' Patience admonished him, then, turning back to Falconer, and trying to look in two directions at once, to include Carmichael, informed them, 'There's a bunch of kids at the college who have decided that the old ways are best, then mixed those up with a load of mumbo jumbo and formed themselves a little cult. There're not a lot of them at the moment, but the numbers are likely to grow, knowing how gullible young people are these days.'

'I bet it's them,' growled Noah, darkly.

'Do you have any idea who might be involved in this 'cult'?' asked Falconer.

'Sorry, no.' It was Patience who answered, and Noah and Dimity both shook their heads, while Carmichael scribbled a quick note in his pad to record the information.

'Well, thank you very much for the tea and coffee, and the

biscuits: but thank you, most of all, for the lovely warm-up in front of your fire. We really needed that, after standing in that draughty old chapel,' Falconer said, rising from his seat, and indicating to Carmichael, with a look, that they'd better be leaving and get back to the station.

'Lovely to see you all again,' added Carmichael, his voice becoming slightly indistinct again, as he crammed a final biscuit into his mouth.

Chapter Two

Friday 29th October – later

Back at the station, Bob Bryant, the desk sergeant, indicated that he'd like a word with them, before they went up to their office, and they changed direction away from the staircase in answer to his hissed summons.

'What's up?' asked Falconer, hoping there wasn't another murder for them. It was 'brass monkeys' outside, and, yes, he did know the origin of the expression.

'You've got a new one, upstairs.' he whispered, his head bowed down towards the desk top in conspiracy.

Catching his drift, Falconer lowered his own head, and put it close to Bob's. 'A new what? Is it something exciting?' he hissed, the sibilants echoing round the cavernous entrance like a nest of snakes.

'A new DC. He's been seconded from Manchester, apparently,' Bob hissed back.

'Why?' asked Carmichael, in a normal speaking voice, and the other two men jumped, with the difference in volume.

'It's compassionate,' the desk sergeant explained, his voice returned, now, to a normal volume. 'His mother lives in Market Darley, and she's just had a stroke: needs some help for a while. Rather than take unpaid leave, he requested to be stationed here for a few weeks, so that he can give her a hand with getting used to life with less mobility.

'Don't worry,' he added, catching the look on Falconer's face, 'Social Services are involved too, and they'll be installing equipment and stuff to make life easier for her. This lad's just here to help her get used to it. He'll soon be out of your hair.'

'And where is he, at the moment?' asked the inspector, a

suspicious look on his face at the thought of this stranger going through the papers on their desks and in their drawers.

'I've put him in the canteen, and settled him with a cup of coffee, a doughnut, and a newspaper. Don't worry; he's only been there about half an hour.'

'I'm not worried, Bob. I'm merely concerned about the confidentiality of the papers left out on view when we were called out like that.'

When they reached it, they found the canteen deserted, the only figure in it with his face shrouded by an open newspaper, and an empty plate and mug on the table in front of him.

Approaching the table where the anonymous figure sat, Falconer called out, 'Hello; I'm DI Falconer, and this is DS Carmichael. Welcome to Market Darley.'

The figure still sat, immobile and silent, and it was only when Falconer looked round the paper barrier, that he discovered that their new DC, whoever he was, was fast asleep. Had it been Carmichael, he would have given a yell to wake him up, but as he didn't know this man from Adam, he shook him gently by the shoulder, until he showed signs of joining the waking world.

When the man appeared to have shaken the sleep out of his head, Falconer repeated the introductions he had made just a few moments ago, and held out his hand. It was taken in a half-hearted shake, and as the man shook Carmichael's hand, the inspector surveyed what had been foisted upon him for the foreseeable future.

The DC seemed to be about medium height – perhaps he wouldn't get so many cricks in his neck, as he did when working with the mighty Carmichael – with short, slightly curly hair in a shade of mid-brown, blue eyes, and the beginnings of a beard. The facial hair was just too long to be designer stubble, and just too short to be a proper beard. He seemed to be reasonably well-muscled, and his skin had a slight tan, as if he had not long returned from holiday somewhere hot.

'I'm Chris Roberts,' he informed them, standing up in the

presence of superior officers, although this seemed to be an awful struggle for him.

'You haven't come all the way from Manchester this morning, have you?' Falconer asked sympathetically.

'No, I came down last night, actually,' he replied, covering his mouth with a hand as he yawned enormously.

'In digs? Not sleep well?' Falconer was still giving him the benefit of the doubt.

'No, I slept like a log, and I'm back at my mother's, so I've just moved back in to my old room,' he informed them, his eyelids drooping.

We've got a right one here, thought Falconer, and then had what he thought was a brainwave. 'How old are you, Roberts?' he asked.

'Thirty-four,' DC Roberts replied, innocently.

'Ever been a student?' the inspector asked him.

'Oh, yeah. I was a student for far longer than I should have been. Just didn't know what to do with my life. When I couldn't sit around taking up space in education any longer, I decided to join the force. That was about two years ago.' He was waking up now.

'Let's go to the office, DC Roberts,' suggested Falconer, the spider inviting the fly to his web for a little chin-wag. 'I've got a proposition to put to you. Have you ever been undercover before?'

Carmichael wasn't born yesterday, and he smiled as they walked along the corridor to the office. He'd twigged what Falconer was up to, and he thoroughly approved of the idea. That should not only get them quick results, but keep him out of their hair at the same time.

'Can I impersonate a student?' asked Roberts, in disbelief. 'I'm a student through and through. I could pass for a student in my sleep, standing on my head, or with one hand tied behind my back. Of course I can impersonate a student, even if it is a mature one now.'

This was the most animation the DC had shown since they

had introduced themselves, and Falconer was pleased that his little idea was being so warmly received.

'What exactly am I going to be looking for? Drugs, is it? It usually is, with students – not that I've ever tried them myself, of course.'

'No, nothing like that. I need you to ferret out a cult.'

'Pardon?'

'A cult. C-u-l-t.'

'Sorry, I must have misheard you.'

'Don't apologise.'

'Do we have any of the names of the cult members?'

'No,' stated Falconer, baldly.

'A name for the cult?'

'No.'

'So, how am I supposed to find them?' asked Roberts, a bit bewildered.

Falconer finished playing with the DC and explained about the trespass and damage at the chapel and what the Butterys had told him about people from the college. 'I suggest that you start with religious groups within the college. You know, the sort of thing that might be on a student noticeboard, looking to recruit new members.'

'And what, exactly, am I supposed to be studying?'

Pulling a couple of likely subjects out of the air, Falconer suggested that he try Comparative Religion and Philosophy. 'I'll get a brochure, to see that both courses are available and have places on them, but I want you in deep cover. I don't want any members of staff to know about you either. You've only missed the first term, so you should be able to catch up quickly enough.' Then he added somewhat maliciously, 'With all that experience you've already had at college.'

'Thanks, guv,' replied Roberts, looking rather crestfallen.

'And don't call me "guv". 'Sir' will do nicely, if you don't mind. I'll get in touch with the college, pretend to be your father, and get you enrolled, if you'll be so kind as to give me your local address, and if you don't hear from me in the meantime, get yourself off to the place, first thing in the morning. Scrub that! I want you in my office at sparrow-fart, so that I can give you some notes – which I shall prepare tonight – describing your background, and your religious upbringing, so that you'll have some idea of the character you're going to be playing, OK?

'I want regular updates from you, so no swanning off home when the lectures finish. I shall expect you here every day to tell me what you've learned, and if anything unexpected happens, get in touch straight away. Here's my card with my office and mobile number on it. I'll write my home number on the back of it, so there are no excuses for not ringing.'

'What shall I do for the rest of the day, guv – sorry – sir?' asked Roberts, not quite sure how he felt about his new role.

'Look on the internet, and see if you can find any information posted there on the Strict and Particular followers – anything that might give you a clue as to who you are passing yourself off as. Now, off with you. I don't want to see you again until tomorrow morning – early, mind!'

When he'd gone, Falconer found Carmichael sniggering to himself. 'And don't you go feeling all superior, either, Sergeant. If he hadn't arrived, that would have been you going back to school.'

'Sorry, sir, but he did look rather as if his get-up-and-go had got up and gone, didn't he?'

'I couldn't agree more. Now tell me, how is Kerry getting on? Have they sorted out her due date, yet? I know there was some difficulty in working out exactly when you should expect the new member of your family to arrive,' enquired Falconer, back to their usual, easy-going relationship, now that there wasn't a new third member of the gang eavesdropping on them.

'They now reckon it should be about the fourth of January, sir!' answered Carmichael, his face alight at the mention of his wife Kerry's pregnancy.

'It might even be a slightly early anniversary present for you, then,' commented Falconer, as Carmichael and Kerry's first wedding anniversary fell on New Year's Eve.

If it were possible, Carmichael's face shone even more with

17

happiness. 'Wouldn't that be grand, sir?'

'Only if you stick to soft drinks, and don't expect to be able to summon a taxi,' was Falconer's answer.

'I won't touch a drop, sir, but they do say that first babies are always late.'

'This may be your first child, Carmichael, but it's Kerry's third, don't forget.'

'God, how stupid of me! I just didn't think! Thanks for the tip, sir,' Carmichael answered, the first signs of puzzlement that had crossed his face dissolving, as he beamed with the thought of meeting his child a few days earlier than he had anticipated.

'Do you know what sex it is yet?' Falconer was curious, and wondered what a little girl would look like if she took after Carmichael.

'No idea, sir. We said we didn't want to know. That way it would be a surprise for us, and for the boys.'

'Best way, in my opinion,' said Falconer, closing the subject for now.

Chapter Three

Falconer had contacted the college the previous afternoon after he had dismissed Roberts and was in the office at a quarter-past eight, waiting for him to arrive for his briefing. The inspector had spent some time at home the evening before, preparing notes of all that he had learnt about the denomination, and had also consulted the internet to make sure that Roberts had done his homework.

He didn't want the DC to get into hot water because of lack of preparation, and have his cover blown. There was no telling what he may unearth at the college; things that may be totally unconnected with the graffito and the sect may come to his ears, and may prove very interesting indeed.

When Roberts finally made an appearance at half-past nine, pleading an out-of-order alarm clock, Falconer had been drumming his fingers on the desktop for the last half an hour. When he had said 'early', he hadn't meant a quarter to tea-break.

'What time do you call this, Roberts?' he asked in a sarcastic tone, looking pointedly at his watch.

'Half-past nine, guv,' replied Roberts, totally unconcerned, and not having the sensitivity to catch the atmosphere. Carmichael was sitting at his desk, his body twisted round to watch the confrontation.

'I told you to come in early, and early is what I meant. I've been sitting here for an hour and a half, and I didn't expect to wait very long for you to appear. A broken alarm clock is one of the lamest excuses I have ever heard since alarms could be set on mobile phones, and don't you dare call me 'guv'! I've

19

told you not to before, and I don't expect you to forget. You're a policeman, dammit! You're supposed to have a good memory: it's part and parcel of the job.'

Carmichael ducked his head as if avoiding a missile while Falconer delivered this little speech, then turned silently back to his work, glad he was not the one on the receiving end of it. Roberts merely looked astonished at being upbraided so.

'This is only a case of vandalism – sir,' he pointed out, in calm and reasonable tones. 'It's hardly murder: just some kids with a pot of paint and a knowledge of Greek. It's no worse than spraying 'Up the Arsenal' or 'Man United for the Cup' on a wall.'

This attitude, of course, got right up Falconer's nose. He liked to run a tight ship, and he didn't appreciate this sloppy attitude, either to the act of vandalism itself or to good time-keeping. 'I think you'll find it's my job to decide what's important and what's not. That's why I'm the inspector and you're the constable.

'If I say a thing needs further investigation, and consider that it might lead to something more serious, then what I say goes. I also dictate whether or not I want you in my office early. I have signed you on for a course in comparative religion at the college, posing as your father, and I shall expect you to visit the college this weekend, and start attending the course, first thing on Monday morning. Do I make myself clear to you?'

'Yes, guv – sorry, sir,' replied Roberts, surprised and nonplussed by, in his opinion, his superior's nit-picking attitude. Why waste police time on an act of petty defacement? 'You couldn't get me on the philosophy course, then?'

'It was full, but then, that's life,' the inspector replied, not realising how neatly he had summed up the subject, in his reply. 'And what's more,' he added, 'the act of vandalism in the chapel might not mean much to one of you big city policemen, but I know how much hard work has gone into collecting the funds to carry out the work on the chapel, and how much energy has been expended on the work, by those locals who can be of use in its refurbishment.

20

'It might just be an unimportant little building to you, with your miles and miles of concrete in Manchester, but in the villages around here, small things *are* important. We may not have many big-time villains in the villages, but we look after our own here, and investigate anything we think is of importance to the residents, no matter how petty you may consider the matter to be.'

'Yes, sir,' agreed Roberts, getting the hang of it now.

'So, what did you glean from the internet yesterday?' asked Falconer, calming down a little.

'Er, I didn't actually have the time to check out anything. My mother needed some heavy housework doing, and I had my room to get in order, and my clothes to iron. As today was Saturday, I didn't think there'd be any real hurry.'

'Oh, you didn't, did you? Did it not occur to you that the college has events and some classes at the weekends? Did you think it would be locked up and empty? Well, let me assure you that that is not the case. I wanted you prepared to go in today to start putting yourself about as a new student, and now you tell me you did absolutely no research yesterday, despite what I asked you to do?'

'Sorry, sir,' replied Roberts, realising that this time spent on secondment wasn't going to be the piece of cake he had surmised it to be. There was always something big going down where he usually worked, and he'd seen a secondment to a rural station almost as a holiday where nothing much would happen, and he could spend his time on a little light office work and skiving off whenever the opportunity presented itself.

It would seem that he had had completely the wrong idea of this little sojourn, and he would be kept busy by this detail-crazy inspector, who was willing to weave an investigation out of virtually nothing at the slightest provocation. 'What shall I do then, sir?' he asked, uncertain of his next move.

'You will take this print-out of all the notes I made and the information I gathered last night; at home; in my own time; for free, and you will study them, until you feel capable of starting your job as an undercover officer. Do you understand?'

'Yes, sir. Shall I work in the main office?'

'Yes. Find yourself a free desk, and go through what I've prepared for you, then come and see me again so that I can check out how much of the information you've retained.'

'Yes, sir.' Robert was now feeling very subdued. Falconer had pricked his pretty balloon, and he was feeling not only rebuked but caught out as well. He wasn't a great fan of hard work, and he'd been rumbled, here, in this little station, within twenty-four hours of his arrival. Maybe there was something to be said for the anonymity of a busy urban station after all.

When he had made his humiliated exit, Carmichael twisted his body round from his desk again, and commented, 'Cor, sir! You gave him a real scorcher!'

'He deserved it, Carmichael,' replied Falconer, full of self-righteousness after this encounter.

'And you sure delivered it, sir. I'm glad that wasn't me on the receiving end of it.'

'It could never have been you, Sergeant. One thing you have never been is lazy. Or work-shy,' the inspector added. Outrageously dressed, behaving in a thoroughly child-like manner, having the appetite of a gannet – all those things, he could accuse Carmichael of being, but lazy or workshy – never. He was a hard-working young man, surprisingly old-fashioned in his attitudes to life, and exceedingly well-mannered. Carmichael always pulled his weight, and that was no light-weight matter, either, thought Falconer, realising how much he had got to know his partner since they had begun working together in the summer of the previous year.

After lunch, Roberts knocked on Falconer's door and said he felt ready to go to the college. Falconer bade him enter and sit down, then said, 'Right, DC Roberts, I'm not going to throw a lot of questions at you. I want you to tell me, in your own words, what you know of the beliefs and practises of the members of the congregations of the Strict and Particular Chapels.'

This, in itself, stunned Roberts. He had facts and figures at his fingertips to answer any question that was thrown at him, but this was a different matter altogether. He was going to have to tell his new boss the story of this tiny denomination, and he simply wasn't very good at telling stories.

'Uh, they were formed in the first half of the nineteenth century. Um, they were one hundred per cent strict on the Ten Commandments. Manners and morals were very important to them. And, um, they believed in the punishment of their own, for anything immoral or, ah, what they thought was bad, but not serious enough to involve the law. Er, they dressed very conservatively, and, um … they didn't like mixing with people from the other churches, because they … they, uh, considered them impure.' His face reddened, as he finished the end of his tale.

'Very good, Roberts. You don't seem to have much trouble with your memory, as long as it just doesn't evaporate as quickly as you assimilated it.' Falconer was fair, and always gave praise where praise had been earned.

'Now, we have to discuss your appearance.'

'My appearance – sir?' The DC added this last, as he remembered how strict Falconer had appeared on the use of this mode of address.

'Well, your hair's a bit long, so don't have it cut; and your designer stubble's a bit untidy too, so leave that as it is. It all adds to the verisimilitude of your appearance, but you have to dress like a student, too, albeit a mature one,' the inspector explained, only to have an interruption to his train of thought, from Carmichael.

'I could tell him how to dress like one of them from up the college,' the DS offered.

'That's very kind of you, Carmichael, but I don't think that DC Roberts needs any sartorial advice from you. I have my own ideas about how I would like him to present himself,' Falconer answered with alacrity, remembering some of the outfits the sergeant had arrived in for work since he had left the uniformed branch and become anything but plainclothes division.

'Roberts, I don't know what kit you've brought with you for this placement, but may I suggest jeans and trainers – not new ones – would be satisfactory, and if you have a T-shirt which is a bit anti-establishment or rebellious, that might cover the top half,' suggested Falconer.

'Well, I've got an F.C.U.K. T-shirt,' he offered, and when Carmichael suddenly exploded with, 'That's rude!' explained hurriedly that the letters stood for 'French Connection U.K.', just in case the boss man thought he was deliberately being offensive.

Carmichael looked scandalised, but Falconer took it in his stride, saying, 'I do know what the letters stand for, and I think that would be perfect, considering that none of them at that college can spell.'

But this wasn't quite true. One of them could spell perfectly in Greek, a very difficult language in which to spell, as it had five letters or combinations of letters that made the sound 'ee', and two letters that were both pronounced 'o'. To use them correctly showed a considerable mastery and understanding of the language.

'What about a coat, sir? It has turned very cold for the time of year?' Roberts obviously felt the cold. 'Would an old parka be OK?'

'Provided it looks its age, it sounds perfect to me. Now, I suggest you get yourself off, familiarise yourself with the campus, and take a look at any student noticeboards you can find. Mooch around a bit, see if there are any students about, and see if you can locate anyone else who might be on the comparative religion course – that sort of thing. Any questions?'

'When and how do I report to you, er, sir?' asked the DC.

'By e-mail, for the record, and by telephone if it's anything urgent. It doesn't matter too much about telephoning, as long as you're not overheard by anyone who will blow your cover. Got it?'

'Got it, sir.'

'Off you go, then, Roberts, and no lolly-gagging at home.

Get changed straightaway, and get yourself over to that campus. There shouldn't be much doing tomorrow, though, with it being Sunday, so if you're rostered for duty you might as well come into the station.'

'Yes, sir.'

'Although, come to think of it, I've got tomorrow off. What about you, Carmichael?'

'I'm off, too,' said Carmichael, smiling at the thought of a day with his family.

'I believe I'm not actually scheduled to work, either,' added Roberts.

'In that case, do what you can today – no skiving, mind – and I'll see you bright and early on Monday morning.

'Yes, sir.'

DC Roberts exited Falconer's office, determined to do a good job. Something about the inspector had inspired him, and he would act on this inspiration to be a more dedicated officer. Goodness knows how long this would last, but he'd better take advantage of it while it did.

When he'd gone, Falconer looked at Carmichael, to see him looking unusually morose. 'You're not jealous of the new boy, are you, Carmichael?' he asked, with a smile.

'What, sir? No, sir. It's not that. It's something completely different that's playing on my mind.'

'Tell Uncle Harry then,' ordered Falconer, unusually informal, for once.

'There's this bloke, moved into Castle Farthing about six months or so ago – not very long after Kerry and I got married – and he's been an absolute pain in the wotsit, to everyone. Oh, I don't mean that he's foul-mouthed, or violent, or anything like that, but he likes to pick on something a person might be sensitive about, and then, I suppose you might call it, teases them whenever he sees them. I don't think he realises how much he's upsetting people. He just looks on it as this great big joke.'

'Like what?' asked Falconer.

'Well, do you remember the Brigadier?'

'How could I forget him? That was on our first case together,' Falconer replied, smiling at the memory of the bluff military man.

'Every time he sees him he stands to attention and hums the theme tune from *Dad's Army*. Whenever he goes into the general store – that's called 'Allsorts', if you remember – he asks whoever's on the till where they've hidden all the liquorice. When he goes into the pub – that's The Fisherman's Flies, sir – he calls out, asking if the fisherman's flies are open or not. That's the sort of thing he does, and he tries to take over anything that's being organised.

'He was a right pain in the arse over the Harvest Festival, if you'll pardon my French, and I thought the locum vicar was going to lump him one, not long before the day of the service. It's that sort of thing. Nothing awful, individually, but put together, he's a very unpopular man, although he seems to think he's the life and soul of the village.'

'This isn't like you, Carmichael, to get all bent out of shape by something like this,' Falconer commented.

'No, it's not, sir, but he caught me on the raw, this morning.'

'How?'

'I took the little doggies out for their morning walk, and he was on his way to the shop. They were having a sniff around on the green, checking the tree trunks for other canine visitors. You know what dogs are like, sir? They do like to pick up their messages.

'Anyway, he was just about to pass by, when he stopped dead and burst out laughing. I looked up to see what he was laughing about, and he was staring at me and the two pups – well, I suppose they're not pups any more, really – so I asked him what he was laughing at.

'He only went and said he was laughing at me. Young Longshanks, he called me! And he said that the dogs looked like a couple of cotton wool balls on strings. 'There goes Young Longshanks and his two fluff-balls on a string,' was what he actually said, and then he added that he always had a good laugh when he saw me taking them out.'

'And that's all?' Falconer was amazed at how thin-skinned Carmichael appeared to be over this matter.

'It's not what he says, sir, it's the way he says it. He's got up just about everybody's nose. Someone's going to have to have a word with him, before too long. I don't suppose you fancy …?'

'No, I don't! Get your mother over, and get her to give him a good verbal mauling. That'll shut him up for good.' Falconer had met Mrs Carmichael senior at Carmichael and Kerry's wedding, and he was terrified of her.

For once, Roberts acted exactly according to his instructions and, by just after three o'clock, was passing through the large glass doors of the entrance to the Market Darley College of Further and Higher Education.

Straight ahead of him, a corridor ran off into the distant indoor darkness, but either side of this corridor, on the wall facing him, were two enormous noticeboards covered with various notices and messages relating to different aspects of college life.

One had a cluster of missives, both in print and handwritten, notifying anyone who cared to read the board of meetings of the Local History Society, and advertising for new members. Another part of the board – the main portion – concerned sporting events, both within the college itself and in the surrounding area. There were also reminders about practises for various sporting activities, and team lists for fixtures.

The other board had a small section reserved for the philosophy students, which was only half full. Philosophy did not appear to be a publicised subject at this particular college, even though the course was full. The remainder of the board concerned social events for the students, and notices for the department of comparative religion. One caught his eye straight away.

Leaning forward to read it, he saw that it was for the discussion group that applied itself to local religious beliefs, practices, and history, and appeared to be run by someone called Jocasta Gray, who had signed herself as Head of

Comparative Religious Studies. That would certainly be worth a look, he thought, pulling out a piece of paper and a stub of pencil from the pocket of his thoroughly disreputable parka.

The notice stated that there was to be a meeting on Monday evening, here at the college, and he made a mental note to attend. There might be some useful information to be gleaned from the students who attended, but he'd have to be subtle in his questioning. If anyone from the college had an interest in the Strict and Particular Chapel in Steynham St Michael, it was bound to be this group.

From this starting point in the huge entrance space, he took himself off to the information desk, to see if there was anyone on duty who could be of use to him on this quiet day in the educational week.

The desk was unattended, and a 'closed' sign sat prominently in the middle of it, but he espied a chubby girl with her lank hair in a plait quite close by, stuffing some leaflets into an information stand, and he wandered over to her to see if she could be of any help to him.

She blushed an unbecoming shade of crimson when he greeted her, a look that definitely didn't complement the broad band of acne sprinkled across her nose and cheeks. On her forehead, three or four large spots were vying for supremacy.

'I'm sorry to disturb your work,' he apologised very prettily, 'but I'm starting late on the comparative religion course on Monday, and wondered if you knew anything about it, or the other people on the course.'

At this point, the girl turned an even darker shade, approaching beetroot, this time, and answered, 'Actually, I'm on the course, myself. I'm Elspeth Martin, by the way.'

'Pleased to meet you, Elspeth Martin,' Roberts said, holding out his hand to shake hers, then realising her age, remembered what an old-fogeyish thing this would be to do, as a student, and briefly retracted it, as she stared at it in incomprehension.

'I'm Chris Roberts. So, how are you finding the course?' he asked, sounding like his late father, to his own ears.

'Oh, it's marvellous!' she gushed. 'And the tutor's

absolutely fabulous.'

'Would that be Jocasta Gray?' he asked, remembering her name from the noticeboard.

'Yes,' replied Elspeth, looking a bit heroine-struck. 'She makes the course so interesting and absorbing.'

'And she's going to run this meeting on local religious beliefs and practices on Monday evening?' he continued with his questioning.

'She is. The one's we've had so far have been – well, just wonderful. So fascinating and, well, sometimes, unbelievable.'

'That sounds great!' he replied. 'I think I'll go to it, myself, if they're that good.'

'Oh, do come along,' Elspeth encouraged him. 'The more the merrier, as far as Jocasta's concerned.'

'It's a date!' he concluded, causing her to return to the beetroot shade that had just begun to fade from her features. Seeing her discomposure, he added, 'Well, not a date, date. But I'll see you there, I expect.'

'Of course. Of course,' the poor flustered girl replied, adding, 'There is something ton ...' and then clammed up, like an oyster, clapping her hands to her mouth, as her eyes stared at him in horror.

'What was that?' he asked. 'I didn't quite catch it.'

'Nothing! Absolutely nothing!' she declared in a small, fearful voice, and turned away from him to resume her work, re-stocking the college's information stand.

'That was a bit odd,' he thought, but then he put it to the back of his mind. She was evidently painfully shy, and socially immature, and it probably didn't mean anything.

As the place seemed more or less deserted, DC Roberts, aka Chris the student, decided to go home and resume his poking around on Monday. He'd already picked up some bits and pieces that could prove useful, and his former conscientiousness had faded rather.

It was Saturday, and he felt like he deserved a night out on the town in Market Darley. His mother was managing quite well at the moment, with the help of equipment from the Social

Services Department, and he should be able to arrange things in the house that would allow him to get a bit of R&R and not be at anybody's beck and call.

As he left the college campus, he was surprised to see an ice-cream van parked outside the gates, apparently doing a roaring trade, customers snaking back from it in a long queue, and not one of them a day under eighteen.

How odd, for ice-cream to have that sort of appeal, when the outside temperature was as low as it was, and all of the van's customers old enough to vote. Market Darley certainly lacked the sophistication of the streets of Manchester, in his opinion, and his lips moved in a small sneer of superiority.

Chapter Four

Sunday 31st October – Hallowe'en

Market Darley and all its surrounding villages were bedecked with pumpkins carved into gruesome faces, just waiting to be lit that evening. All over the area, excited children were preparing for that exquisite experience of 'Trick or Treat', a reasonably recent import from the USA, but none the less popular for that.

Falconer, due mostly to his experience in past years, but also because of his (infrequent) contact with Carmichael's boys, for whom he had been asked to be a godfather sometime in the dim and distant future, kept little treats in the house in case trick-or-treaters came a-calling, and had also gone to the trouble of carving out a pumpkin and placing it in his front window with a night-light burning in it, to show that the little horrors were welcome to come to his door.

This was his only contribution to what he thought of as a very American affair, but at least it stopped him from getting eggs thrown at his windows, his wheelie bin overturned, or worse. There had been none of this organised begging when he was a child, and he in the main disapproved of it, but knew that it was a case of 'if you can't beat 'em, join 'em', so he had.

In his opinion, children had more than their fair share of treats these days, and, as a policeman, he knew that there were some little ones whose parents didn't give a fig, and would let their children go trotting off to ring and knock at the front doors of total strangers, putting themselves in God knew what danger.

A uniformed member from the station usually went round the local primary schools, telling the children not to go out on this activity unless accompanied by a parent or other adult, but he didn't know how much good this did. It was the parents who

31

needed to be given a kick up the behind, because it would be these lackadaisical individuals who would be the first to complain and go to the press should something calamitous befall their child.

Many parents today, sapped by working full-time as well as having a family to bring up, rarely knew where their children were, if they were out, what they were doing, and with whom. And it was these same parents who made the most fuss, if their little (or not so little) one got into trouble, and were brought home by the police after having committed an offence. It never crossed their minds that their children were their responsibility, be they home or out, and that their misdeeds were in no way the fault of the police.

He planned to spend a quiet evening at home with his four cats, Mycroft, Ruby, Tar Baby, and Perfect Cadence, the latter now having learnt the nickname of 'Meep', because of the way she meowed. This sleek grey cat seemed to have some sort of feline speech impediment, and even hissed with a lisp, which always made him laugh, and her sulk at the indignity of being laughed at.

Thus, he settled down in front of the fire – for it had turned very cold – with his book, cats draped over various parts of his chair, to await whatever callers the evening would bring him, a bowl of goodies and a bowl of fruit for the more discerning child sitting on his dining table, ready to be transported to the front door should the need arise.

In Carmichael's house, all was chaos. Carmichael had volunteered to carve the pumpkin, but there had been so much opposition to this that Kerry had eventually purchased one large and two smaller pumpkins, so that her husband and her two sons could have a pumpkin each to prepare for that evening's festivities.

She had made the costumes for their own outings long ago, so as not to be caught out when the date arrived. In fact, she vividly remembered Inspector Falconer calling to collect Davey one day when she had him standing on a chair, pinning the hem of his outfit when the doorbell had rung These seasonal disguises now hung, freshly pressed, on hangers on the outside of wardrobe doors. 'Daddy Davey', as Carmichael was addressed by his two step-sons, had helped them with the manufacture of their *papier-mâché* masks, and these, too, appended from the hangers upstairs in their bedroom.

Kerry spent the afternoon collecting the discarded chunks from the inside of the pumpkins, fastidiously removing the seeds, and popping the chunks of vegetable into a huge saucepan to make soup for supper after they had been out in their costumes, and the delicious smell of pumpkin soup permeated the house for the rest of the day.

Carmichael wandered in and out of the kitchen to see if she was tired, being on her feet for such a long job, and that everything was OK. She was heavily pregnant with Carmichael's first child, her third, and the baby was due in just over two months' time. He noticed with a growing sense of pride the size of her bulging belly, as it grew with the fruit of his loins inside her.

He still found it difficult to believe that he was actually going to have a child of his own: a child he had made. Although he loved Kerry's two sons dearly, and felt like they were his own, he had not been there when they had been born, nor heard them speak their first word, or take their first steps. At times, he found it almost impossible to believe how lucky he was.

The dogs, Fang and Mr Knuckles, seemed to have caught the excitement in the atmosphere, for they capered around, chasing invisible insects and begging for pieces of pumpkin, which they sampled with an initial chew or two, before opening their mouths to let the raw vegetable fall to the floor in disapproval at the taste, and Carmichael was in his element, not only being a child again, but being grown-up enough to warn the boys not to give any of the pieces of pumpkin from the floor to Mummy for the soup, as they might have doggie spit on them.

At half-past six, when all three gruesome orange faces glowed from the front window ledge, the three men of the house disappeared upstairs to don their fancy-dress, and Kerry removed from their hiding place (in case the boys should have spotted them, and demand their share) the sweets and treats she had bought earlier in the week for visitors to their door tonight. Opening and discarding packets, she poured the whole mélange into a bowl, big enough for a cluster of little hands to delve to secure their treat.

There was a lot of giggling and much laughter from upstairs as the three prepared themselves, and at just before seven o'clock they trooped downstairs for Kerry's inspection. On seeing them, she clapped her hands with delight. Two young boys and a very large man had gone up the stairs. What had come down again, were a vampire, a ghost, and an extremely tall witch, hooked nose and warts visible on its face.

As they neared the bottom of the staircase, the vampire (Dean) fingered his fangs, the ghost (Kyle) made whoo-ooing noises and waved its sheeted arms, and the witch cackled most convincingly as it reached for its twig broom at the foot of the stairs.

'Glory! You do look convincing!' Kerry exclaimed, amazed at how good her handiwork looked in full light. She had done a good job with their outfits, and they should get some positive reactions from those they called upon.

'We're going to visit the houses from the Carsfold Road at the other end of the village, then work our way up to The Old Manor House to finish off with, then we're coming home', Carmichael informed her. 'That should be plenty for tonight, and what have we got next week, boys?'

'Guy Fawkes' Night!' the two boys shouted in unison. Carmichael was determined that they would celebrate this date with all the traditions of his own childhood. Of course, he and Kerry would take them to an organised display as well, but he wanted them to know the excitement of fireworks being let off in their own garden, and the smell of the gunpowder at close quarters – safely organised and conscientiously policed by Kerry and him.

Three ghastly figures fled out into the night in Castle Farthing, and Kerry sat down and put her feet up, the soup now ready just to re-heat and serve, knowing that she had earned her period of rest, her bowl of treats at the ready for when children other than hers rang the doorbell.

Chris Roberts had noticed that there was a fancy-dress party at one of the larger pubs in Market Darley that evening and had managed to put together quite a gruesome costume using a rubber mask he had managed to purchase in the town. With this, and a pair of jeans and a very old T-shirt, suitably stained with red paint, he looked like the victim of a vicious attack, with the face of a politician currently in high office. Little did he know that tonight, his appearance would turn out to be fiction mocking fact (but without the political theme).

He was in blissful ignorance of this, however, as he set out, in high hopes of a good time, at half-past eight, with instructions for his mother not to wait up for him, as he didn't know what time he'd be back.

The pub was quite near the college, and had advertised low drinks prices on a board outside, probably intended to lure students inside to spend their unearned student loans. He set off in the certainty that some of the students from the college would be there – maybe even Elspeth Martin, who might be kind enough to introduce him to any friends on her course – *their* course, now. That really would give him a head start for tomorrow, although he must make sure he didn't stay out too late, as his undercover work really commenced in the morning.

Inspector Falconer ought to be proud of him, he thought, selflessly giving up his Sunday night to seek out others with whom he might be studying (and questioning) in the future. At this thought, he felt quite proud of himself, never for one moment considering that the real reason he was going was just to have a good time and a couple of drinks in convivial company. He looked much younger than his years, and would easily fit in with the student crowd.

Chapter Five

Carmichael arrived at the station just after Falconer the next morning, but didn't go straight to his desk, merely dropping off his coat and disappearing immediately, saying he'd be back in a minute, for he had something to show the inspector.

Falconer was puzzled, but dismissed it from his mind, as just another 'Carmichaelism'. There had been reports of 'Mr Spliffy', the drug-peddling ice-cream man, seen out on the road again, and he needed to find out where the van operated from. In the past, tracing the vehicle license number had proved useless, as it seemed that the van had different number plates every time it went out. He needed that van followed to its den before he could do anything about making an arrest – feeling a collar, as it were.

While he was sticking pins into a map of the town, which was affixed to the wall to mark sightings of the rogue van, there was a discreet knock at his door. 'Come in,' he called, and turned to see who it was.

His eyes couldn't believe what was standing before them, and his mouth let out an involuntary scream. There appeared to be a six-and-a-half foot old hag in his office, and it was a couple of seconds before he realised that it was just Carmichael, evidently in his fancy-dress costume from the night before.

'You frightened the life out of me, Carmichael!' he exclaimed, his right hand rising to clutch his chest. 'I'm sure that apparition has taken six months off my life. Whatever do you think you're playing at?'

'I just thought I'd let you see the finished costume, sir, seeing as how you called round for me once when Kerry was fitting it for me. Don't you remember?' came the reply, the witch's face looking crestfallen, its plastic nose drooping towards it chin, and its hastily applied warts threatening to drop off.

'I appreciate the thought, Sergeant. I just wished you'd warned me first. You must have scared the bejesus out of all the little kids last night, turning up on their doorsteps looking like that,' Falconer replied, his heart-rate now slowing down.

'I did, a bit, actually. One of the little nippers wouldn't stop screaming until I left the garden,' Carmichael declared.

'I'm not surprised. If I'd seen an apparition like that when I was a kid, I'd have had nightmares for months afterwards,' Falconer chided him, suddenly remembering Nanny Vogel, about whom he still had bad dreams, and he was now forty-one. 'Jolly fine effort, though. Very lifelike! Now, go and take it off, there's a good chap. We've had some more sightings of Mr Spliffy, and I'm just marking them on the map to see if we can identify an area that he might originate from.'

Carmichael perked up at this titbit of praise, and headed back to the gents', so that he could take off his Hallowe'en weeds, and return to the office, ready for work. If Mr Spliffy was out there again, they'd find him and nail him, this time.

Chris Roberts had had a fine time at the Hallowe'en 'do' on Sunday night, but had not bumped into Elspeth Martin or, in fact, anybody who had introduced themselves as being a student at the local college, and so, on Monday morning, he turned up bright and punctual to find his place on the course, knowing that he would run into Elspeth there.

He had decided that he was going to enjoy being undercover – it was akin, almost, to being his own boss, with no one to answer to every minute of the day. He'd dressed as advised, and the scruffiness of his garments was perfect for blending in with the younger students.

The woman, now on duty behind the information desk, confirmed that he had been booked in for the comparative religion course, and helped him to fill in a student registration card. On being asked whether he had anything to identify him as a student, such as a student rail card, an ID card for pubs and clubs, or a National Student Union membership card, he apologised at being so badly remiss, and claimed that he had yet to get hold of the former and the latter, as taking this course had been a last-minute decision. As he was a mature student, he wouldn't need an ID card, and offered his driving license as proof of identity, and this was accepted without question.

She then directed him to room 101, as his course home-room, and sent him on his way without a hint of suspicion that he might not be exactly what he had claimed to be. This was all to the good and, as he traversed corridor after corridor, in pursuit of where he would be spending a lot of his time in the near future, he pondered what this future would hold for him.

In a large cottage in Dairy Lane, Steynham St Michael, named curtly and simply 'Honeysuckle', were foregathered a group of residents who had formed the committee that had organised the village's Hallowe'en party the night before in the village hall. They had spent this morning clearing away the detritus of the celebrations, and had now adjourned to Bryony Buckleigh's home for some well-earned refreshments.

Apart from Bryony herself, there were also Patience Buttery (who had taken a day's annual leave so that she could help out), Dimity Pryor, who had left her volunteer assistant in temporary charge of the charity shop, Elizabeth Sinden, and her new beau, Craig Crawford, who was a self-employed accountant, and could do as he pleased with regard to his working hours.

Bryony offered cups of steaming coffee from a tray, while Dimity followed behind with a plate of biscuits and a plate of tiny cucumber sandwiches, so that there should be a choice of sweet or savoury nibbles.

Bryony, being retired, had taken the chair of the committee and, when she finally had the chance to sit down, thanked her helpers most heartily for their efforts before, during, and after the event. A special thank you was given to Craig Crawford, who had manfully hauled tables and chairs around, placing them wherever directed without a single grumble.

Craig bowed his head in acknowledgement of this unexpected accolade, and said, 'I've always been very biddable. My parents were very lenient with me when I was growing up, but I wasn't the sort of child who rebelled against authority. I was quite happy –'

'With your train sets,' burst from each and every woman present, not quite in unison, but he understood what they meant. He had an enormous layout of trains, stations, and miniature countryside in his house which many a grown man would envy. It had been his hobby throughout his childhood, and his enthusiasm had never waned. Many mocked him as childish, but those who were men did so with a secret envy, knowing that their wives would never stand for so much of the floor space being taken up by this sort of hobby.

His new girlfriend, Elizabeth Sinden, the one-time goodtime girl of the village, had turned over a new leaf when a murder had occurred in the village at the beginning of the year, and instead of entertaining a new man friend every week had accepted a courteous offer to go on a chaste date with Craig.

She had not regretted that decision, thoroughly enjoyed playing with his trains with him, and felt that they were headed for something more permanent. It was so lovely to be treated as a whole person – a lady – and not just as a piece of meat, and Craig was a perfect gentleman, with all the old-fashioned courtesies that didn't seem to exist any more in people of his age and younger.

Craig was thirty-nine years of age, and had never been married. Elizabeth, at thirty-five, and divorced, had had what seemed a lonely life stretching in front of her, with no one in particular to spend it with. Now, though, it sparkled with possibilities, and she harboured a secret hope that they might even marry, and she might be granted her wish of motherhood. Buffy had been an old-fashioned girl at heart herself, before her divorce. Craig had steered her back to the straight and narrow, and only just in time, in her opinion. She had become Elizabeth again, as she had been when she was young.

40

Everyone who knew her was very pleased about her current circumstances, and there was many a secret wish harboured that this fairy-tale would have a happy ending for them both.

'I love Craig's train sets,' Elizabeth burst out, and everyone laughed at the expression of indignation on her face.

'Don't you take any notice of us,' advised Dimity. 'We're all very happy for you both. More power to your elbow.'

'Elbow?' Craig mouthed, but Elizabeth dug him in the ribs, and he very sensibly kept quiet.

'When we've all had sufficient here,' suggested Bryony, 'I wonder if we might go on up to the chapel, to see if it's no longer a crime scene, and if so, whether Mr Hillman and Mr Warwick have had time to paint over that terrible disfigurement on the wall?'

'I think that's a splendid idea,' agreed Dimity, and the others nodded. Although the chapel would be able to be used again for services should anyone wish to resume them, it would also be a curio; a tourist attraction for those who visited the village and had sufficient interest to take a step down Tuppenny Lane to visit it. They had been promised an official sign from the Tourist Board when it was finished, and had been inspected and passed as of sufficient local historical interest.

As Bryony collected cups and saucers on her tray, the others donned their outdoor gear, which was now more substantial than it had been just a couple of weeks ago as the weather was unseasonably cold, and a bad winter was confidently expected. Hats were pulled on, gloves were donned, and scarves were wound around necks as they prepared to go out and face the hostile elements, even though it was only the first of November.

Dimity and Patience led the way down Dairy Lane, turning left into Farriers Lane, and then left again into Tuppenny Lane, where the chapel was situated between the chip shop and the now sadly closed down library, and Patience gave it a regretful look as they walked past its locked doors, not to be opened again until it was stripped of its stock and fittings, to be sold off to some other body for some other purpose.

The doors were unlocked, the blue and white tape that had

declared the chapel a crime scene gone, so there must be somebody there, and the five villagers hurried into the building's shelter from the cutting wind. It was what was usually referred to as a 'lazy wind': that is, one that could not be bothered to go round one, but went right through one instead.

Once inside, the first thing of which they were aware was that the red painted Greek graffito had, indeed, been painted over. Someone must have worked overtime to get that done by today. Within a small fraction of a second, their minds became aware that the red writing had been replaced by some other message, this one also in red paint, on top of the fresh layer of white. This was in English, and read: '*Vengeance is mine, sayeth the Lord.*'

'Oh, my dear goodness!' exclaimed Dimity, clapping her hands to her mouth in horror. 'What on earth's going on here?'

There were gasps from her companions, and smothered oaths as their brains took in all that had happened since they had last been in the building.

A lone voice asked, 'What's that, up there on the altar?' Elizabeth Sinden had been the first to drag her eyes away from the new desecration, and she now alerted them all to the fact that things were even more wrong than they had thought.

They turned to her, to find her pointing at the crude stone table that had served the chapel as an altar, and would do so again, when it was reopened. Its rough surface now bore a burden – a lumpen shape covered with what looked like, in the dim winter's light, an old table cloth of some sort.

'What on earth is that?' asked Bryony, the first one to find her voice. 'Come on, let's go and take a look. If this is someone's idea of a joke, I must say that I am not in the least amused, considering what's already happened this year in the village.' Murmurs of consent greeted this remark, and they followed her down the aisle to see what awaited them at the east window.

It was Dimity who was bold enough to reach out a hand and twitch the cloth – which did indeed prove to be an old red chenille tablecloth – aside, and reveal what lay underneath its folds in anonymity. On being greeted with the gaze of dead eyes, one of them slightly bruised and swollen, Dimity gave a little scream of surprise, and dropped the cloth back into its all-enveloping position.

Bryony reached out a hand and twitched away the tablecloth again from what lay beneath it, and revealed the dead body of Steve Warwick, the plasterer and painter who had been working at the chapel. This was much worse than the appearance of a new graffito, and the reactions of those present reflected this.

Dimity toddled, in a rather drunken fashion, towards the front pew, and dropped down on it before she passed out. Elizabeth stood transfixed, and Craig put his arm around her shoulder and led her away from the offending sight. Bryony stared with horrified interest at the features of the dead man, one side of his face bruised and swollen, the opposite side of his head at the right temple caved in like the shell of a boiled egg hit with a spoon, but it was Patience who was the most practical of the bunch.

'We've got to report this to the police. This is obviously murder, and we need to get in touch with them as soon as possible. Does anyone have their mobile phone on them?' she asked.

A chorus, indicating that no one had thought to bring this particularly useful piece of modern equipment, greeted this question.

'Has anyone got a key to the church?' she asked, with a little more confidence in her second question.

'I have,' volunteered Dimity. 'It's in my pocket. I made sure I had it with me this morning, because I intended to come here this afternoon and didn't expect to find the doors unlocked.'

'Right!' said Patience, marshalling her thoughts. 'I suggest that we all adjourn to Bryony's again, if she has no objection, and telephone the police from there. This man seems to have been dead for some time, so it would be a waste of time summoning medical help. Perhaps Bryony would be so good as to make us another cup of her excellent coffee, for the shock.'

Bryony Buckleigh indicated that the plan was acceptable to

her with relief, as she had not really wanted to return to an empty house after what she had just seen. There was probably a murderer on the loose, and she lived alone, so the thought of company was a cheerful and comforting one.

As they regrouped for leaving, Elizabeth suddenly said, 'Did I just hear a movement up in the organist's loft, or am I imagining things? I thought there was a sort of rustling sound. Shh, everybody.'

There was absolute silence in the little chapel for about ten seconds, then it was broken by Craig's voice, declaring that anything Elizabeth thought she had heard was probably the result of shock and an over-active imagination. This remark was greeted by an embarrassed little titter from the others present, and they left the chapel, Dimity conscientiously locking the front doors behind them and re-pocketing the key before they set off for 'Honeysuckle' once more.

In the organ loft, a figure raised itself to an upright position in the gloom, and looked down at the broken body below. With a sharp intake of breath, the figure left the loft, descending the winding little staircase that led up to it, and let itself out through a small door on the north side of the chapel that no one had even bothered to check.

At the college, Chris Roberts had been greeted politely by Elspeth Martin, who seemed to be in a rather strange mood. Although her eyes looked anxious, there were high spots of colour in her cheeks, indicating some sort of excitement. Surely it couldn't be at seeing him again? he thought arrogantly.

Before the class was called to order she managed to introduce him to Antonia Knightly and Jamie Huntley, her particular friends on this course. 'And the tutor's Jocasta Gray, but I told you that when I met you, didn't I? Here she comes now. We'd better get ourselves sat down and settled: she doesn't like unruly students. Says it destroys the positive thoughts she has gathered together for the teaching session.'

The woman who entered the room was tall and slender, with prematurely grey/white hair, worn in a bun on the top of her head, wisps and tendrils escaping to soften the lines of her lean face. She wore the black gown to which she was entitled, and discreet make-up which enhanced her features rather than changing their colour. Chris thought her beautiful, and could understand why Elspeth was suffering from a severe case of heroine-worship.

Jocasta Gray had been perceptive and conscientious enough to get together all the class notes and hand-outs that Chris had missed due to his late registration in the limited time available to her, and made a point of singling him out before she began the lecture to offer these to him. She told him that if he had any questions, she was always ready and willing to talk to him, and he suddenly felt like he'd won the lottery.

Her voice was musical and hypnotic, and he found that, by the time they broke for coffee, he had not written a single word on his notepad, but had merely doodled a couple of hearts, and written Jocasta six times. He knew that he was making a bad start, but, so bewitched was he that for the moment he didn't care.

Elspeth led him to the refectory so that they could get some refreshment, and there she introduced him to three other students, Amelia Harrison, who was studying history, Aaron Trussler, who was studying physical education, and Daniel Burrows, one of the philosophy students, and the only one to offer his hand to be shaken. Chris noticed that he winced as he took the hand, looking down at it to see one of the knuckles grazed and all of them slightly bruised and swollen.

'How did you hurt your hand?' he enquired, earning himself a frown from Burrows.

'Jack slipped when I was changing a wheel on my car,' he retorted curtly, and turned to Aaron Trussler, giving Chris the cold shoulder.

Aaron Trussler, conscious of the snub, leaned over to tell Chris that Daniel should have come to him. He was doing a car maintenance course at the weekends, and could have done the job much more quickly and efficiently. 'I've got an old van,' he informed Chris. 'Always breaking down, so I thought I'd better find out how to fix the thing, so that it doesn't cost me a fortune every time something simple goes wrong.'

Wonder what all that was about, thought Chris, but, like most things that didn't immediately make sense, he sent it off to the back of his mind, where his subconscious could work at it and see if it could come up with an explanation.

These six seemed to have formed a little clique, and it wasn't long before he found out what they had in common: they were all members of the group he had seen advertised on the college noticeboard who met to discuss local religious beliefs, practices, and history. 'Of course, there are a lot more of us, but we've gelled as a group, so we hang out together, timetables permitting,' explained Elspeth.

'Oh, I saw that on the noticeboard, and thought I'd give it a try. There's a meeting tonight, isn't there?'

'Yes!' answered Elspeth, with enthusiasm. 'That would be lovely, wouldn't it guys?' she asked the others, who didn't seem quite as enthusiastic as she was, but nevertheless, nodded their heads in agreement. 'Ooh, look! Here comes Jocasta now,' she suddenly informed them, then blushed at the very sound of the tutor's forename.

And, indeed, Jocasta Gray was approaching their table, cup of coffee in her hand, and a smile of greeting on her face. 'I see you've rounded up our new boy,' she exclaimed, pausing at the table. 'Good for you. I've a feeling it won't be too long before he's one of us,' she stated, mysteriously, while the others nodded their heads in apparent understanding.

'I hope I'll soon be one of you, too,' replied Chris, smiling back at them all, and wondering what he'd just let himself in for.

'Can't stay long,' declared Jocasta Gray, as she took a place at the table and placed her hot cup of coffee on its surface. 'I've got an appointment later, and I don't want to be late, but I'll see you all tonight anyway. Are you going to come to our little discussion group, Chris?' she asked, and Chris blushed to the roots of his slightly-too-long curly hair.

'I'd seen the notice about it when I popped in to the college on Saturday, and I'd certainly thought it might be very interesting,' he replied, feeling like a schoolboy again with his first crush.

'That's marvellous!' said Jocasta, and left him grinning like a fool as she turned to one of the others and started asking him questions about the arrangements for printing the agenda that evening.

'I simply don't believe it!' roared Falconer as he crashed down the telephone handset.

'What's that, sir?' asked Carmichael, bewildered as to what could have set off the inspector in such a way.

'You know we've been over to Steynham St Michael about that paint job in the chapel?' he asked.

'Yes, sir. What is it? More defacement?'

'It's murder! That's what it bloody well is!' yelled Falconer, not a man who swore lightly. 'There's been another bloody murder there! Get your coat. We're off. Christmas will meet us at the chapel.'

Carmichael grabbed his long black coat from the coat-rack and followed the inspector, fighting to get his arms into its sleeves as they left at a trot.

'Why are you so cross, sir?' asked Carmichael, diligently doing up the buttons on his coat.

'I seem to have dealt almost exclusively with murders since I've been here. I thought we might just work our way through the various villages, and that would be that, but we're going out to murder number two in Steynham St Michael, and we haven't even finished all the villages yet for their *first* murders. If we have to keep going out to repeat visits, I'll spend the rest of my life investigating murders in banjo country. That's why I'm so cross! And where the hell did you get that coat, Sergeant?'

Carmichael had felt overwhelmed by this unexpected tirade, from his usually even-tempered boss, and the question at the end had really thrown him.

I can't remember, sir. I've had it years, but I haven't worn it for ages, because it hasn't really been cold enough for it. Why?'

'Because you look like a scarecrow in it – a right tatty-bogle!' replied Falconer, still feeling out of sorts, and taking this murder personally.

'Kerry likes it!' he shot back.

'I'm sure she does. Oh, take no notice of me. I'm just in a bad mood. Let's go back to Steynham St Michael, and see what's waiting for us. At least we know some of the villagers there, and can be sure of a reasonably warm welcome after solving that previous case there.'

'They were pretty nice to us the other day,' commented Carmichael.

'Yes, they were,' agreed Falconer. 'I'm sorry about what I said about your coat. I didn't mean it.'

'That's all right, sir. Everybody has off-days.'

'That's very understanding of you, Carmichael.'

'My pleasure, sir.'

Chapter Six

Monday 1st November – later

They took Carmichael's car, because Falconer was feeling so tetchy that he didn't want to risk driving in that mood. On the way, Carmichael suggested that they stopped at the mobile café, just a mile or so outside the village, to get a cup of tea. They were liable to get very chilled in the chapel, and a cup of tea would warm them up just before they had to stand around in the cold. 'And it might cheer you up a bit, sir,' he added.

'OK! I'm sorry. Come on, let's get a couple of cuppas and sit in the car and get it nice and fuggy.'

At the serving hatch, Falconer scanned the price list, and applauded Carmichael's choice of tea as that was only £1 a cup, whereas coffee was £1.50. 'Two teas,' he called out to the rather portly man serving, and took them from him, giving one to Carmichael, who immediately began to help himself to sugar from the container provided in the hatchway.

The man behind the counter looked on in wonder as Carmichael put spoonful after spoonful into his polystyrene container, and finally began to stir the sticky mixture with his plastic spoon.

'That'll be two pounds fifty,' declared the man in the serving hatch, and Falconer looked at him with some surprise.

'Surely that should be two pounds?' he queried. 'It says that tea's a pound a cup.'

'Not the way your mate takes sugar, it's not. That's extra! If everyone took sugar like 'e does, I'd be out of business in a fortnight. Now, pay up, and less of yer moaning.'

'We're policemen, you know!' Falconer stated, with dignity.

'Then you should know when one of yer innocent public's

bein' robbed. And that's me, with all that sugar wot 'e's put in 'is tea. Now, give us yer money and get orf, outta my sight. And if yer comes back again, bring yer own bleedin' sugar. I can't be givin' out the whole year's supply from a small Caribbean island to customers like 'im every time 'e wants a cuppa. Tell 'im 'e's to bring 'is own next time!'

Falconer 'got orf', indicating for Carmichael to follow him, not knowing whether to lose his temper at the bare-faced cheek of the vendor or laugh his head off. He'd have to see what mood he was in before he decided.

'That'll be fifty pence, Carmichael,' he declared. 'I don't mind paying for your cuppa, but I'm damned if I'm going to pay for your sugar as well.'

Carmichael solemnly rummaged around in his pocket and produced a fifty-pence piece, which he handed to the inspector in silence.

'Thank you,' he growled, feeling a bit embarrassed at his petty meanness now that Carmichael had actually paid him the supplement.

About fifteen minutes later they drew up outside 'Honeysuckle' in Dairy Lane. Word had got round, as it does in a village, and Vernon Warlock and Charles Rainbird were also waiting for them, having left 'back in ten minutes' signs on their shop doors. Gossip was much more important that lacklustre sales.

As the two policemen were ushered in, Charles Rainbird announced, in a rather theatrical voice, 'An inspector calls! Well, the writing's *really* on the wall, now.' There was a groan from the assembled villagers, who turned their attention away from this feeble witticism and towards the two figures representing law and order who had just entered the now rather crowded room.

'Oh, thank the Lord you're here!' exclaimed Dimity, rising from her seat.

'The cavalry to the rescue, as usual!' declared Bryony. No one else spoke.

'I understand that there's a corpse in your chapel?' Falconer

50

asked, anxious to get whatever details he could before visiting the locus.

'It's that man who was working there, who did the plastering and painting,' volunteered Patience. 'I think his name's Steven Warwick.'

'He looked like he'd been thumped in the face, and he had a very nasty wound on his right temple,' offered Craig.

'And there was an old tablecloth covering him. Whoever did it left him lying there, on the altar. That's disrespectful, that is,' Elizabeth exclaimed, in the rush of information.

The two shopkeepers, Vernon Warlock and Charles Rainbird, remained silent. They hadn't been there, and had seen nothing. They were only at Bryony's cottage because of the efficiency of the village grapevine, and had gone there to lend their support to the ladies, neither of them considering that Craig Crawford was much of a man, what with his schoolboy train sets and model countryside.

'Does anyone have a key to the chapel?' Falconer asked, at once practical and wanting to get on with the job.

'I have,' said Dimity, leaning over the back of her chair, to extract it from her coat pocket.

'Thank you very much, Miss Pryor,' he said, taking the proffered lump of cold metal. 'DC Carmichael and I will visit the scene of the crime, consult with the police surgeon – or Forensic Medical Examiner, as he's taken to calling himself now he's got all those nice shiny new qualifications – then return here, to take statements. Should any of you wish to go home in the meantime, I'm sure we'll find you without too much trouble.'

Without any further ado, they left, and made their way (by car, because of the temperature) to the chapel, with Falconer muttering away to himself, 'Forensic Medical Examiner! Blasted new-fangled terminology! That man's getting ideas above his station. Paddington!'

Carmichael, who was only semi-tuned-in to what the inspector was mumbling, suddenly asked, 'The bear?'

'What bear?' asked Falconer, suddenly jolted out of his little rant.

'Paddington,' stated Carmichael, trying his best to get the gist of things.

'No! The station! Don't you listen to anything I say?'

'Sorry, sir.'

Arriving at the chapel they found Dr Christmas newly arrived and twisting and turning the ring of the door handle in hopes of getting inside and away from the wicked north wind.

'Hurry up, Harry!' the doctor cajoled the inspector. 'I'm dying of hypothermia here!'

Falconer obliged, and, still muttering away to himself under his breath, all three were soon standing at the far end of the aisle, looking down to the altar, where something lay covered with an old table cloth. It was difficult to discern the colour at this distance and in this light, and they soon began to make their way towards the thing underneath its surface.

The inspector gave a low whistle, and said, 'Well, the writing *really* is on the wall, as has just been pointed out to me.'

Falconer produced a large evidence bag from the small attaché case he had brought with him and, after pulling on a pair of protective gloves, so as not to contaminate the evidence, Dr Christmas lowered the cloth carefully inside the waiting receptacle.

What this action revealed was the corpse, orientated north to south, its head pointing north. This probably signified nothing, but Carmichael drew out his notebook and made a note of it just in case. Christmas declared life extinct, and made a note of the time, before taking a closer look at the injuries visible. Although the less serious of the two wounds, it was the one to the face that drew their attention. The man had evidently sustained a fairly powerful blow to the face.

'This was done about the same time as that wound on the head was inflicted,' declared the doctor. 'There was little time for the tissue to swell and bruise. I think the eye socket may be cracked – can't be sure until I get him back to the mortuary – but if it is, I'd have expected maybe just a little more swelling and bruising than we've got.'

'What about that blow to the head?' asked Falconer, as Christmas moved his face as close as he dared to the damage area without actually touching it.

'I can't say anything for certain now, but you know that. My initial gut reaction is that the blow was inflicted by our old friend, the blunt instrument. I can't see any traces of splinters of wood in the wound, and I'm going to make an initial guess, given the power behind it, that whatever he was hit with was made of metal, or some-such non-brittle material.

'Now, I know that's not very helpful, or particularly clever, but I can't do anything until after the SOCO team have taken all their photographs, fingerprints, and samples, so you'll just have to be patient, Harry.'

'Any idea when he died?' Falconer asked, knowing he was pushing his luck, and might end up with the rectal thermometer inserted into his own body.

Dr Christmas put a hand on the body's chest, where the winter-weight shirt was slightly open, then gently tried to manipulate one of the hands without disturbing its position.

'You're pushing your luck, old boy, but I'd make a fair guess, without any official confirmation, that this happened sometime last night.'

'Thanks for that, Philip. We really appreciate it. We'll leave you to wait for the SOCO boys and girls now, and go off to see if we can glean any information from the neighbours. Oh, no!' he suddenly cried out, slapping one hand to his forehead.

'What is it, sir?' asked Carmichael, concerned once again about the mood of his superior.

'You know who the nearest neighbours are, don't you Carmichael?' the inspector asked, his face a mask of tragedy.

'Forgotten!' answered Carmichael, economically, not wanting to waste words when he could see the heat escaping from all their bodies into the air in the form of clouds of vapour every time someone spoke.

'The drunken Littlemores!' exclaimed Falconer, and Carmichael gave a groan.

'Malcolm and Amy, Olympic drinkers,' he said, shaking his

head in despair. 'We'll never get any sense out of them,' he concluded.

'Especially as someone commented that they were still on the sauce when we were here about the Greek graffito,' Falconer replied, in agreement. 'They have a problem remembering which way is up most days, and on bad ones, they couldn't find their own arses with both hands and a mirror.'

'Sir!' burst out Carmichael in admonishment.

'Well I feel like that today,' was Falconer's rather weak excuse, and it was left to Dr Christmas to restore some sort of normality – given the circumstances of them being there together – to the situation.

'I'll get this done as soon as possible, and let you know the results *tout suite*,' he promised.

'Make sure you do,' replied Falconer, still seething with the injustice of having to return to Steynham St Michael only months after having worked on a murder case here before.

Monica Raynor returned to her estate agency on the Market Darley Road rather later than she had planned after lunch, only to find the office locked and deserted. That was odd, because Quentin had promised that he would cover for her until her return, and here he was, gone. He could've let her know on her mobile that he was going out, she thought, then remembered that she had switched it off before she left the office.

On her desk was a note that read simply, 'Gone out. B back B4 5', with Quentin scrawled under this message. She checked his diary, but there were no entries for appointments or viewings this afternoon, and she wondered where he'd gone. He didn't respond to his mobile either, but she could hardly complain about that, as she hadn't had hers switched on either.

He was either in need of complete peace and quiet or up to something, or both. At the moment she didn't care which it was, and sat down at her desk and removed a half bottle of vodka from her bottom drawer; the one she always kept locked.

Taking a deep slug straight from the bottle, she thought, what the hell! Badger's Sett's only just down the road. I can get a lift from Quentin, if he's back, or I can simply walk. It's only a few yards away, and at this comforting idea, she raised the bottle to her lips again, and drank deeply of its contents.

Falconer and Carmichael approached the Littlemores' home, Forge Cottage, on foot as it was only just across Tuppenny Lane. The light was fading fast at this time of year and with the overcast conditions that had prevailed throughout the day, and as they crossed the road, they could see the cottage, ablaze with lights, like an ocean liner at sea during the dark of night, and hear music seeping out of every crevice, which must mean it was very loud indeed when one considered that they had double glazing throughout the property.

Carmichael rang the bell as Falconer stood back to avoid getting caught in anything that might issue from that front door with unfriendly intent at being interrupted mid-binge.

It was Amy who answered the summons after only the third ring, her hair dishevelled, the top two buttons of her blouse undone beneath her cardigan, and a strong smell of ouzo emanating from her. It was only then that Falconer identified the blaring music as Greek.

'Good afternoon, Mrs Littlemore,' Falconer greeted her, suddenly realising how appropriate the couple's surname was – 'just a little more, please'. 'We'd like a word with you and your husband ...'

At this point she interrupted him, holding one hand up to an ear, and shouting, 'Whassat? Can' 'ear yer!'

'Could you turn the music down, please, Mrs Littlemore?' he requested, only to get a similar response, this time with the other hand cupping the other ear,

'Speak up, love. Can' ear yer 'cos of this bloody loud music!'

'Mrs Littlemore, may we come in for a minute? We need to speak to you and your husband,' the inspector shouted.

''Ang on a minute. I've go' ter turn this bloody music dahn. Can't 'ear a bloody thing,' she announced, and disappeared back into the house, inadvertently shutting the front door on them.

They waited for two or three minutes, and when she hadn't returned, Falconer turned to Carmichael with a deep sigh of displeasure. 'She's forgotten about us, drunken old sot. Give that bell another long push, Carmichael. We'll have to see if we can get her to come back to the door.'

This time, it was Malcolm Littlemore who greeted them, leaning forward, trying to hear what Falconer was saying, but being defeated, as had been his wife, by the volume of the music coming from inside the house. ''Ang on a mini',' he said. 'I've gotta turn tha' bloody music dahn. Can' 'ear myself fink, with that racket blarin' out,' and he too, disappeared back inside the house.

Fortunately, he didn't close the door on them, and they entered, without permission, to try to rouse the inebriated couple sufficiently to ask them if they'd heard anything the night before. Just before they entered the living room, as noisy as a night club, now that they were closer to the source of the music, Falconer turned to Carmichael and mouthed, 'Fat chance!' before entering the room and turning off the music himself, his ear-drums protesting as he approached the equipment.

'Oh, 'ello again. Oo le' you in, then?' asked Malcolm, smiling a welcome at them. 'Come in an' 'ave a li'l drinky wiv us. We're 'avin' a late 'Allowe'en par'y. Yer welcome ter join us, if yer wan' to.'

''Ave a li'l drinky-winky,' echoed Amy, standing at practically a forty-five degree angle at the other end of the room, as she fought to keep her balance.

'We've come about the murder over the road, at the chapel,' Falconer announced, in a slightly louder voice than normal, assuming that their ears would probably be a little jaded by the volume of what they had been listening to.

'No needs ter shou', old boy,' slurred Malcolm, and waved an arm at the empty sofa, a gesture indicating that they should take a seat.

'You do realise there's been a murder in the chapel, don't

you, Mr Littlemore, Mrs Littlemore?'

'Whassat?' asked Amy, finally losing her battle with gravity and toppling over to the floor, glass still in her hand.

'Steady on, ol' girl,' chided Malcolm, moving to her aid. 'Bi' unsteady on 'er pins, is our Amy. Go' sumfink wrong wiv 'er inner-ear,' he informed them, tapping his right index finger against his nose and winking.

'Mr Littlemore,' bellowed Falconer. 'Will you be opening up your shop tomorrow?' he asked, realising that they were fighting a losing battle with these two today.

'Shouldn't fink so. Know wha' I mean, squire?' Malcolm slurred, looking at them both through bleary eyes.

Good God! thought Falconer. It's only late afternoon, and they're absolutely rat-arsed.

'P'r'aps in the ar'ernoon,' Malcolm added, hopefully.

'We'll come back and see you then,' the inspector announced. 'Thank you very much for your time *this afternoon*.' He stressed the last two words, in the hope that it may make them realise what a state they were in so early in the day, but it was like water off a duck's back to these two, he supposed, and nodded for Carmichael to follow him out of the house, to get back to interviewing people who were stone cold sober.

Malcolm Littlemore staggered politely to the door, fulfilling his role as host, as he perceived it, in his drunken state, and waved them off cheerily, calling, 'Do come back soon!'

When they arrived back at 'Honeysuckle', the same crowd was still present, and as Bryony let them in they could hear that conversation had turned, temporarily, to the Hallowe'en party of the night before, and Dimity was holding forth about times gone by.

'When I was young, we didn't have any celebrations – whatever you like to call them – for Hallowe'en, although we children always tried to pay a sneaky visit to the graveyard, to see if, indeed, the dead would walk; but if Guy Fawkes' Night fell on a Sunday, the fireworks were let off on the Saturday night before. To let off fireworks and have a bonfire on the Sabbath was taboo. But now, anything goes, it seems,' she ended, her voice sad and wistful.

'No respect for anything these days, the younger generation.' This was pronounced in Vernon Warlock's slightly lugubrious tones, and, having met the man, Falconer wondered if he had ever been young. He had got the impression that Warlock was born old and cranky.

As the two policemen entered the room, the sound of conversation fizzled and died, and all eyes were swivelled in their direction.

'Anything to report?' asked Charles Rainbird, a dreadful old gossip, and always willing to put himself forward if it meant learning something interesting.

'Nothing, except to confirm that the dead man is Steven Warwick. I was able to do that, because he was pointed out to me, when we visited before, to view the graffito. I think at this point that you know as much as we do. I've left the scene in the care of Dr Christmas, to see to the SOCO team, and the only thing for me to do now, before I leave the village, is to have a word with all of you who found the body today.'

'Do we have to go now?' asked Charles Rainbird, referring to himself and Vernon Warlock.

'You weren't involved in the discovery of the body, were you?' Falconer made it a question, rather than a statement. It was best to keep every resident he could on his side.

'I'm afraid not, but we could tell you where and when we last saw the chap. That might help, mightn't it?' Charles wasn't giving up on being at the epicentre of the action without a fight.

'If you'd like to go into the dining room – if that's all right with Mrs Buckleigh?' he queried.

'Quite all right, Inspector. Use whichever room seems the most appropriate,' called back a voice from the kitchen, where Bryony was brewing yet more coffee and tea, and wondering, now that the afternoon had moved on a little, whether it might be more appropriate to offer sherry.

'Thank you. Mr Rainbird and Mr Warlock, if you would

care to precede DS Carmichael into the dining room, he'll take any relevant information from you for a statement.'

The two men exited the room, followed by Carmichael, who had to duck to get through the doorways in this cottage, so low were they, and so tall was he. When he left the living room and entered the dining room with a double duck, Falconer was reminded of those lanky toy birds that used to dip backwards and forwards into a small pot of water as if drinking.

That left him with the original party of discovery and, while he waited for Carmichael to note down anything pertinent that the two men may have to tell him, he told the others the order in which he would like to speak to them.

'I'll speak to you first, Miss Pryor. We can use the dining room, after DS Carmichael's finished in there. Then I'll speak to you, Mrs Buckleigh, if that's agreeable. Then I'd like to interview you, Mrs Buttery; then Miss Sinden, and finally, Mr Crawford.

'You're free to leave after I've spoken to you, but if anyone would like a lift, as it's dark now, will they please wait in here, and DS Carmichael and I will see to it when we've finished.

There was, however, very little for them to learn, and it was only forty-five minutes later that they took their leave, everyone having left in a bunch, to drop people off on the way, even if it took them on a rather strange route home.

On the way back to Market Darley, conversation in the car was desultory, and Falconer kept his eyes front, looking at the countryside as they drove through it. The last few autumn leaves were falling from the skeletons of the trees along the sides of the road, fluttering like ghosts in the headlights of Carmichael's Skoda, only to disappear from sight, tiny phantoms of the summer that they were, as suddenly as they had appeared.

Falconer shivered, not because the interior of the vehicle was cold, but at the thought of the dark, sunlight-starved days of the approaching winter. He didn't mind that particular season when the sky was clear and the weather was crisp, but the dull, cloudy days that usually numbered its days made him feel both oppressed and depressed. The cloud cover seemed to him like a vast opaque glass lid that had been set over the countryside, and it always left him feeling sad and slightly out of sorts with his world.

Once back at the station, Falconer heaved a huge sigh, and stated bleakly, 'We're going to have to spend the whole day tomorrow interviewing that chap's workmates, and tracing his family to inform them of what's happened.'

'I know, sir, but there might be a bit of luck in there, if we find ourselves a suspect,' Carmichael comforted him.

'Don't hold your breath, Carmichael. I can feel it in my bones that it's not going to turn out to be that simple. I've just got a gut feeling that this is going to prove a tricky one, and that we're not finished yet: not by a long chalk.'

Chapter Seven

Chris Roberts equipped himself with a notebook and pen for his first meeting with the discussion group. He also had a Black Sabbath T-shirt, its origins lost in the mists of his past, which he donned for the evening's outing. Giving his hair a last ruffle so that it would not look too tidy and respectable, he got into his car and headed for the college.

He felt not only apprehensive, but excited as well. Would he be accepted for what he was? Would he show enough general knowledge on the subjects that would arise not to give himself away? What would happen if his cover was blown on this first evening? There were no answers to these questions at the moment, and he pulled up in the college car park a little unsure of himself, but trying to put on a confident front.

A notice in the foyer directed him to room 101. At least that was a good omen. He knew how to get there, as it was his home room. Although he was a little early, he caught up with Elspeth Martin and Antonia Knightly on his trek through the corridors, and the three arrived at the appointed room together.

There were people already assembled there, including Jamie Huntley, also in his class, Amelia Harrison, and Aaron Trussler. At the last minute, a panting Daniel Burrows took his place in the room, and at eight o'clock on the dot, Jocasta Gray joined them, appearing suddenly in their midst like a black-draped jack-in-the-box.

'Settle down, everybody!' she called, clapping her hands for order, and the buzz of conversation suddenly ceased. She had this lot in the palm of her hand, thought Chris. They were as obedient as Pavlov-trained dogs.

'Tonight,' Jocasta announced, 'we are going to discuss the beliefs of the Strict and Particulars, with regard to punishment – law or community. Would anyone like to start the discussion? Yes! You, Elspeth. The floor is yours.'

Elspeth Martin had been waving her arm in the air like a schoolgirl hoping to be chosen as milk monitor. With a smile and a blush, she rose to her feet, came to the front of the room, and turned to face her peers.

'The beliefs of the Strict and Particulars towards punishment were that it should take place in the community in which the offence had taken place ...'

'Or misdeed, Elspeth,' interrupted the tutor.

'Sorry! Or misdeed. And that the punishment should be meted out by either the person or persons who had suffered by what had taken place, the miscreant's family, or, in extreme cases, by the entire community,' she continued.

'And what about more serious cases? What happened about those?' asked Jocasta, interrupting again, in prompt.

'More serious cases were, we believe, handed over to the appropriate authorities, to be dealt with by the law of the land. There are, however, stories that exist to this day, that this was not always so.'

'Thank you very much, Elspeth. You may re-take your place,' Miss Gray informed her student, then turned to the rest of those gathered there. 'Are there any comments, questions, or areas of discussion you would like to raise?' she asked them, scanning the room with bright eyes for volunteers. Chris put up his own hand in trepidation.

'Yes – Chris, isn't it? What would you like to contribute to tonight's discussion?'

'Only that I don't really know anything about this Strict and Particular denomination, because I'm not from round here, and I wondered if you'd mind filling me in about exactly what their beliefs and customs were; including these stories that Elspeth alluded to in her introduction.'

'How nice, to have a really enquiring, fresh mind in our midst. Antonia, will you tell Chris about some of the other beliefs and practices, before we go back to the stories that Chris requested be told?'

Antonia Knightly rose and went to the front of the room. 'The Strict and Particulars dressed very conservatively, the women never showing uncovered arms, legs, or hair. They wore no jewellery, except for a plain gold band when they married, did not adorn their faces, and were absolutely obedient to their husbands, or fathers if they were unmarried.

'They didn't partake of snuff, tobacco, or strong drink, as these were seen as the temptations of the devil. For some time they educated their own children, the emphasis being on the teachings of the Bible.

'Social activities consisted of Bible readings, religious discussion groups, community hymn-singing, and prayer.

'They did not eat rich foods and banned the eating of meat on Fridays, like the Old Religion.'

Jocasta interrupted here to explain that Antonia was referring to the Roman Catholic Church when she named the Old Religion.

Antonia smiled at her tutor, and continued, 'No work whatsoever was allowed on the Sabbath, and food had to be prepared the day before for consumption on this day. The children were not even allowed to play, but had to sit reading their Bible, the only interruptions to this activity being three church services – early morning, mid-morning, and evening: a bit like Eucharist, Matins, and Evensong now,' she explained, 'and the family meals, of course.

'They wore a very limited range of colours, their clothes being black, brown, or very dark blue, the only exception being when a bride was married, when she was permitted to wear cream. White was not permitted, not to cast a slur on the bride's morals, but to acknowledge that we are all sinners, and have no right to don the purest of colours.'

'Phew!' exclaimed Chris. 'Life certainly wasn't a bowl of cherries for them, was it?'

'It was a very hard life indeed,' offered Amelia Harrison. 'I'm a history student here, and I've done some research on the subject in the county archives. At their formation, they were shunned by the local employers because they had set themselves out as different, and that was resented by the other villagers. It took some time for them to be accepted into the local community, but they never fully integrated.

'Some who joined the denomination left their families, and were forbidden to contact them because it was considered that the members of their family must lead sinful lives, and the new recruits just accepted this without demur. Today, with the strictness of the rules they had then, they would be referred to as a cult, but their ways did relax a little as the twentieth century dawned, and by the time the First World War had the whole country in its grip they became a little more outgoing and willing to mix. Their young men went to war as well as those from the village.'

'What do you think about that, Chris?' asked Jocasta, interested in his views, not only as a new member of the group, but as a new resident of the area as well.

'I'm just glad my family's always been C of E,' he said. 'Which, in effect, means that they never go to church, although both sets of my grandparents were frequent attenders at service on a Sunday. I think a lot of people got out of the habit after the First and Second World Wars, but that's only my opinion.

'I know my granddad said he lost his faith, seeing men die as he did. He was on the Expeditionary Force to France, and he still won't talk about what he saw then, and his father had been in the trenches in the First World War. My late father said that no God could be that ruthless and cruel, and, therefore, there could be no God.'

'That's very interesting, Chris. Do any of you others have similar stories in your families?' Jocasta asked, of the room at large.

This question produced a lot of discussion of the attitudes of parents and grandparents to organised religion, and it was half-past nine before the meeting wound up.

'Just before you go – and I'm sorry we didn't find time to break for coffee this evening – I'd just like to ask my advanced discussion group to meet me tomorrow morning in the refectory, before registration. Safe journeys home, you lot and, if I don't see you in class or round the college, I'll see you next Monday night at the same time.'

The group, which numbered about twenty-five, left in a gaggle, with only a few stragglers, which included Chris and Elspeth, the latter staying on to have a few words with Jocasta before she went home. Chris took his time over collecting his various bits and pieces together, and dawdled out into the car park. He had a reason for this, and hoped that Elspeth didn't walk or cycle home, otherwise his cunning plot would be a complete washout.

On exiting the building, he was surprised to hear again the tinny strains of an ice-cream van, and was just able to catch sight of it, disappearing down the road and into the night. That was the second time he'd seen it near the college, but, this being Chris, he didn't think any more of it.

He sat in his car until Elspeth appeared, exiting the building, and made noises with the car engine, turning it on, revving it, then switching the engine off as if it had cut out. About ten yards from his vehicle sat another lone car, and he hoped against hope that this would prove to be hers and not Jocasta's. He wasn't ready to tackle her yet, not having mastered the strong feelings he experienced whenever he saw or spoke to her.

Elspeth did indeed seem to be headed for the other car, but turned her head, as he did a particularly enthusiastic rev, then switched off the engine, and got out of the car to lift the lid of the bonnet. He hadn't played the part of Oliver Twist in the school play in vain all those years ago, and felt that he was still a fair actor.

Yes! Elspeth was approaching his car. She was going to ask if she could help. It was working, this ruse of his.

'Hi, Chris. You having a bit of car trouble?' she asked, appearing at his side.

'Certainly am,' he replied. 'I'll have to get it serviced. This is the third time in a week that it's done this to me.'

'Do you think you can get it going again?'

'Not tonight,' he informed her. 'When it's done this before, I've had to leave it overnight to sort out its little brainstorm. I guess I'll just have to walk home.' He said this last in his 'poor little me, whatever am I going to do?' voice, and looked at her in mute appeal.

'Oh, come on, you,' she said, giving him a little smile. 'I know you well enough to know that you're not a serial murderer or a rapist. I'll give you a lift home, if you tell me where you live.'

'If you can just drop me off at the big roundabout just outside town, that'd be great. I said I'd call into a mate's house for a coffee after we'd finished, and I can easily walk from there.' He didn't want her knowing where he lived. If she was at all nosy, she might ask around and find out he was a policeman, and that would never do. That'd blow his cover sky-high!

'The passenger door's open,' she called, as she got into the driver's seat. Chris opened the front door on the other side of the car, and found a pile of what looked like heavy material sitting on the seat. Unthinkingly, he pulled it out to fold it before depositing it on the rear seat so that he could get into the car.

'What the hell do you think you're doing?' Elspeth's tones, normally so mild, had risen to a screech as she realised what he had found. 'How dare you touch that! Give it to me! now!' and she was out of the car like lightning, rushing round to the other side of it to pull whatever it was from his arms and put it in the boot, slamming the lid of the boot on her mysterious cloth-y thing.

'I'm terribly sorry,' Chris apologised. 'I had no idea I was messing with anything private. Please forgive me.'

'I'm sorry too,' said Elspeth, calmer now that the thing, whatever it was, was out of sight. 'I guess I'm just feeling a bit jumpy tonight.'

Changing the subject, Chris asked, 'What was all that about an advanced discussion group at the end?'

'None of your bloody business,' She snapped, then looked contrite. 'There I go again, snapping for no reason. It's just a small group who have been together longer than the main discussion group, and we get together now and again for more advanced discussion. We've already covered all that stuff we did tonight, but we come along to support the newer members so that it doesn't close from lack of numbers.'

When Chris got out of the car at the roundabout he thanked her politely for the lift, and waved as she drove off. It was only a couple of streets to his mother's house, and he had food for thought on the short walk home. That cloth he had found hadn't been a blanket, or anything like that. It had looked to him very much like a dark-coloured monk's habit with a hood, and he wondered if this had anything to do with this advanced discussion group.

'Advanced discussion group, my arse,' he muttered to himself as he tramped through the frosty streets. 'There's definitely something going on, and I'm going to find out about it if it's the last thing I do.' He had not considered that it was never safe to challenge the gods.

For Falconer and Carmichael, it had gone exactly as Falconer had said it would. Both workmen had cast-iron alibis, and the family of the dead man proved to live in County Durham, and were as likely to have turned up in Steynham St Michael that day as pigs were to fly.

The man had had few friends, not having lived in the area for long, and there appeared to be no leads whatsoever from a hard day's questioning. Falconer had declared that side of things a dead end, and speculated that the murderer was either someone from the village, or from 'that weird lot' up at the college, that Roberts had been sent to infiltrate.

Chapter Eight

The next morning Roberts made his first report, by telephone, to Falconer, and held the phone away from his ear as Falconer embarked on the expected bawling-out for not getting in touch the day before.

'I couldn't actually do that, guv,' explained Roberts, and the tirade resumed. 'Sorry,' he said, 'I promise I'll remember to call you 'sir' or 'inspector'. But I really didn't have the opportunity.'

'What about the evening?' questioned Falconer. 'The college isn't open till midnight, is it? You're not up to your eyes until the witching hour, are you?'

'Not exactly, sir,' continued Roberts, anxious to calm Falconer's outburst of temper, and tell him what he had discovered.

'Go on.' Falconer was actually expecting a taradiddle to cover up for a day mostly spent skiving.

'When I went to have a look at the college on Saturday, I met one of the students on the same course as me, and I got talking to her. She told me a bit about the tutor, and I realised she had a schoolgirl crush on the woman.

'I also noticed, on the noticeboard, that there was a discussion group about the history of local religious beliefs and practices, and this girl said she was a member of it.

'I duly went in on Monday morning and met my peer group, and this mysterious tutor, whom, I might tell you, is a definite, star-quality babe, and just about the right age for me.'

'Keep your brains in your head, Roberts, and not in your trousers. You're undercover there, not under-bedcover,'

Falconer interrupted abruptly. He couldn't have the man fluttering his eyelashes and flirting, to the detriment of his objective.

'Keep your hair on, Inspector! I have no dishonourable intentions towards the woman, no matter how devastating she is. I am perfectly aware that I've got a job to do, and I wouldn't even think of approaching her before the investigation is over and I can drop this 'Chris Roberts, student' lark.

'Anyway, in the refectory, this Elspeth girl introduced me to some other students, not all on the same course, but all members of the discussion group and, of course, I said I wanted to come along.'

'Good man!' put in Falconer.

'So, I went to the meeting, and it was really all about the Strict and Particular denomination, but there was something said that indicated there was a hard core of members that had formed, and met as the advanced discussion group. I couldn't really find out anything about that. It was covered up by a story of it being people who'd been in the group for some time, and wanted to take the discussions further than was appropriate for those just being introduced to the subject. My arse, they do.

'I'm going to find a way to either infiltrate that, or spy on their meetings. I don't know what they're actually up to, but I'm determined to find out.

'Then, when I left the college, I saw that Elspeth's was just about the only car left in the front car park, apart from mine, so I pretended to have trouble with my engine, and she fell for it, hook, line, and sinker. She offered me a lift home in her own car, just like I'd intended she would.'

'I hope you didn't let her take you right to the door. There's no knowing what she could find out about you if she had your real address and went round discreetly questioning the neighbours.'

'I thought of that, sir.' Great! He'd remembered to address the inspector as 'sir'! 'I got her to drop me off at the big roundabout just outside the town; claimed I was going to see a mate before I went home.'

'Well done, Roberts!'

'But that's not all, sir.' Yes, he was really getting the hang of it now. It was coming much more naturally to him. 'When I opened the door to get into the car, there was this big pile of heavy dark cloth on the front seat, so I picked it up to fold it and put it on the back seat, and she went ape-shit – excuse the language, sir.'

'How exactly did she do that?'

'She started shouting at me like a mad woman, got out of the car, snatched it out of my hands, and put it in the boot, asking something like how dare I think I had the right to interfere with her possessions? She was really weird about it.'

'That's very interesting, Roberts. Well done! Keep up the good work, and don't forget to report to me *every day*. It's for your own safety, as well as for the progression of the investigation.'

'Yes, guv – I mean, sir,' Roberts concluded, and considered ending the call before he could be chastised again. He was quite enjoying being a student, so far, but he toughed it out. 'And by the way, I've seen this weird ice-cream van – that's twice now – , just leaving the vicinity of the college. I wouldn't normally mention something like that, only it seemed so odd to see something like that doing business outside a college. A school, I could understand, but the students here aren't exactly children, and I'm sure they would rather spend their student loans on beer than ice-cream. God knows what he thought he was going to sell, out there at that time of night, but it's so cold, I didn't really feel like indulging in a 'ninety-nine'. God! I remember the good old days, when 99 was a higher number than the price of the things!'

The call ended and Falconer was rather pleased. So, there were a couple more pins to go into his map, although in his excitement about hearing about these extra two sightings, he had forgotten to tell Chris to keep his eyes peeled for any more appearances of the highly suspicious van. He just wasn't used to running an undercover officer, and he realised he wasn't doing a really efficient job of it. And he still hadn't given him the details of the murder, to heighten his awareness of the danger of his situation. He couldn't even send him a text or a ring on his mobile, as that might blow his cover, if one of the other students got hold of it. He *must* tell him when he rang again.

As Falconer put down the phone, Carmichael entered the office, a big, goofy grin on his face. 'What's got into you, to make you so happy?' asked Falconer.

'Nothing, sir. It's just that when I was leaving the house this morning, I looked at Kerry – she looks like she's swallowed one of the Hallowe'en pumpkins, whole – and I just felt like bursting with pride. Here I am, a married man, with two lovely stepsons, and my very own first child growing in my wife's belly. How lucky can a man get?'

'Hrmph! That's enough about 'bellies', Carmichael. Could put a man off his coffee,' answered Falconer gruffly. He didn't like to hear anything about women's conditions or the problems peculiar to their sex, and shied away from anything that promised unwanted detail in these areas.

'Dammit!' exclaimed Falconer, apropos of nothing that Carmichael could discern. 'I forgot to ask Roberts about Sunday night, and I didn't tell him about the murder either. I daren't phone him myself: I might blow his cover. I'll just have to wait until he calls in again.'

Changing the subject, he said, 'Do you think you could have a quick word with Bob Bryant on the desk: see if Green and Starr are on duty? I've got a little job I want them to do, and it's probably better done sooner than later.'

PC Merv Green and PC Linda 'Twinkle' Starr appeared in Falconer's office in due course, and he asked them to go to Steynham St Michael to do some door-to-door enquiries round the rectangle formed by the Market Darley Road, Tuppenny Lane, Farriers Lane, and the High Street, and to include Dairy Lane in their visits.

'And no skiving off to canoodle!' he warned them. They had begun going out with each other, and Falconer knew Green was completely smitten to the point where he wasn't looking for a quick leg-over, but treated his new lady friend with some old-fashioned respect. But he didn't want temptation to get the better of them with just the two of them in the car together and all those handy little rural hidey-holes.

He wanted them to find out if anyone had seen any unusual vehicle, or strangers, perhaps acting suspiciously (he really was asking for the moon, here) in the area, anytime between Sunday, late afternoon, and very early Monday morning. Whoever it was might have been observed passing through on their way to the chapel and been noticed by someone who didn't realise the significance of what they'd seen.

He then applied himself to the map he had been creating, of sightings of 'Mr Spliffy' and his ice-cream-and-drugs van. Remembering his conversation with Roberts, he made sure that there were two marker-pins outside the college gates. It might be worthwhile getting Roberts to keep an eye out for the van and take a note of whatever number plate it was displaying on each of any sightings.

From the uniformed branch he already had six different registration numbers, and the one he and Carmichael had noted down themselves when they had first seen it and been suspicious of it.[2] There must be some way they could track it to its lair, and get a warrant to search wherever it was kept.

In Steynham St Michael, Green and Starr were received warmly. Not only did the residents they visited feel indignant that there had been a second murder in their village in less than a year, but were also scandalised that the body had been discovered in their newly refurbished chapel, which was also, hopefully, to become a tourist attraction in the coming season.

Arriving as they did at lunchtime, they found many people at home who would have been at work had their call been an hour later or an hour earlier, and PC Starr was a real hit with Vernon Warlock and Charles Rainbird.

Both men invited them in for a cup of tea, and Vernon

---

[2] See *Music to Die For*

Warlock, often irritable and scratchy, behaved with a great deal of charm, given that he had an attractive young woman in his living room. Merv Green he tended to ignore, but he made up to 'Twinkle' Starr in a charming, almost Edwardian way, she responding with the odd flutter of the eyelashes and a come-hither-ish look.

Charles Rainbird was in his element, having always been a terrible flirt despite his sexuality. He was what some called a 'greedy', not showing a particular preference for which side he batted for, as long as he got what he wanted. Twinkle caught on to his flirtatious nature immediately, and responded to it, in the hopes that he might have something for them, but he was rather more interested in her, and it took Merv taking her tiny hand in his to stop the verbal pursuit of his ladylove by this old rake.

On being questioned later by Starr about this unprofessional show of affection in public, he defended himself by saying that he needed to put the old boy off the scent because she was spoken for. He didn't want Rainbird to make a nuisance of himself at the station, claiming he'd seen things that he hadn't just because he wanted to see her.

'How gallant of you, Merv. And am I spoken for, then?' she asked, looking up at him bashfully.

'You can bet your shirt on it, baby,' replied Green, smiling at her with appreciation, and the fact that she was indeed his.

Having turned the sign to 'closed' at the office because she needed to go home to freshen up, and Quentin had unaccountably disappeared, Monica Raynor was also at home when they called on her, although she had only just arrived there.

When she opened the door to them she nearly swooned, her face drained of colour, and her mouth gaped open.

'Are you all right, madam?' asked Green, stepping forward to take her by the elbow, before she drooped to the floor.

'It's Quentin, isn't it?' asked Monica, her mind responding like lightning to finding two police constables on her doorstep, and dragging up what she could to cover her shock and fear.

'I'm sorry, madam, but I don't know what you're talking

74

about. Who exactly is Quentin?'

Monica's body visibly relaxed, and the colour started to come back to her cheeks. 'Nothing's happened to Quentin, then?' she persisted, then added, 'Quentin is my husband, and he disappeared from the office – the estate agent's office – when I was out. He left no note or message, and I've no idea where he's got to.'

'We have no information whatsoever about your husband, madam. Perhaps he just fancied a breath of fresh air, or he's off on an appointment that wasn't made until after you went out. I shouldn't worry too much. He'll turn up, and there'll be a totally innocent explanation for his absence.'

Her shock having now abated, Monica asked them in and offered them coffee. It was Twinkle who accepted the offer, but only on the condition that they could use their facilities before they left, as they had been lucky enough to be offered refreshments by other households they had visited that morning.

'Have you heard about the dead body that was discovered in the Strict and Particular Chapel in Tuppenny Lane?' Merv asked her, and she nodded, colouring slightly for reasons unfathomed.

'Yes. It's all over the village. Nobody seems to be talking about anything else, and it gets a bit wearing after a while,' she replied, with a slight hardness in her voice.

'Did you ever meet the deceased?' asked Green, Twinkle sitting with her notebook on her knees under the kitchen table, taking discreet notes.

'I did, as a matter of fact,' Monica admitted. 'I wanted a quote for some decorating in the house, and I knew he did painting and decorating as well as plastering. They sort of go together, don't they? When you take off old wallpaper, it often takes some of the plaster with it, and then you need someone else to make good, before the decorator can get going. He seemed perfect, offering both services.'

'When did you last see him, Mrs Raynor?'

'I really can't remember,' Monica replied, taking a big gulp of coffee, then choking on it. It had been the dregs left in her cup that she had so hastily drunk, and she had a mouthful of grounds.

'Did you see anyone you wouldn't expect to see, or anyone strange about the village between Sunday evening and very early Monday morning; or any vehicle that you didn't recognise that caught your eye?'

'Nobody. Nothing, I'm afraid,' she answered, shaking her head to emphasise her answer, now that she was recovered from her little misadventure with the contents of the bottom of her cup.

At this point, Monica was feeling a little more like her old self and, looking Merv up and down, asked him if he was married, a naughty twinkle in her eye. But Merv had his very own Twinkle sitting beside him at the kitchen table, and told Monica that he was already spoken for, adding, 'unfortunately', to his statement, just to tease Starr.

He knew a man-eater when he met one, so he wound up the interview, getting Twinkle to give her a card with the station's number on it, should she remember anything that might be pertinent to their investigation. There was no way he was going to give her a card that was anything to do with him. She'd eat him for breakfast! *And* spit out the bones.

In the late afternoon, Falconer had two communications: one from forensics, and the second from Philip Christmas.

The forensic information was that there had been oil stains detected on the clothing of Steve Warwick. There were also some fibres on his clothes, as yet unidentified, but they would send a detailed report so that CID could look out for any possible matches to them as they went about their investigation.

They'd also taken paint scrapings of the new graffito, and photographs of the writing itself, and the conclusion that had been reached was that it had been a completely different brand of paint from the first defacement, and, even though the alphabets were different, it was obvious that they had not been daubed by the same hand.

The second communication was telephonic. 'Hello there,

Harry,' the familiar tones of Doc Christmas greeted him, as he put the handset to his ear. 'How's it hanging?'

'How's what hanging?' asked Falconer, not being aware of the expression.

'Oh, never mind. Just a figure of speech,' the doctor replied, then continued, 'I've got some information for you on the exact location of the murder.'

'Go on,' Falconer encouraged him.

'It was too damned cold in that chapel to do much, and although I noticed it when the SOCOs had done their job, and the body had been carted off in the meat wagon,' – sometimes he could sound very cold-hearted – 'I realised that he hadn't been killed where we found him, on the altar.'

'You mean the body was moved?'

'Spot on! It looks like he was walloped on the head at the side of that area, near an old bookcase. The carpet's red, but much too red in one area, and I think someone must have struck him from behind while he was standing there. Had there been carpet covering the whole area where the altar stands, the drag marks would have been visible in the tread, and there would have been fibres adhering to the backs of his shoes, but with a flag-stoned floor, I don't doubt the forensic boys have got nix.'

'Aha, well, there you're wrong,' declared Falconer, in triumph. 'They've definitely got some alien fibres that aren't from his clothes. It's just a job of working out where they could have come from. Some will probably be from that carpet where he was killed, but as for any others – needle-in-a-haystack job, really. And now you tell me that the body was moved. That would've taken a bit of muscle-power! He was no light weight for someone to lift up to that stone altar,' he concluded.

Christmas gave Falconer his last little present. 'And the blow to the face: that was definitely inflicted at the same time as he was killed, give or take a very small passage of time, so they're definitely connected. Always happy to pass on good news, Harry boy.' No one else could get away with addressing Detective Inspector Harry Falconer in this off-hand manner: Christmas was an exception. They had hit if off from the start of their professional relationship, and Falconer now thought of the doctor as a regular member of the team.

'Always happy to receive it, *Père Noel*! Just let me know when you're going to have some to pass on,' he replied facetiously, smiling despite his petty little outburst.

'I'm going to have a good rummage round in his insides, now: see what he had for his last supper,' Christmas informed the inspector.

'Oh, what fun you have in your job. I wouldn't do it for all the tea in China.'

'I know you're not overly fond of the gory stuff. And do you remember when your Carmichael threw up in the mortuary when I was in the middle of one of my little treasure hunts?'

'How could I forget? I'll not let him play round at your place again in a hurry.'

'My mum wouldn't let him in,' joked the doctor, then rang off to commence his gruesome task.

When he'd put the phone down, Falconer's face fell. Even if Warwick had been murdered in the chapel, they were still going to have to search for the weapon.

Just to be on the safe side, however, he'd get Green and Starr out to the village again in the morning. The light had gone now, and the red of blood is the first colour to become unidentifiable in poor light. They might just take a stroll round the vicinity of the chapel and the graveyard to see if there were any signs of either a scuffle, or a blood-stained blunt instrument. Fat chance, but it had to be done.

Finally, just before he left the office, Roberts had called in, but had nothing to report, other than that he was trying to ingratiate himself both to Elspeth and Jocasta Gray, in the hope that he might be invited to join the 'inner circle' of the discussion group to find out exactly what they got up to.

Falconer thanked him for his call (much use it had done the investigation!), reminded him to keep a low profile, and to use his ears rather than his mouth, if he wanted to stay undetected. 'Bugger!' he exclaimed loudly. 'I still didn't give him the details of the body found in the chapel. What the hell's wrong with me?' It'd just have to wait until his call tomorrow.' Except that, although he didn't know it, it would be too late by then.

Back home for the evening, Falconer grilled himself a salmon steak, baked a potato in the microwave, and opened a supermarket bag of pre-chopped salad. Really! He was getting lazy about his food. It was probably the shorter days, and the fact that everything fresh had been imported from so far away, that his conscience pricked him if he even thought of buying anything.

Then it struck him that his bag of mixed salad had probably been prepared with ingredients from places as far away as South America, and sighed deeply with resignation. It seemed that there was no escape from decreasing one's use of imported products in the hope of decreasing one's own contribution to the global carbon footprint.

After he had eaten he opened his post, put the paperwork to one side, and tore the envelopes into halves, screwing them up into paper balls. Finding a section of carpet unencumbered with furniture, he got down on all fours with his paper balls, and made kissing noises with his mouth.

No, he hadn't gone mad! This was how he called his cats, and the sound soon had all four of them arrive at a run. They spotted him immediately, and what he had for them, and scampered over eagerly. 'Paper ball' was their favourite game, and he hadn't played it with them for days now.

As Falconer gathered discarded balls back from them and sent them skimming across the carpet again, he thought, 'What the heck! A man's got to have some playtime, hasn't he?' and rolled on to his back, for the cats to use him as their own, personal, feline bouncy castle, a particularly favoured activity of Tar Baby's. He seemed to know how heavy he was, and really seemed to relish pouncing, full weight, on his owner's stomach.

In The Ox and Plough in Steynham St Michael, the village worthies had assembled, as if by telepathy, to discuss what was apparently going on in their midst. Of course, it had probably been the visits of PC Green and PC Starr that had prompted them all to visit this watering hole, but it seemed strange, nonetheless to all involved that they should all have decided to visit the pub on the same night, and at approximately the same hour.

Not one of them had considered giving their custom to The Fox, although this licensed house was more or less the same distance from some of their homes. They had met in The Ox and Plough for a long time, until the beginning of the year but, after the unfortunate events that occurred then, many of them had stopped going out for a drink, for it brought back too many memories.[3]

This evening, however, they had gathered, somewhat embarrassed, round the welcoming log fire, nobody mentioning how they used to meet there, another friend (now absented from them forever) with them, for friendly (usually) games of cards.

It was quiet in the pub, Tuesday night not being a favourite night for visits from its usual habitués, and it was Vernon Warlock who broke their awkward silence. 'Well, we all know why we've come here tonight. We've got another murder in our midst, but at least it wasn't one of ours, this time.'

'This used to be such a sleepy, quiet village before ...' but Dimity couldn't speak the name. She tried to continue, by adding, 'Except for the Littlemores, of course.'

There were noises of agreement, and heads nodded. Sitting together round the fire were Vernon Warlock, Charles Rainbird, Dimity Pryor, Bryony Buckleigh, and Monica and Quentin Raynor. Elizabeth Sinden and Craig Crawford had not made the sojourn out into the cold and darkness and were at this moment curled up in front of the fire in Elizabeth's home, Clematis Cottage.

'I thought I'd lost Quentin this afternoon,' said Monica, eager to break the further silence that had fallen, after Dimity's sudden silence, albeit followed by a coda. 'I got back to the

---

[3] See *Inkier than the Sword* again

office, and there was no sign of him whatsoever. The office wasn't locked, the closed sign wasn't turned round: no message or note, either. He seemed to have disappeared into thin air, and then when the police came to the door, I thought they'd come to tell me he was dead.'

'Silly old thing,' commented Quentin, stirring himself to life. 'I got a call to go out to look at a property that the owner said he wanted to put on the market, but when I got there, there was no one who knew what I was talking about. It must have been some silly sort of hoax,' he declared, his face red from the fire. 'Bloody kids messing about, I suppose, blast their socks!'

'Well, at least it probably stopped us from having another argument,' Monica said, now displaying a much more off-hand manner.

''S right!' agreed Quentin, and turned his attention back to his drink.

'Isn't it nice that Buffy – oops! Elizabeth – and Craig have got together?' asked Bryony Buckleigh. They make such a handsome couple, and such a better life for Elizabeth, after all the racketing around she used to do with a different man each week, it seemed to me.'

'He's just what she needed,' said Dimity, now over her moment of sorrow. 'A nice, steady young man, with a good solid profession behind him.'

'He's not that young,' sniped Monica, who was considerably older than Crawford's thirty-nine years, and a few years longer in the tooth than Quentin, but did her best to disguise her age and would have died rather than reveal her date of birth.

'Meow!' Vernon chided her. 'Put your claws away, dear.'

'Oh, no!' This last exclamation was from Charles Rainbird, who had remained silent throughout the conversation, so far. 'Look who's just come in,' and he nodded his head in the direction of the pub door.

Walking unsteadily through it were Malcolm and Amy Littlemore, the latter the un-steadier of the two. 'Evenin' all,' she shouted across the bar. 'Can we join yer? Got room for a little 'un, and 'er great big keeper?'

Vernon and Charles began to discuss the state of business in the worlds of books and antiques in an English village in November. In fact, it was only Dimity who looked in their direction, and she made up her mind instantly. 'I'm just off home. Just dropped in for a quick one, before having an early night. Help me sleep, you know?' she said, raising her voice slightly, so that her companions would understand her intentions.

There was a general stir of movement within the group and, suddenly, everyone had a perfectly reasonable excuse for why they had to go home early.

Just squiffy enough to be able to ignore a snub the size of an elephant, Amy and Malcolm made for the bar, settled themselves on high stools with only a little difficulty, and ordered their drinks from the barman, Malcolm commenting thoughtlessly, 'I could murder a pint.'

Chapter Nine

Wednesday 3rd November

Carmichael entered the office in a dreadful state the next morning, his clothes resembling those he had worn in his early days in plainclothes, unshaven, his hair sticking up in all directions. Without even a good morning, he slumped into his chair and dropped his head into his hands.

Falconer looked up from his desk, concerned, and asked, 'Whatever's up with you? It's not the baby, is it?'

Carmichael shook his head, but left it buried, still, in his enormous hands.

'Kerry?' Falconer tried again.

Carmichael's head moved from side to side again.

'The boys?' Falconer was running out of things to suggest.

'The dogs?' At this, Carmichael gave a howl of despair, and nodded.

'What's wrong with them?' asked Falconer, who had become, through no fault of his own, Uncle Tasty-Trousers in the eyes of Carmichael's two minute dogs.

Carmichael raised his head slowly, and turned to face the inspector. 'Do you want to know the bad news, or the really bad news, first?' he asked, his face screwed up in incomprehension.

'I think I'll take the bad news first, then we can work our way round to the really bad news afterwards,' replied the inspector, now very concerned for his sergeant.

'Fang's in pup!' Carmichael announced abruptly, looking away from Falconer again.

'He can't be! He's a boy, and you promised me months ago that you'd booked both of them into the vet's to have them done,' exclaimed the inspector.

'I had to cancel the appointment. Something came up,' explained the enormous sergeant, reduced to the age of a schoolboy by the perceived calamity.

'And you didn't remake it?'

'It didn't seem to matter, because they were both boys. They were sold to us as boys, and now it turns out that Fang's a girl.'

'Carmichael!' Falconer exclaimed, with disgust. Did you never look?'

'I didn't like to, sir. It seemed somehow rude to just turn them upside down and look at their privates.

'And Mr Knuckles is the father?'

'We're almost certain he is.'

'So, what's the problem? It'll be great for the boys to have some puppies in the house to play with. If they're big enough for them to find, that is. And you can always find them good homes when they're weaned.'

'I know,' Carmichael replied, looking even more despairing, 'but they won't have gone by the time the baby's born. They'll still be with their mum, and I don't know if it's hygienic to have a load of tiny puppies around with a new-born baby in the house.'

'You'll love them when they're born, and you'll cope. The boys will be delighted to be on puppy guard, and your Kerry can cope with anything.'

Carmichael's face brightened a little at Falconer's confidence in the ability of his family to cope with any situation that life could throw at them.

'And in the future, remember, it's quite simple to sex an animal, Carmichael. You just look at its back end, and if it's a continental plug, it's a female, and if it's a pencil sharpener, it's a male.'

'That rude, sir?' replied Carmichael, looking embarrassed.

'No it's not, Sergeant. It's simple common sense. There is one thing you'll have to do, though,' said Falconer thoughtfully.

'What's that, sir?'

'Change that dog's name to Mistress Fang. We can't have a dog in her condition having a masculine-sounding name. Now, what's the really bad news?'

Carmichael's face crumpled again, and he dropped his face back into his hands, mumbling through his fingers, 'It's my ma!'

'She's not ill, is she?' asked Falconer, concerned, because he realised how fond of his mother Carmichael was.

'Sort of,' Carmichael replied, still muttering through his fingers.

'Take your head out of your hands so I can hear you properly,' he barked, in a very headmaster-ish manner. 'What's wrong with her?'

'She's in pup, too, sir. Or, well … you know what I mean. I know she's not over the hill, but I thought all that sort of thing was over, and now I find out I'm going to have a brother younger than my own little one. What am I going to do about it?'

Falconer almost burst out laughing, but suppressed it for the sake of Carmichael's feelings. 'Congratulate her, Sergeant. There's no point in getting all bent out of shape about it. So, your sibling will be younger than your son or daughter. So what! So, your parents are still having sexual relations. So what! It does happen between older people, you know, and I bet this wasn't planned.'

'I'm sure it wasn't sir, but I remember what my ma told me about her pelvic floor – remember I told you as how she reckoned it were riddled with woodworm?'

'Yes,' agreed the inspector, with a little moue of distaste, at the mention of such a portion of Mrs Carmichael Senior's sturdy body.

'Well, what if he falls out in the Co-op?'

'Oh, Carmichael, grow up! What if it does? As long as it's healthy, it doesn't matter a jot where she 'drops' it. Actually, you said 'he'. Has she had a scan?'

'She had to. The doctor thought she might have a growth.'

'Well, surely, this is much better news than that she may have cancer. Isn't it?'

'Yes, sir. You're quite right, sir.'

'Now, go and wash your face, and comb your hair while you're at it. Get yourself a cup of tea in the canteen. I'll see you back here in half an hour, and we won't mention this conversation again,' Falconer ordered him.

'Yes, sir. Thank you, sir.'

Dear God! thought the inspector. He seemed to spend more of his working hours doing social work these days, what with that overgrown child masquerading as a DC, Chris Roberts, and Carmichael coming over all emotional on him. It would be nice to get the chance to do a little detecting, instead of sorting out other people's problems for them.

This was Chris Roberts' third day at the college, and already he was getting used to the rhythms of student life. He got up just that little bit later and went to bed much later than he would usually. He was also surprised to realise that he was supposed to do the coursework, his tutor not knowing anything about his undercover placement, and that really was a pain.

There was to be no skiving off written work in Jocasta Gray's tutor group, and he had to spend quite a lot of what he had envisaged would be free time writing essays and making coherent notes from what he had jotted down in lectures.

He continued to be a bit of a hit with Elspeth, however, and was slowly being drawn into her little clique, which consisted of her best friend, Antonia Knightly; Jamie Huntley, also on the same course; Amelia Harrison, the history student; Aaron Trussler, the physical education student, and Daniel Burrows, the philosophy student.

Apart from that one little spat with Daniel Burrows a couple of days ago, everything seemed to be going well for him being accepted as a regular member of their little gang, and he felt he had managed to place himself very nicely for finding out about the 'special' group that he was here to uncover. After all, hadn't he already found a monk's habit with cowl in Elspeth's car?

He centred his attentions on her and managed to get her to agree to go for a coffee in town with him after the morning lecture ended, suggesting that they go to one of Market Darley's branches of the multitudinous coffee houses that had sprung up in recent years, because he wanted to get her away from her peers and see what he could winkle out of her when he'd got her on her own.

She was cautious when he first suggested it to her at registration, but as he worked on her over the morning she finally gave in and, at half-past eleven, they were sat in armchairs in front of a low table in Enrico's with lattes in front of them, she in a much more relaxed mood.

'You're a very mysterious girl.' he complimented her. 'You're really deep and unfathomable.' He was good at this sort of thing when he wanted to be, and didn't even feel the need to cross his fingers behind his back. 'There's a lot more to you than meets the eye,' he went on, noticing how her eyes were shining at this praise.

'Don't be silly!' she admonished him, but a blush was spreading steadily across her acne.

'No, I mean it. Not just the ordinary things like where do you come from, and how many brothers and sisters you have. You're deep, spiritually, and I want to know more about that side of you.'

'Come off it,' she said, turning her face away in embarrassment, at the onslaught of such welcome compliments.

'Look!' he said, deciding to get a bit artistic about the whole thing, 'If people were made of water, most of the people I know would just be puddles, if we looked at them spiritually. But, you – you'd be an ocean. You feel things I've never even dreamt of, and I want to know about them. I don't want to spend my life as a puddle. I want, at least, to aspire to a small lake.'

'Oh, Chris, you do have a nice turn of phrase, sometimes,' she spluttered.

'I want to share the things you believe in. I want to feel the things you feel. I want to penetrate the secret Elspeth, and feel her triumph,' he declared, now getting quite heated in his invention.

The word 'penetrate' had obviously got to her, because she

slid her hand across the table, and put it over his, pulling it away swiftly, as she realised what she had done without thinking.

'I'm sorry! I'm sorry!' she said, looking horror-stricken.

'Whatever are you sorry about?' asked Chris, struck by this sudden change in atmosphere.

'I touched your hand. Touching's not allowed, as it encourages sins of the flesh and fornication,' she explained.

'Then we'll just forget it happened,' he countered.

'Can we?' she asked, with unexpected hope in her voice.

'It'll be our little secret,' replied Chris, hoping that this was what she wanted to hear.

'Oh, Chris, you are wonderful,' she whispered, then looked away again, in embarrassment.

'Look,' he began, 'I know we can't touch, or kiss, or cuddle, or do any of those other things that we might want to do.' He was really excelling himself here. 'But we could be close in other ways, that no one could object to,' he cajoled her.

She thought about this for a moment, her gaze far away and dreamy, and it was all Chris could do not to laugh. 'Like what?' she eventually asked, gazing at him adoringly, then added, inconsequentially, 'I do love beards!'

'Now, this is probably going to sound a little racy to you,' he began, 'but if I can't physically get inside you, you could let me into your head; let me penetrate your thoughts. It would be our little secret.' He had purposely stressed the word 'penetrate' again and, although she leaned away from him looking shocked, he realised that he had phrased it correctly, and that she understood the offer to mean that mental fornication held a promise of physical things to come.

'Only if you promise to keep it deathly secret.' She was whispering again.

'Of course I will,' he whispered back. 'It will be our own special sort of intimacy.' Now he really was laying it on thick, but she was very naïve, and might just fall for it.

Clunk!

She had.

Very quietly and discreetly, she shuffled her armchair closer to his, and leant over, beginning to whisper in his ear, her eyes bright with excitement and daring. 'I've never done this kind of thing before,' she began, and he believed her; by his reckoning, it wasn't the only thing she'd never done before, either.

When Carmichael got home that night, he was still feeling a little emotional, when Dean, now a robust seven-year-old, and Kyle, a grown-up eight, came up to him with serious faces, and asked if they could ask him a question which was very 'importenant'.

'Of course you can, boys,' replied Carmichael, wondering what was coming, and whether he'd have to call Kerry to help him deal with it.

'Will we still call you Daddy Davey when the baby's borned,' asked Dean, his thumb rising to his mouth without thought, and showing that this was something very 'importenant' indeed to both of them.

'If you want to. Why?' replied Carmichael, not quite aware of where this conversation was going, now that it had started.

'What will the baby call you?' asked the elder of the two, looking worried.

'Why, Daddy, of course.'

Both their faces fell, and Dean looked like he was going to cry.

'Whatever's up with you two? I don't understand,' said Carmichael softly, now totally out of his depth.

'C-c-can't we call you Daddy, too?' whispered Dean, tears forming in the corners of his eyes, and threatening to spill down his cheeks.

Carmichael gathered them into his arms and hugged them close. 'Of course you can, you silly sausages. I'll always be your daddy. Of course you can call me Daddy. I'd like that very much. It would make me very happy!'

A small sniffling on his shoulders indicated that the boys wished to be released, and he let go his hold of them reluctantly.

They were all smiles now, Dean wiping his eyes and nose enthusiastically on the cuff of his jumper.

'Thanks, DADDY!' they cried out in unison, and skipped off to the kitchen to tell their mother of the momentous event that had just occurred. Carmichael, with all that had happened lately in his own family, was completely overcome, and had to make a dash for the bathroom where he could dry his tears without witness. That they were tears of joy was unquestionable, and a rush of love for his family overwhelmed him as he hid away from its other members for a few moments.

Chris could hardly believe his luck. Not only had Elspeth spilled the beans about the 'inner circle'; the advanced discussion group, but she had also invited him along for its meeting tonight, provided he came to her place first in the halls of residence because there was some preparation to do before they could be seen at the meeting. He hadn't a clue what she meant by preparation, but he was too elated to worry about little things like that, and presented himself at her room at ten o'clock, having left a note for his mother that he probably wouldn't be in before midnight.

She had let him through the outside door and was very circumspect, leading him up to her room. 'We're not supposed to have gentleman callers after ten,' she whispered in explanation, before yanking him through her door by the arm with quite a determined grip. He'd have to watch her, he thought, as he assessed her strength. If he wasn't careful, she might take advantage of him, and that didn't bear thinking about. How would he ever live that one down?

Fumbling under the single bed, she pulled out a medium-sized suitcase, and opened it to reveal the monk's habit he had seen the other day on the seat of her car. Underneath it was another one, identical. 'These are what we wear for the meetings,' she informed him, 'but we'll have to get changed in the car when we get there. I don't want anyone here seeing us. You'll just have to keep absolutely silent till I introduce you, otherwise there might be a bit of a ruckus. All right?'

'All right!' he agreed, feeling the atmosphere of secrecy and conspiracy flowing off her body in waves. 'I won't say a word, until you tell me it's OK.' Oh, boy! This was really the business. It looked like he was going to penetrate right to the centre of the group suspected of defacing the chapel in Steynham St Michael. What a triumph that would be for him!

'We'll go now,' she suddenly announced, lifting the suitcase ready for departure.

'You mean that I only came up here so that you could collect a suitcase?' he asked, puzzled. 'I could have met you outside, if you'd just come down alone with that thing.'

With an embarrassed glance at him, she made for the door without a word, and Chris realised that she had probably never had a man in her room before, and had taken the opportunity to at least have one step over the threshold in her conversations with others, when it offered itself.

'I'll follow you in my car,' he announced, realising that tonight he would witness whatever high jinks they got up to, although he realised, with a twinge of chagrin, that there was unlikely to be an orgy on the agenda.

In bed that night, Carmichael wept again as he told Kerry what had happened earlier, with the boys. 'I think they thought I might love the baby more than I loved them,' he told her, between heaving great sobs that shook his entire body.

With her arms round him, she reassured him that she believed that would be impossible. 'They came to the kitchen to tell me, but I knew something had really happened,' she said, 'when I heard them call you Daddy, when we were eating our supper. And when I put them to bed, they had such grins pasted on their faces, I suspected that something had made them more than usually happy. They really love you, Davey, and so do I, for that matter.'

Carmichael's fit of weeping gradually tailed off, and he laid there, his head on Kerry's shoulder, wondering afresh at how his life had changed over the last year and a half.

Chapter Ten

Thursday 4th November

Falconer arrived in his office the next morning to find several messages waiting for him. One was a report of a not quite sober phone call, late the evening before, of the presence of hooded figures in Steynham St Michael, but as this was from Amy Littlemore, he didn't put visiting her at the top of his priority list.

The second message had been from Chris Roberts' mother, reporting that, although Chris had left a note declaring that he would not be back until midnight or so, he hadn't come home at all, or phoned, and she was worried about him. He wasn't answering his mobile phone, and his car was still not back.

The third was a report of a car found burnt out in a field, about a mile north of Steynham St Michael. It had not been recovered yet and therefore not identified, but it was thought to be a Mini, colour, possibly green. There had been no reports of stolen vehicles, and this, together with Mrs Roberts report, made Falconer feel very uneasy.

A fourth message was from Monica Raynor, who reported that her husband Quentin had not come back home the night before. She had no idea where he was, and wanted to report him as a missing person. It looked like the misadventures of 'Mr Spliffy' would have to be put on hold while he sorted out this tangled web of events.

He was not given a moment, however, to collect his thoughts, because his telephone rang and, on answering it, he found that a doctor from the local hospital was on the other end of the line, informing them that they had a patient in a very bad way, admitted in the small hours, having suffered what appeared to be a very severe beating. The man had no clues to his identity on him, and they wondered if the police would care to take a look at him, to see if they could solve the mystery of his identity.

'Prioritise!' he thought. The mysterious hooded figures could wait, as they were probably only a symptom of DTs, brought on by an over-active imagination on the part of Amy Littlemore, off on another of her frequent alcoholic binges.

The burnt-out car could also wait, although he was aware that DC Roberts drove a green Mini. Quentin Raynor had probably stayed out all night with one of his frequent 'lovelies', if he was currently playing his wife at her own game.

The patient in the hospital was a different matter, however, and his sudden feeling of impending disaster was compounded by the fact of that burnt-out car.

As Carmichael swept into the office, Falconer instructed him, 'Don't bother to take off your coat. We're off to the hospital to visit a chap who was badly beaten last night, and hasn't been identified yet. I've got a bad feeling about today. I feel as if we're on the brink of disaster, and if I were superstitious, I'd probably be touching wood like mad by now.'

As they left the officer, Carmichael did lean over and touch the wooden frame of an old upright chair. It wasn't that he was at all superstitious. He just liked to cover all possibilities.

A Dr Singh conducted them to the ITU, and over to a bed where a figure was covered to the neck with just an arm outside the sheet, showing the needle where medication dripped into the body from several bottles suspended from a metal stand. The head was swathed with bandages and, for the moment, a ventilator was breathing for it.

'This is the man I telephoned about,' announced Dr Singh, indicating the figure in the bed. 'He had nothing on him from which we could identify him.'

Approaching the bed apprehensively, Falconer and Carmichael became aware that they did recognise the figure, and that it was DC Chris Roberts, last seen going undercover at the college.

'It's all right, Doctor: we know him. I'd like to know all you can tell me about how he came to be admitted, and what his current status is, medically,' Falconer informed the slightly built man in the white coat standing beside him.

'Why don't you come along to my office, and we'll see what sort of story we can patch together,' suggested Dr Singh, and they followed him out through the double doors on the tortuous journey to his designated office.

Once sat down, Dr Singh pecked at the keyboard of his computer until he was satisfied that he had gathered all the information that was available, then turned his attention to the two whey-faced policeman, who stared at him anxiously from the other side of his desk.

'It would seem,' he started, as Carmichael remembered to get out his notebook, 'that the gentleman was admitted by ambulance about 2.30 a.m. His body seems to have been dumped by the side of the Steynham St Michael to Market Darley road, and left for dead.

'A passing driver noticed it and stopped, then immediately dialled 999 to summon an ambulance. He had a blanket in his car, fortunately for the patient, with which he covered him, or he might have died of hypothermia. It was a very cold night last night, and we don't know how long he'd been lying there.'

'Do you have a record of who reported it?' asked Falconer, wondering who the passing Samaritan might have been.

'Unusually, yes we do. It was a Dr Philip Christmas, whom I believe is known to you. He said he'd been called out to a patient about one o'clock, and was on his way home.'

Falconer turned to Carmichael. 'Did Doc Christmas meet DC Roberts or not? I can't remember. My head's in a complete spin.

'I can't remember either, sir,' Carmichael replied, mirroring the anxious expression of the inspector.

'Even if he had met the patient before, it's possible he wouldn't have recognised him,' Dr Singh informed them. 'Our staff have made a good job of cleaning him up, and what with

95

the lack of light, and the lateness of the hour, I don't think that his own mother would have recognised him. He looks considerably better now, even though the swelling is, naturally, more pronounced than it was.'

'But how is he?' Falconer asked. 'What are his injuries, and have you any idea how they were caused?'

'I expect an opinion from an expert like the uniquely experienced Dr Christmas would answer your second question with more accuracy than I,' he replied. 'And, as for his injuries, he has several broken ribs, a broken wrist, a small fracture of the skull, and severe bruising all over his body. We hope he will be able to be taken off the ventilator in the next forty-eight hours, but a lot depends on his head injury.

'He'll be going for a CAT scan within the hour, so that we can see whether there is any bleeding or swelling to the brain, and we'll just have to take things from there. I'm sorry I can be of no further help to you, gentlemen. A lot depends on the scan as to how we assess his chances of making a full recovery.'

After thanking the doctor for his time and trouble, they left his office in a somewhat subdued mood, Falconer announcing that he would give Doc Christmas a ring as soon as they were outside, and ask him if he could call in to see Roberts after his morning duties were completed.

The drive back to the station was accomplished in complete silence; Carmichael again counting his blessings and contrasting his life to that of the poor figure that was inhabiting that hospital bed in the ITU; Falconer, because he knew he would have to break the news to Mrs Roberts. DC Roberts was, to his knowledge, an only child, and his mother was widowed, she herself recovering from a stroke. What would her life be like without her son? he wondered. And he knew he'd have to be the one to visit her, because he was the one responsible for her son being undercover as a student. In essence, it was his fault that Chris had been so badly beaten, and he'd just have to take his lumps – though not physical, like the ones Chris had suffered – and get on with it.

When he got back to the office, he found that the landlord of the Ox and Plough, Mike Welland, had phoned. Apparently his German Shepherd had wanted to go out to conduct some 'private business' at about eleven o'clock, and he had taken it down Tuppenny Lane to use the bit of waste ground next to the now-closed library.

As he turned down Tuppenny Lane and passed the chip shop, he could have sworn he'd seen a cowled figure drifting through the graveyard of the chapel. It had made the hairs on the back of his neck stand up at the time, because the weather had developed into a freezing fog, which made the scene appear supernatural.

He soon pulled himself together, however, and, keeping a tight rein on the dog, went to investigate. When he reached the chapel, though, there was no one to be seen, and he had dismissed it at first as a figment of his imagination, then changed his mind as his dog began to growl, its hackles rising.

That was enough for him, and he dragged the poor animal straight back to the pub, where it was subjected to the indignity of having to do its 'business' at the back of the pub, for Mike to clear away and dispose of. He had then heard about Amy's 'hallucination', when she came in for a quick snifter before she opened the craft shop in the High Street, and began to wonder if what he had seen had been real.

That was when he had decided to report it. They'd found a dead body in that chapel, and if he could be of any assistance in finding the workman's murderer, he would do anything he could to achieve that end.

That afternoon, after his very distressing visit to Mrs Roberts, Falconer informed Carmichael that they were off to Steynham St Michael again. 'We need to have another look at that chapel, and the graveyard, to see if there are signs of anyone having been there as recently as last night, and we need to have a word with both Mrs Littlemore and Mike Welland from the Ox and Plough about what they reported they saw. And I suppose we'll have to call in on Monica Raynor, to see if Quentin's shown-up, no doubt looking shame-faced and acting very apologetically,' he informed his sergeant.

'How did Mrs Roberts take it?' asked Carmichael, somewhat tactlessly.

'How do you think she took it, Carmichael? I turned up on her doorstep, and informed her that the son, who had come down here from Manchester to help look after her while she recovered from a stroke, had been beaten almost to death and left for dead by the side of the road. She took it very badly, if you really want to know, and I had to fetch in a neighbour to sit with her. That's how it went, Carmichael, thank you very much for asking.'

'Sorry, sir,' apologised Carmichael, who had become aware of his *faux pas* just an instant after the question was out of his mouth, his brain being a bit slow today after all the emotion of the day before.

'I'm sure you didn't mean anything by it,' Falconer replied. 'It's only natural curiosity. It's just that it was a very uncomfortable visit, and I suppose I'm a bit edgy after it. I'm sorry I snapped at you.'

'No worries, sir,' said Carmichael, in complete understanding.

Their first visit was to Badgers Sett in response to the call from Monica Raynor but, getting no answer from the house, they moved up the Market Darley Road to the estate agent's office, wondering at her going into work when Quentin had, to all intents and purposes, disappeared into thin air.

The windows of the outer office were fogged with condensation, the building not yet possessing double glazing, and their minds were set at rest immediately when they discerned two figures, both sat at desks, one on the telephone, the other with its eyes glued to a computer screen.

After entering, Falconer waited for Monica to put down the phone, before he allowed his temper to show itself. 'I see the wanderer is back, Mrs Raynor. You might have had the courtesy to let us know, before we set a manhunt in motion.'

'I'm so sorry, Inspector,' she replied. 'I meant to phone as soon as he came wandering in, an hour after I phoned the station, but he was so distressed and cold that I completely forgot about it.'

'So what happened, then?' asked Falconer. 'He looks perfectly OK, now,' he added, reining back his displeasure for long enough to hear her story.

At this point Quentin took up the tale, seeing as he was the sole protagonist in it. 'I went out to measure up a house just north of Market Darley,' he explained, 'and as it was brass monkeys outside, and the house was empty and unheated, I decided to drop into the pub in the town, and get warm, before I drove home – The Royal Oak it was, just opposite the main post office.

'Well, one thing led to another, and I decided to stay on for a bite to eat. The next thing I knew, it was closing time, so I thought I'd better get on my way, or Monica would be worried about me. I only got just over a mile, though, when the ruddy car broke down.

'I had a look under the bonnet, but I don't know a thing about cars. I checked the oil, and that seemed all right, and I checked the petrol, and it wasn't that, so I didn't know what to do. That was when I found out my phone battery was out of juice. I was going to phone Monica, and have her come out and fetch me, or get the AA to come out to sort it out, but I couldn't contact anybody.

'There was no way I fancied walking all the way back to the pub at that hour of night, on an unlighted road in the freezing cold, and with that fog. Of course, I gave it a go, but within a couple of yards it was so slippery I fell flat on my back and completely winded myself. I could hardly see my hand in front of my face, and I thought, if something big comes down this little road, in these weather conditions, I'm going to be minced – I must admit to not being the most adventurous and courageous of men, Inspector – so I went back to the car, got the emergency blanket,' (*for one of his 'lovelies', no doubt!*) 'and decided it was safer to stay where I was and hope to attract the attentions of a passing motorist, and hope one passed before the morning.

'By golly, it was a cold night. Fortunately I'd taken an overcoat and scarf with me, and I had the extra blanket from the boot, so I wrapped up as best as I could, and spent a wakeful night, wishing I could turn the blasted engine on when it got too cold, and trying to doze in between times.'

'He was absolutely frozen when he got in,' put in Monica, for once, showing genuine concern for her husband. 'I told him to take a hot shower and go straight to bed, but he insisted in coming in to work, even if it was just for the morning.'

'So, who did eventually come to your rescue, then?' Falconer queried.

'There was a passing milk-float, about six o'clock. He didn't have a mobile with him, but he said he'd pop into the first pub he came to on his rounds, and promised to stop there when he delivered the milk and get the landlord to send out the AA. It took over two hours for someone to find me and get the problem fixed, and by then I was chilled to the bone,' he concluded.

'And where was he headed?' asked Falconer.

'Oh my God!' exclaimed Quentin, slapping a hand to his forehead. 'He must have been on his way here, to Steynham St Michael. I was so cold I wasn't thinking straight. I could have got a lift with him back home, albeit it a slow one, and not had to carry on my vigil, waiting for the AA to show up. What a dick I am!'

'I presume, then, that he stopped at the Ox and Plough,' commented Falconer, trying to suppress a smile. At this detail, Monica's hearty laughter echoed round the office, filling it with the sound of her realisation of exactly what Quentin had done. 'He could've dropped you off right outside our door,' she spluttered.

Ignoring her, her husband responded to Falconer's comment. 'No doubt you're right on the button, and that's just across the road from home. How am I ever going to live this one down? I'll be the laughing stock of the village!'

'Thank you,' said Falconer, still fighting his mirth. 'We'll have a word with the landlord of the Ox and Plough, and the milkman, if you can remember which dairy it was from, to save us time, just to confirm what you have told us. It was the Royal Oak you visited in Market Darley, wasn't it?'

'Yes, but that's a bit strong, isn't it?' asked Quentin. 'I was only broken down, not robbing the Bank of England.'

'Not really, Mr Raynor. Last night was a busy night, and a number of incidents occurred in the vicinity, which it is our job to investigate. If, however, your story is the unembroidered truth, then you have nothing to worry about, have you? I shall have to go now, as I have a number of other calls to make. Did you say which dairy the milk-float came from?'

'I'm sorry, I didn't notice,' mumbled Quentin, feeling very embarrassed.

'Never mind: we'll track it down for you,' said Falconer, not knowing whether Quentin would see this as a threat or a relief. What if Quentin had been with one of his 'bits of skirt'? No, he was making fiction out of fact. He didn't really believe that Quentin was lying. It was just such a coincidence, so many things happening on the same road in one night: what with the car being burnt out just near it, Quentin breaking down, and Doc Christmas finding Chris's unconscious body.

It was a wonder the doctor hadn't noticed Mr Raynor's broken-down car, but then a man can't be expected to be aware of every detail in his peripheral vision as he concentrates on the road ahead, and it had been a foul night, what with the freezing fog and the plummeting of the temperature to leave the countryside dusted with a thick frost. It would have been enough of a job just to keep to the right side of the road, and not slip on any of the black ice that had developed as the night wore on.

They called next into the Ox and Plough to speak to Mike Welland, landlord of that licensed premises. The pub was closed now for the afternoon, as it wasn't one that had opted for all-day opening, but a side door bore an electric doorbell, which Falconer duly rang in the hope of raising some attention from inside.

Within a few seconds, the door was opened by a large man with sparse greying hair combed across his bald patch, and his belly hanging over the belt of his trousers. 'Mr Welland?' enquired Falconer, sizing up the man and deciding how perfectly built he was to cope with any trouble that arose when about his business of providing alcoholic beverages for his customers should they get a bit exuberant in drink.

He bade them enter, and offered them, surprisingly, a cup of coffee, which they gladly accepted. Sitting in the deserted bar, sipping their scalding drinks, Mr Welland confirmed that the milkman had asked him to send an SOS to the AA for a man, early that morning, and he had obligingly done so. That was the extent of his knowledge, having no idea whether the AA had responded or not. Without hesitation, he confirmed that the milk float had been from the Home Farm Dairy, a Market Darley-based supplier, who had always provided the pub's milk during his tenure there.

When asked about the events of the previous night, however, he put his coffee cup down on the table with a shaky hand, spilling a few drops as he did so. 'That was damned scary,' he informed them. 'I was just taking Jake – that's my dog – for a little walk, seeing as he had something on his mind that wouldn't wait till morning. Well, I often go down Tuppenny Lane, and let him do his 'business' on that bit of waste ground beside the library. Patience was always at me to clear it up and take it home with me, but I can't stand the feel of it through the plastic bag. It makes me want to throw up.

'Anyway, off I went last night, turned into Tuppenny Lane as usual, but after a few steps – I was just passing the chip shop – I thought I saw movement in the churchyard beside the chapel, and I stopped dead. The light wasn't good, and that foul freezing fog had begun to come down so visibility wasn't great, but it looked to me as if there were a monk or something, creeping round the gravestones.

'It damned near made me do what I'd brought Jake out to do, I can tell you,' he informed them, with a rather false laugh. 'Then, I thought, big man like me, I ought to take a look, so I walked on a bit further, peering through the mist to try to catch sight of it again, but it had gone; like it had just disappeared into thin air. Jake growled a bit, but I didn't hang around. I'd seen enough for one night, so I gave a tug on the lead, and we headed back here, and I let him do his 'doin's' in the backyard.'

'And you're absolutely sure of what you saw, Mr Welland?' asked Falconer.

'If I wasn't, Jake's growling would've confirmed it for me. I might not have been positive that there was someone there made of flesh and blood, but he was.'

'That's been very helpful, Mr Welland. Thank you for your time,' said Falconer, concluding their visit.

'Can I get you another coffee before you go?' the landlord asked.

'No, thank you. We have other calls to make, and I don't want to take up any more of your time,' Falconer replied, heading for the side door through which they'd entered.

Before they could take their leave of the pub, however, a vast hairy figure bounded out of a now-open door, and landed with its paws on Falconer's shoulders, drooling happily. 'That's our Jake, announced Mr Welland proudly, close on their heels. 'He's a friendly fellah, ain't you, boy?'

The dog looked lovingly into Falconer's eyes and panted its approval of its new playmate. 'I wonder if you could just ...' Falconer pleaded.

'Come on down, Jake. The gentleman doesn't have time to play. Maybe he'll come back another day and throw a stick for you.'

As Welland explained evidence of Jake's friendliness, Jake was getting rather too friendly with Falconer's crotch, sniffing deliriously and wagging his tail, while Falconer did a sort of rumba with his hips, trying to avoid the prods of the dog's large nose. Jake's owner, of course, noticed nothing.

When they were finally outside, Carmichael grinned at the inspector's discomfiture, and said innocently, 'I didn't know you could dance, sir!'

'Carmichael.'

'Yes, sir?'

'Shut up!'

'Sorry, sir.'

Straight back to the business in hand, Falconer said, 'I suppose we'd better pay a visit to Mrs Littlemore now, then. What do you think, Carmichael?'

'I think her surname's very apt,' replied Carmichael in a gloomy voice at the prospect of more time spent in the company of an habitual drunk.

'How's that?' asked the inspector.

'Well, I bet every time someone asks her if she'd like anything more to drink, she always says, 'Oh, just a little more,' and that's her, isn't it, sir? – A Littlemore!'

'How very perceptive and witty of you, Carmichael. I shall have to watch you, or you'll be turning into Noel Coward.' Falconer declined to mention his own similar observation of earlier.

'I dunno who he is, sir, but I'm very happy being me at the moment, and I don't want to change anything,' replied Carmichael with great sincerity, if not complete understanding of what the inspector had said to him.

There was no reply to their ringing and knocking at the door of the Littlemores' residence, and it suddenly dawned on Falconer that they might actually be at work in their craft shop. He'd usually had contact with them outside business hours, and wasn't sure how strictly they adhered to these. Today, though, they might just be at work, and in a fit state to answer questions. That would certainly make their job a good deal easier.

The craft shop was, indeed, open, although it had no customers at the moment, and the two policemen had the place to themselves. Both Littlemores had mugs of something hot and steaming in front of them, and when offered similar refreshment, Falconer assented to their offer without a second thought.

It was only when he took a hearty swill from the mug that Amy had handed to him, that he realised what they had been given, and nearly choked. 'Goodness, that's strong!' he declared, and motioned to Carmichael not to drink his. 'He's driving!' he explained, setting his mug down on the counter, determined not to have another mouthful. It may have once been hot chocolate, but it was now about forty per cent brandy if his taste buds were any judge. So much for finding the couple perfectly sober!

'Business seems to be very quiet,' Falconer commented, as a sort of polite introduction to their visit.

'Always is, these days,' replied Malcolm, taking a swig from his mug.

'We was thinkin' of retirin' and, per'aps, openin' a little country pub,' Amy chimed in.

Falconer nearly choked on his drink, and Carmichael had to pretend to be looking at the stock in the window display, while he blew his nose noisily into his handkerchief, to smother his laughter. A pub? These two? It didn't bear thinking about. They'd have drunk the business dry in no time.

Regrouping his thoughts, Falconer said, 'I'd like to talk to you, Mrs Littlemore, about what you reported seeing last night in the area of Tuppenny Lane.'

This was her moment to shine for the police. Puffing her chest out in pride, Amy launched herself on her dramatic story. 'I dunno what time it was, but Malcolm and I had just had a little discussion,' she began. Argument, more like, thought Falconer) 'Anyway, I went outdoors for a breath of fresh air, and to clear me 'ead a bit, 'cos I'd 'ad a few glasses of wine. Anyway, I was toddlin'' (*Staggering*!) 'round the garden, when I seen this shape – 'orrible it was – like somethin' outta one o' them 'Ammer 'Orror films. It was like old Rasputin 'isself 'ad come back to life, an' was stalkin' the village.

'Then, when I took another look, there was a whole crowd of 'em, all in that there cemetery, millin' around as if they was 'avin' a party, like. Well, I'd seen enough, at that point, so I shot back indoors, and told Malcolm about it, but he didn't believe me. By the time I'd convinced 'im to come out an' 'ave a butcher's, they'd all gone, and 'e said I must 'ave imagined it, but I didn't, Inspector. They was real!'

'I believe you, Mrs Littlemore,' he informed her, causing her husband's mouth to drop open in surprise. 'You weren't the only one to see something of the sort in the environs of the chapel last night, and I believe every word you've told me,' he informed her, followed by the thought; except for the number of figures she had thought she'd seen. He'd probably have to halve that, to take into account the double vision with which she was probably suffering at the time.

'And you really don't know what time it was that you went outside?' he asked, hopefully.

'The ten o'clock news was over, when I wen' out. I know that, 'cos we watched the weather forecast. It wasn't too long after that, but, as I said, I'm not too sure of the actual time.'

That would more or less confirm Mike Welland's story that there had been something going on in the chapel grounds the night before, but Mrs Littlemore claimed to have seen several cowled figures, and Mike Welland only one. Had one stayed on for some other purpose, or was this figure just the last to leave whatever they were up to in the chapel grounds?

'Perhaps we ought to go and look in the chapel, sir: see if there's any new defacement of the walls,' suggested Carmichael.

'I think we'll leave that to the good ladies and gentlemen who have been working so hard to get the chapel refurbished, to make that discovery. To tell you the truth, Carmichael, I've had enough of this village for today. I'd rather get back to Market Darley, and see how Roberts is doing, wouldn't you?' The inspector was still feeling twinges of guilt about Roberts' condition.

'Definitely, sir. He's one of ours, after all, and what's that compared to a bit of paint on an old chapel wall?'

Halfway back to the market town, Falconer took a quick glance in Carmichael's direction, and just murmured, 'A pub!', then had to pull off the road, because they were both laughing so much at the thought of the Littlemores running a licensed establishment. It would be like putting a fox in charge of the hen-house.

Chapter Eleven

Friday 5th November

The next morning it was confirmed that the burnt-out car did, in fact, belong to Chris Roberts, and the hospital had confirmed that he was now fighting his way towards consciousness. The CAT scan had revealed nothing sinister with regard to inter-cranial bleeding, swelling of the brain, or possible permanent damage, and he had been taken off the ventilator first thing that morning and was now breathing for himself.

Sightings of the ice-cream van now referred to as 'Mr Spliffy' had been reported by a number of patrol vehicles, and there was a pattern emerging on Falconer's wall map now. Although the sightings, literally pin-pointed over a period of time during the day were wildly at random, there seemed to be a general area where they started in the morning and ended, sometimes very late in the evening.

Falconer felt that he was moving in on whoever was peddling dope under the cover of selling ice-cream, and wondered if the vendor actually kept some real ice-cream and lollies on board, in case he got some kosher customers. He supposed that whoever it was would have to, otherwise someone would have been bound to complain, and it would have come to the ears of the local community police officers and passed on to the station.

Given the date, Carmichael's thoughts were on a totally different subject, and he was hardly able to conceal his excitement as he contemplated the happy hours he would spend in his garden, lighting a bonfire and burning the guy he and the boys had made, then letting off the fireworks he had purchased specially for the occasion, and safely stored in the loft, away from prying eyes and hands. Kerry had promised that they could bake potatoes in the embers of the bonfire, and cook sausages held to the flames on long twigs, and he felt as if he were seven years old again.

When Monica Raynor called to say that Quentin had disappeared again overnight, Falconer was not in the best of moods, and suggested that, as Quentin was an adult, it was not advisable to start a search for him until he had been gone for forty-eight hours, and asked if he had charged his phone, and made sure the car was in working order before he'd left.

At that point, he had hung up on her, exasperated by Carmichael's capers round the office, and his continued guilt at the beating Roberts had suffered. If he had let the call last a little longer, he would have discovered that Quentin had not taken his car. It was still outside the house, and his mobile phone was sitting on the kitchen table, not even switched on, but Monica made no second call, lulled into a false sense of security at the mention of waiting a little longer before doing anything official.

In the end he sent Carmichael home early, asking him to pass a little time by visiting Roberts' bedside again, and not to let him, Falconer, set eyes on him until the following morning, when his gunpowder plot would have been executed.

He, as the only sane half of the partnership left today, would have to carry on the investigation on his own. Roberts would have kept notes, and they would probably be at his mother's house. If he called there, he could take a look at what the detective constable had written up so far, and that might give him an idea of whom he should interview at the college.

It would seem that Roberts' cover had been blown somehow, and the only way to tackle things now was to get some names and start conducting interviews at the college himself. Much as he had no appetite for looking Mrs Roberts in the eye, he knew his duty, and set off for her home feeling like a heel. His discussion with her would not be a pleasant one, but he had to face up to it if he wanted to get his hands on her son's notes.

It was still a toss-up in his mind whether this murder was down to this 'cult thingy' that had grown at the college, or whether it was a purely village affair. He couldn't make up his mind which he favoured after the events of earlier that year, but thinking about that time certainly took his mind off his coming ordeal on his drive to Chris's home.

The front door was answered by a neighbour, who said she had been looking in on Mrs Roberts since Chris's accident, and Falconer's guilt returned with a discernible thump in the region of his solar plexus. This was all his fault, and now he had to accept what was coming to him.

In the event, Mrs Roberts was very gracious about the matter, telling him that her son had understood that the job might prove dangerous at times, and that he had accepted this before joining the force. This, of course, only compounded Falconer's guilt, but he pressed on regardless, and she gave him permission to search for the notebook or books in Chris's room.

Although a relatively untidy person in his appearance, it seemed that Chris was impeccable in his living space, and the bedroom was as immaculate as a monk's cell, the two notebooks he had used sitting tidily on his bedside cabinet for easy access in the mornings. As he took them, Falconer wondered how long it would be before Chris woke up in his own bed again, and not just his own bed here, but his own bed where he actually lived, in Manchester.

He left the house with relief, firstly because his meeting with Mrs Roberts was over, and secondly because he knew he would find useful information in Chris's notes; and he couldn't wait to get back to the station to read them.

He spent the rest of the afternoon deciphering the hieroglyphics which the detective constable used for his notes, but did manage to glean confirmation of the names Chris had mentioned to him in one of his telephone reports, and he noted them down in his own notebook for interviews on the morrow: Elspeth Martin, Antonia Knightly, Amelia Harrison, Jamie Huntley, Aaron Trussler, and Daniel Burrows.

He'd ring the college in the morning to check their

timetables, and if it was not possible to find them at the college, which was likely, tomorrow being the weekend, to obtain either home addresses and telephone numbers. He'd had enough for today, however, and closed down his computer and left the building, becoming aware, as he walked to his car, of the bangs and whizzes of fireworks being let off in the early darkness of this time of year.

Saturday 6th November

Although Falconer was not officially down to work today, he had deemed it necessary to come in to follow up those names from DC Roberts' notebooks. No sooner had he reached his office, though, when the phone rang for him, twice: firstly Quentin Raynor, lost, and then Quentin Raynor found.

The first call was from Monica Raynor, to let him know that Quentin had still not shown up, and that he had not taken his car or his mobile phone with him when he went, and she wanted to officially report him as a missing person.

The second was from Vernon Warlock, who was at his home in Steynham St Michael, and had a very distressed Dimity Pryor with him. She had arrived almost hysterical at his front door about half an hour ago, and it had taken him all of that time to get her to tell him a coherent story.

'She's just been to the chapel, Inspector Falconer,' Vernon informed him. Vernon's house, Vine Cottage, was only two doors from Dimity's, and she had taken shelter with him, rather than go home on her own and report what she had discovered.

'It seems that no one had officially been to the chapel for days and, as she has the key, she thought she'd just look in on it. They were expecting the site manager, Dave Hillman, and the electrician, Bob 'Sparks' Stillman to turn up sometime, the electrician to do a final check on the re-wiring, and the site manager to sign off the job as completed, but they hadn't shown up, to her knowledge.

'When she got there, she put on the lights, it being so dark at this time of year, and the chapel being so dimly provided with daylight, and what she saw nearly caused her to faint clean away.'

'And what was it she saw, Mr Warlock?' asked Falconer, getting a bit fed up with the extraneous names and details with which Mr Warlock was providing him – no doubt just for dramatic effect.

'It was really very upsetting for someone of Dimity's sheltered upbringing,' he continued, but Falconer wasn't going to suffer too much of this embroidery.

'Just tell me what she found, sir, then I can get on with doing something about it,' he chided him.

'She found another body!' snapped Vernon Warlock, cross at his dramatic speech being thus foreshortened.

'Whose?' snapped Falconer, now all ears.

'Quentin Raynor's,' answered Warlock, pettishly. 'She said it was on the stone altar table, like the other one, but this one didn't have its head bashed in. It looked, in her opinion, as if Quentin had been badly beaten and died as a result – beaten to death, was how she described it to me.'

'Did she lock the chapel door when she left?' the inspector enquired anxiously.

There was a muffled moment as Vernon covered the mouthpiece with his hand, then his voice sounded clearly on the line. 'She said she did it automatically, before panicking completely and rushing round here.' Sounds of disagreement with this last statement came faintly over the line, but Falconer wasn't listening.

'I'll get there as soon as I can,' he promised, cutting the caller short, but before he had a chance to ring Carmichael, the internal telephone tinkled, and Bob Bryant informed him that Superintendent 'Jelly' Chivers had come in that morning, and would like to see him immediately, in his office.

As Carmichael wasn't in, Falconer allowed himself a fairly loud 'damn!' before leaving his office for that of the superintendent. What had he done, now? He couldn't think of anything for which he could be hauled over the coals, but if there had been the slightest hint that he had stepped out of line,

Chivers would find out about it and give him a good going over for it. Just for a split-second, he knew how Roberts felt, and then dismissed this thought as unworthy, given the physical injuries that the DC had sustained.

At his knock, a terse voice bade him enter. He opened the door, stepped into the lion's den, and then was turned to stone. Sitting opposite Chivers was someone he had only had brief glimpses of the last time he had investigated a case in Steynham St Michael, and whom he had hoped to meet properly for some time.

'Come in, do, man, and stop standing there like a rabbit caught in the headlights,' Chivers barked at him, and Falconer was suddenly aware that he had effectively become a statue. His limbs felt like lead, as he walked across the floor to the super's desk, his eyes glued to the figure seated opposite him.

'May I introduce you to Dr Hortense Dubois,' Chivers almost purred. It sounded like he appreciated the view as well. 'Dr Dubois has worked with us before, and is gaining a reputation as a psychological profiler,' Chivers explained.

'Dr Dubois, may I introduce you to Detective Inspector Harry Falconer, one of my most promising officers,' he concluded, and Dr Dubois rose to shake Falconer's hand.

He felt as if he were in a dream. Here, before him, stood the woman who had been the object of his desire for almost a year now, and he was actually shaking hands with her. She was tall: tall enough to look him in the eye, and he found the experience very unnerving. Her hair was plaited in near-black corn-rows, and her slim body was encased in a canary yellow wool suit, worn with a simple white silk blouse.

'Pleased to meet you,' she said, in a beautiful, slightly deep voice. 'I believe we almost met once before, on a previous case,' she stated, and he nodded dumbly, too thunder-struck to speak. 'And please call me 'Honey'. Everyone else does.'

Her voice was that of an angel, and her clothes contrasted so beautifully with her dark, perfect skin that he felt he would faint with ecstasy just being in her company. Her eyes were like liquid plain chocolate, her teeth as white as pearls, and her skin, oh! her skin; it was like superbly carved ebony. He honestly didn't believe that he'd ever seen someone so stunning.

For a very brief moment, he thought guiltily of Serena, whom he had met the year before, and from whom he had inherited Ruby and Tar Baby, and then dismissed such thoughts from his mind as irrelevant, now, given what had happened.[4]

So lost was he, in reverie, that it took Chivers' rather grating voice to rouse him to the present. 'Well, take a seat, man! I don't know what's wrong with you today, dithering at the door, and now standing in front of my desk, dithering again like an old woman.'

Falconer sat abruptly in the empty chair next to Dr Dubois', and tried to muster his wits. 'Dr Dubois is going to be working closely with you, to try to identify the type of person we're looking for in this case,' Chivers informed him.

He was in Heaven. He must have died and gone straight there. Was he really hearing the words that informed him that he was to be working closely with this vision of loveliness? With a shake of his head, he became instantly the professional that he was, announced that there had been another death in Steynham St Michael, and that he was just about to alert the necessary personnel to attend the scene.

'Off you go then. I only wanted to introduce you to Dr Dubois. You'll start working together on Monday morning,' Chivers informed him, and Falconer crossed the fingers of both hands under the desk in hope that they would not have solved the case by then, and thus deprive him of the chance to work alongside this enchanting creature.

When he returned to his own office he found that not only were his hands shaking, but his legs were as well. Boy, had she had an effect on him! Now, he must phone Carmichael, and get Bob Bryant to rustle up suitable personnel to kick this second death into action (which didn't sound right in his mind, but *he* knew what he meant).

When he got through to Carmichael and told him about the

---

[4] See *Choked Off*

second body in the chapel, something in his voice must have betrayed his mood, because Carmichael asked him, in a slightly puzzled voice, 'If Quentin Raynor is dead – murdered – why do you sound so happy, sir?'

'It must be a bad line, Carmichael,' he said, and hung up before he broke out into peals of joyous laughter. He'd keep himself in control long enough to meet Carmichael at the chapel as soon as he could get there, but for now, he was chuckling away like a madman at his unexpected good fortune.

Falconer drove to Steynham St Michael like a recently qualified driver, so disconcerted was he by what had happened just before he left the station, and Carmichael was already waiting for him when he arrived, as was Dr Christmas. The speedy arrival of the SOCO officers meant that they were already inside, doing what they needed to do to gather evidence and assess the scene.

'What took you so long, sir?' asked Carmichael, as Falconer locked his car.

'Traffic,' was the inspector's completely untrue answer to this enquiry.

Carmichael's next question was very close to the bone, however. 'You *are* happy! You said it was just the telephone line, but you're grinning from ear to ear like the Cheshire Cat. Sir,' Carmichael added at the last minute.

'Nothing to do with this death,' Falconer told him, trying to resume a more normal countenance. 'When can we have a look? It's freezing out here.'

'They're just coming out now, sir. They must be finished inside. Mind you, they've still got to go through the graveyard to see if there's anything helpful to be found there.'

'In this light?'

'They've brought their own lighting, sir, just like at the theatre,' Carmichael answered, and Falconer became aware that Philip Christmas was also standing there, and that he had totally ignored him in his excited state of mind.

'Hello there, Doc. We meet again,' he greeted him, holding

114

out his hand to him.

'A damned sight too often for my liking,' replied the doctor, pulling a face. Although he loved his job, he had to grumble a little, just for verisimilitude. 'It looks like we can go in now; see what all the fuss is about, eh?' he concluded, practically rubbing his hands together at the thought of another body.

Inside the chapel was, if possible, even colder than outside. The lights were switched on, but the place was far from bright. At the far end of it they could see something lying across the altar table, like an over-sized turkey that just wouldn't fit on the carving dish, but there was also some fresh writing on the wall, for the first time in black paint, and in English: *Be sure your sins will find you out.*

'Well, better get this over with,' pronounced Christmas, with enough relish to garnish a whole turkey in itself. 'See what we've got, eh?'

Falconer and Carmichael followed him slowly down the aisle, not rushing to see what they had got like kids at Christmas. Falconer would be willing to bet that a young Philip Christmas would have had all the wrapping paper off his presents well before dawn on Christmas Day.

'This is a merry amalgamation we've got here,' announced Christmas. 'A positive marriage of methods. Look!' and he pointed to the face of the body – the thing that had been Quentin Raynor.

The face was bloodied and beaten, and some of the limbs seemed to sit at unnatural angles. 'Placed on the altar, just like the first victim,' pronounced Christmas, 'but beaten to death, as had obviously been the intention with your poor DC Roberts. And it looks like the same weapon was used for both beatings,' he concluded, pointing to something very small embedded in the facial tissue.

'If I'm not mistaken, that looks like a tiny spicule of wood, and I'd say it was something very like, or identical to, a baseball bat, that was used on him: nice and long for force, and thick enough to do some real damage.'

'How do you sleep at night?' Falconer asked the medical

man, now completely sobered-up from his earlier intoxication, his mind back on the job at hand.

'Like a baby, Harry,' confirmed the doctor. 'Like a baby.'

'Do you mind if I go outside, sir?' asked Carmichael, turning a whey-faced countenance on the inspector.

'You go and get some fresh air, Carmichael. I'll do everything that's necessary in here.'

With a sigh of relief, Carmichael turned and fled down the aisle, like a bride who has changed her mind at the very last minute, and hurtled into the cold clean air outside the chapel. He sometimes suffered from a weak stomach and he could feel a 'chuck' coming on just looking at that battered, bruised, and swollen countenance inside, but he didn't have long to wait before Falconer joined him.

'Come on,' said the inspector. Let's get ourselves off to interview poor Dimity Pryor.'

They found Dimity still at Vernon's cottage, sipping a hot toddy, which the cottage's owner had suggested, both against the cold and for shock. She was sitting in an armchair beside the fire, a rug tucked across her lap and under her knees.

'Good morning,' Falconer greeted her. 'I'm sorry you've had such a shock. Are you sure you'll be all right?' he asked.

'I'll be fine, provided I can sit in here with Vernon for company for the next hour or so, then I'll have to get myself off home. Housework doesn't do itself, no matter what anyone says,' she replied, giving him a weak smile. 'It was that nice doctor that called in for the keys,' she informed him, and Falconer was grateful that Philip had thought things through and worked out where Dimity was, for although he had told the doctor that Dimity had discovered the body, he had not told her that she was at Vernon's cottage.

'Can I get you anything, gentlemen?' asked Vernon, at his most obsequious.

'I don't think so, Mr Warlock, but a bit of privacy would be appreciated while we interview Miss Pryor here. I know it's a bit of a cheek, this being your home ...' He let the sentence trail off, and it worked.

'That's quite all right, Inspector. I've got plenty of chores to deal with in the kitchen, so I'll leave you to get on with your job,' he informed them. And, no doubt, one of those things was eavesdropping at a not-quite-closed door, thought Falconer, as he rose to make sure that the adjoining door was tightly fastened.

He turned back to find Carmichael squatting at Dimity's side, looking at her compassionately. 'Poor Miss Dimity,' he murmured, and took her small, birdlike hands in his enormous paws; his way of offering comfort. How was it, thought Falconer, that Carmichael always reacted instinctively like this, yet such a thing would never have crossed his own mind? He didn't know the answer to this one; he just knew that, for all his size, Carmichael had a calming effect on people who were upset or shocked.

The inspector saw Dimity's face break into a watery smile, as she gazed into Carmichael's concerned face, and he took a seat opposite her, nodding his head to Carmichael to seat himself, ready to take notes, and fixed his gaze on the now-calmer woman sitting on the other side of the fireplace.

'I know how ghastly this must be for you, Miss Pryor, but sadly you're an old hand at this sort of thing now, and you know the procedure. I have to ask you about what happened earlier, and you need to give me as much detail as possible so that we can catch whoever it is who's committing these terrible murders,' he stated.

'He was one of our own,' she began, 'One of the villagers. It's like it's happening all over again, Inspector Falconer, and I don't think I could stand that: not after the last time.'

'I don't know if you're aware of it, but a young detective constable has been beaten senseless too, and left at the side of the road on a freezing night to die.'

He heard a sharp intake of breath at this information, and continued, 'I believe that the attack on him was carried out by the same person who has left those bodies in your chapel, and we want this person put away where the public won't be in danger any more. I'm sure you understand my sentiments.'

'I do, indeed. I shan't sleep sound in my bed again until whoever is doing this is in police custody,' she declared, two spots of red appearing on her cheeks as her anger at the situation over-rode her shock. 'I've got to be brave and tell you everything, so, here goes!

'I hadn't been to the chapel for days. I was waiting for the site manager and the electrician to make a call to confirm that everything was safe to be used, and sign off the job. What with this cold weather, I haven't been out much, except for work and a trip to the Ox and Plough recently, and I realised that it was time to check the building if they weren't going to come until next week.

'I had initial fears that there might be a third lot of writing on the wall to be painted over, and my first glance inside told me that this was indeed so. And how are they getting in there, to plant all those dead bodies, and paint nonsensical religious messages on the wall? That's what I'd like to know. To my knowledge, there are only three keys. I've got one, the vicar's got one, and the builders had the third, and it hasn't been returned yet either, I might tell you!

'Then, when I looked towards the altar, I could see there was something on it, but, before I turned on the lights, I assumed it was a pile of decorator's sheets, and just tutted a bit at how they had been so carelessly discarded.

'That was my only thought as I walked down the aisle, because lightning's not supposed to strike twice, is it? Then, as I got closer, I realised I had been mistaken, and I slowed my pace, fearing what I would find there. I wanted to close my eyes and run out screaming, but I was brought up to be strong, and to face reality, so I walked on until I was right in front of it.

'Oh, that poor man! The pain he must have suffered! He was almost unrecognisable. I must admit that, at that moment, I rather lost my nerve. I was going to run straight home and telephone the police from there, but when I got to Vernon's door, just a couple away from mine, I cracked, and hammered on his door as if all the hounds of hell were after me.

'I needed some company, and I knew I could trust Vernon not to treat me like a silly old biddy. He'd wait until I was ready to talk, then treat me sympathetically.

'Well, I blurted out the bare bones of what I'd found, and Vernon, dear man that he can be sometimes, sat me down in front of the fire, covered me with a rug, and rang you immediately. Then he made me a hot toddy, and just let me ramble, until you arrived. There isn't any more I can tell you, I'm afraid. I haven't seen anyone suspicious in the area, because I simply haven't been out much.'

'Thank you very much, Miss Pryor. That was most succinct. And now, we'd better be off. You make sure that Mr Warlock takes good care of you,' Falconer instructed her.

'I will,' a voice floated out from the kitchen and, turning, Falconer could just discern that the door to this room was just, ever so slightly, ajar again.

The visit just next door to Monica Raynor was considerably more distressing. No one, not even the runners of the village grapevine, had had sufficient courage to break the news to Monica, and she was totally unaware of Quentin's fate until she opened the door to Falconer and Carmichael and saw their faces.

'Oh, nooo!' she wailed, her eyes widening, her hands flying up to her open mouth.

'May we come in, please?', requested Falconer, and took her by the elbow and steered her into the cottage so that they could all be shielded from public view. He led her to the kitchen, where he knew she spent a lot of time, and lowered her into a wooden chair at the table.

Monica immediately reaching for a pack of cigarettes and a lighter, said in a very quiet monotone, 'He's dead, isn't he?'

Not wishing to prevaricate, Falconer's answer was curt, and to the point. 'Yes,' he said.

'How?' asked Monica, her hands shaking so much as she tried to light her cigarette that Carmichael had to take charge of the lighter and hold it for her. 'Where? When?' she continued, drawing in a deep inhalation of smoke.

'There's no nice way of saying this, so I'll just give you the facts. Beaten to death, as far as we can see for now. The chapel is where we found him. Sometime last night, is the preliminary estimate of time of death. We can give you no more accurate information than that until after the post mortem. There was another phrase painted on the wall – *be sure your sins will find you out*, it reads. Does that phrase have any particular meaning to you?'

'Absolutely none, except that I obviously recognise it,' she replied.

This was one call where cold rationality and facts were called for, thought Falconer. If she cracked up later in the visit, he'd let Carmichael take over.

She had two more questions to ask. 'Who did it?' was the first.

'We're working on that one. This is the third attack, to our knowledge, and that should narrow things down considerably. We just need a little more time,' he answered, watching, fascinated, as she blew smoke rings without even being aware that she was doing so.

Her final enquiry was, 'Will I have to identify his body?'

'That would be in line with normal procedure, Mrs Raynor. We'll make it as easy for you as possible, and he'll be tidied up and covered to the neck with a white sheet. There's nothing to be afraid of.'

And that's when her veneer of control cracked, and she began to scream at them at the top of her voice. 'Nothing to be afraid of? *Nothing to be afraid of*? There's a mad killer out there who's killed my husband and left me a widow. What if he comes for me? I don't know why all this is happening, and I'm frightened. And how am I going to manage as a widow? Oh, what a filthy word that is! Oh, Quentin, whatever did you get yourself into? This isn't real! It can't be real! I want to wake up and find it's all just a ghastly nightmare!'

Carmichael looked at Falconer in mute appeal. This wasn't something he knew how to deal with, but Falconer did. Filling a glass from the draining board with cold water, he threw it in her face. That silenced her!

'How dare you,' she began to yell at him, then fell absolutely silent. 'Thank you,' she said, in a more normal voice. 'I needed that. I was a bit hysterical.'

'Is there someone we can call for you?' asked Carmichael, now recovered from his shock at the violence of her reaction.

'Perhaps you could get in touch with Roma Kerr. She runs the ladies' dress shop in the High Street, if you remember. Maybe she could sit with me for an hour or so, while I digest this. Her home and work numbers are on the pad by the telephone,' she said in a quiet, pleading voice.

She may have had a fling with Roma's husband, Rodney, but Roma knew nothing about it, but she knew that she had had her ups-and-downs with Quentin, just as she had had with Rodney. A man's woman, suddenly she felt in need of some sisterly support.

Carmichael managed to track Roma Kerr down at his second attempt, and she promised to closes the shop for a couple of hours while she came to Monica's aid.

Back in the car once more, Falconer confessed himself beaten, for the moment. 'We've still got no idea if this is something to do with that bunch of revivalists from the college, or whether it's a purely village affair, and tied up with old beliefs of desecration and goodness knows what.

'I'll tell you what we're going to do now. I know it's cold, but you'd better get your mittens on, because we're going to go right round that graveyard, and take down all the family names we can find, and check them out, to see if there are any descendants locally. That Strict and Particular lot had some very strong views about morality and punishment, and I want to make sure that it's nothing to do with lingering beliefs along those lines that are responsible for what's been happening.'

'In this light, sir? It's a very dark day,' asked Carmichael. 'I bet that'll be another dead end.'

'Ha ha! Very witty, Carmichael! But we've got torches, and

121

we might be able to cadge the lights from the SOCO team, if they haven't already packed up and left.'

'It'll cost you a double hot chocolate in the canteen when we get back, sir. I'm already chilled to the marrow. That last place wasn't very warm, and if I'm going to spend goodness knows how long creeping round a cemetery, then I think I should be rewarded for it.'

'You're on!' replied Falconer. 'And the same for me; with double marshmallows, too!'

It didn't take long for Roma Kerr to shut up shop and arrive on Monica's doorstep. Roma may have a useless husband herself, and knew that Monica hadn't held Quentin in high esteem, but the shock must have been awful, and she wanted to show her support.

Monica opened the door, her eyes red and swollen, the tears having arrived just after Falconer and Carmichael left. She held the door with one hand, while in the other was a crumpled bundle of paper handkerchiefs. Without a word, Roma opened her arms, and Monica fell into them. What she really craved right now was a mother's love, but as that was not possible, so maybe she could be a bit mothered by a friend.

She would normally have called Tilly Gifford, who was her closest friend in Steynham St Michael, but Tilly was also the most accomplished gossip of her generation, in Monica's opinion, and she didn't want the way she was feeling now all over the village, with whistles and bells added to it. Besides, she remembered, Tilly was away on holiday. Roma was at least discreet, and would only let on what she had been given permission to discuss.

They sat in the kitchen for an hour and a half, Monica talking and chain-smoking, Roma just listening, interjecting with a short question now and again. At the end of their session, Monica felt much better; it was if she had cleansed herself of something, but there was one other thing that she had to lay on the table, to give this meeting of support any integrity.

'There's something I want to tell you, but before I do, I also want you to know how very sorry I am that it ever happened,' she said, her voice low and serious.

'Go on,' Roma urged her, though she thought she knew what was coming.

'I'm very much afraid that I had a fling with your Rodney,' Monica almost whispered, and then was sent totally off-balance, as Roma burst out into peals and peals of amused laughter.

'What is it?' she asked, worried. 'What have I said? I thought you'd be furious.'

'Didn't you think at the time that it was rather easy to get Quentin out of the way when you slunk off to meet Rodney?' asked Roma, wiping tears of mirth from her eyes. It must be the intense emotion surrounding this latest murder that had inspired her to such heights of hysterical laughter. Normally she wouldn't be so easily amused.

'I hadn't really thought about it,' Monica replied, waiting for enlightenment, and then she saw the light. 'What? You and Quentin?'

'Yes!' yelled Roma. 'All the time you thought you were getting Quentin out of the way, you were actually giving him leave to see me. So, you see, we're both as guilty as one another.'

The forensic team had already left when they got there. In the churchyard, Carmichael had produced a penknife from the depths of one of his coat pockets, and he and Falconer were taking it in turns to scrape away the lichen from the worn names on the simple headstones, while the other held a torch.

There were no Victorian Gothic offerings here. Each soul had for a grave marker simply a plain oblong of stone, engraved with the name of the occupant, the date of birth, and the date of death. There was no pomp or sentimentality in pious inscriptions here, just a bare statement of facts. The work was painstaking, but easier than it might have been because there had already been an initial clean-up of the burial ground by the volunteers.

It was still cold, however, and although it was still early in the season, there was now sleet in the air. This was definitely not the weather to be working out in the open air.

'Come on, Carmichael,' said Falconer, 'I think we've had enough of the great outdoors for one day. It is Saturday. Let's quit, and come back here on Monday. Maybe the Doc will have some information for us by then, or forensics, and perhaps Roberts will have regained consciousness enough to tell us why he was so badly beaten. He must have learnt far too much for his own good to be treated like that.'

'Good idea, sir. I'm looking forward to my hot chocolate even more, after this.'

'I'm just wondering ...' Falconer said, and drifted off into silence.

'What's that, sir?'

'Well, we've had two murders and an attempted murder so far, and Chivers has called in a psychological profiler. Do you think we ought to get the Regional Serious Crimes Squad involved?'

'Oh, no: Mrs Frazer wouldn't like that at all!'

'What was that?' snapped Falconer, wondering how a complete stranger had made their way into the conversation.

'I said that Chivers wouldn't like that at all, sir.'

'No you didn't!' stated Falconer, accusingly.

'I did, sir! It must be the cold wind, affecting your ears.'

'It isn't!'

'Oh, I think it is!'

'Isn't!'

'Is!'

'Isn't! Oh, let's just drop it. I'm too cold to argue. Come on! Let's just get back in the car, and try to thaw out on the way back.'

Very quietly, 'Is!'

Chapter Twelve

By Monday morning, Falconer had drawn up a list of those he wished to interview at the college and in the village, and announced that they would soon be on their way out as Carmichael arrived.

The inspector had already been in touch with the college to extract the information he needed to contact those on his list, and had spent some time going through the records of the inhabitants of Steynham St Michael to see if he could round up any 'hidden' suspects within their ranks, but with little success.

He'd decided to start with the students actually on the comparative religion course, who would have known Chris better than any of the others, then move on to the course tutor, finishing up with the three students who were in the 'inner circle' discussion group, but studying other subjects. Chris had left a quick character assessment of them all, along with a note of which courses they were registered on, and these might prove helpful to give him a tiny insight into their characters before he actually met them.

Jocasta Gray had considerably eased this job by promising to have the three students from her course available at the mid-morning break in the empty home room, and to attend herself, so that he could tackle all four of them without wasting too much time. It had seemed kind of her, but later reflection caused him to reconsider this, and decide that it was more of a 'we've got nothing to hide' attitude, meant to lull him into a false sense of security.

The college itself was a sixties monstrosity, constructed in concrete and already beginning to crumble away. Finding a space in the car park proved difficult, and made him reflect on how much more disposable money students had these days if so many of them could afford cars to get to and from college.

At reception he and Carmichael were directed to room 101 and, now five minutes late because of the difficulty in finding a parking place, they found all three students waiting patiently with their tutor.

Having introduced themselves to those foregathered, Falconer asked if the other three could wait in the corridor while he interviewed each one, and announced his intention to begin with Elspeth Martin, the one whom Chris seemed to have spent the most time with.

Oh, but she was a plain girl; not easy on the eye, and difficult to feel any affinity with. Although she was close to twenty, she seemed more like a girl of thirteen or fourteen. and it was clear to see why Chris had suspected her of having a bit of a 'pash' on her tutor. She denied any knowledge of what had been found in Steynham St Michael, and said it was nothing to do with her, or with anyone she knew. She had not, though, heard about Chris' beating, and this really threw her into an unexpected show of emotion.

'No!' she cried, her face crumpling. 'No, that can't be right! He can't be in hospital!'

'I'm afraid he is, Miss Martin,' replied Falconer, calmly.

'When did it happen?' she asked, her eyes filling with unshed tears.

'Either late last Wednesday evening, or in the early hours of Thursday morning,' he informed her.

'But that's not possible. I saw him on ...' She stopped speaking abruptly, evidently searching to change what she had being going to say. 'I saw him on Wednesday, at college,' she finally offered, lamely.

'Are you sure you didn't see him on Wednesday evening, too?' probed Falconer.

'No, of course not. I'd have said if I had, wouldn't I?' she asked, acting the innocent, but openly displaying her discomfiture at lying by blushing and twisting her fingers round and round each other.

'You may like to revise that claim, when the investigation is further advanced, Miss Martin,' he warned her, then proceeded to ask, 'And where exactly were you on Wednesday evening?'

'I was at home – in my room in the Halls,' she replied tersely.

'Do you have any witnesses to that?'

'I was alone.'

'The whole evening?'

'The whole evening,' she replied to this last, trying to meet his eye, but not quite managing it.

'What was your relationship with Chris Roberts?'

'We were friends, that's all.'

'Are you sure that was all it was?'

'Of course!' She was now slightly cross, and explained the beliefs of purity and strong moral principles that she held so dearly.

'And are there others who also harbour these ideals?' he asked, chancing his arm with this rather shy and immature gargoyle of a girl. If she'd had any more spots, you could've ordered extra garlic bread to go with them.

'A few of us,' was her curt answer, but at least she had given one.

'May I ask who these are?'

'You know jolly well who they are, because you've got them all waiting outside in the corridor, so that you can interrogate them, too.'

'There aren't any that I don't know about?'

'No, that's all of us. You'll have no need to look any further. And I want the person who beat Chris caught and punished.'

'So do we, Miss Martin, and, knowing some of your group's views on punishment, I think it's probably better if we find whoever it is first, don't you?'

'Definitely!'

'You're fond of Mr Roberts, aren't you Elspeth?'

'He's a very kind man, and I liked him very much.'

He spoke to Antonia Knightly next, but learnt nothing new. If anything, Antonia was even more tight-lipped than Elspeth, and the interview was brief and unproductive. She was a little bit more hard-boiled than Elspeth, and it showed.

Jamie Huntley was next into the room and, apart from appearing rather like an archetypal a Roman Catholic theology student, he also had little to say, and denied all knowledge of the incident even going so far as to ask Falconer if he was sure that Chris had been beaten and not hit by a car and flung to the side of the road by the momentum of the impact.

'Oh, I'm absolutely sure, Mr Huntley. I don't know whether you're aware of the fact, but Chris Roberts was actually DC Roberts, undercover here carrying out an investigation of his own.' This may not have been the most truthful way to explain why Chris had been undercover, but at least it did not admit that he had been directly investigating this little group of Holy Joes.

'I had heard,' he replied, but when Falconer asked him from whom he had received this information, he clammed up and said he couldn't remember, which was suspicious in itself. The revelation of a beating of this magnitude and the fact that Chris was a policeman, would have stuck in his mind like a burr in the fur of a cat's bum.

'Where were you late on Wednesday evening through to the early hours of Thursday morning?' Falconer asked the question with no preamble, hoping to catch the young man off-guard, but it did him not a jot of good

'I was in my room in the Halls, writing up my course notes,' he replied, cool as a cucumber, and Falconer felt like throwing something at his smugly confident, pious face.

Amelia Harrison, the history student, was extremely garrulous, attempting to inform him of the entire history of the Strict and Particular movement, and he had to work hard to stem her flow of high-speed information, which threatened to drown him in facts that he had no interest in whatsoever, but he did manage, in the end, to discover that, *quelle surprise*, she had also been on her own at the time of the attack on Chris, and had no witnesses, as she didn't like to study in company.

That left him with only the physical education and the philosophy students, to be followed by the tutor, and although he knew he wasn't wasting his time in being here, he bethought himself that he would probably gain nothing by his questioning today. They were all shut up tight as clams, like their religious counterparts from the past. He knew that Chris had suffered a 'punishment beating', but he didn't have the faintest idea how he was going to prove it.

Aaron Trussler, the physical education student, also admitted to attending a car maintenance course at the weekends, and claimed he should in fact be in the workshops at this precise moment, doing some catch-up work despite it being a Monday. He offered this information in a sullen voice, then just sat opposite Falconer, scowling at him in an intimidating way. He was a well-built young man, and Falconer was glad to have Carmichael taking notes in case Trussler should take exception to any of the questions he should be asked.

Trussler's answers were monosyllabic whenever they could be, and he had no air of cooperation about him: he just wanted to go back to pulling engines apart and getting his hands dirty.

In stark contrast, Daniel Burrows was so laid-back he was almost comatose, waking up only to challenge Falconer about there being any meaning to life at all. 'After all,' explained the student, 'the only consensus we can come to is that there is no absolute proof, and no way of obtaining any, that there is a supreme being; that God actually exists. The only reason the idea exists in any society is because man cannot believe in his own futility, and must believe in something greater than himself to carry on with his life without going mad. God is just a creation of hope and blind faith.'

'And yet you are part of this revivalist religious group, which follows the practices and beliefs of the Strict and Particulars?' asked Falconer, sure now that there would be no denial of the group's existence, merely of its actual practices.

'I don't want to be one of the unfortunates who go mad,' he replied, with infuriating logic.

Falconer glanced over at Carmichael, who gave the inspector what could only be described as an 'ooh, get 'im!' look, with which he totally concurred, and he speeded up his questioning to get the irritating young man through the process, and out of his sight.

Finally through with the students, he asked Jocasta Gray to join him in the tutor room. When she came in and sat down, unlike DC Roberts, he did not find her instantly fascinating, but rather repulsive, so slim was she that she was positively bony under her flowing gown. Once seated, she reached round to remove this garment, as the room was well-heated, and she was already warm.

Sitting in front of him, her thin, bare arms exposed to his gaze, he had to quell a shudder of revulsion at the whiteness of her skin, as well as the stick-like quality of her arms. It reminded him of veal, and his stomach lurched threateningly.

When he had been quite young, he had been given veal to eat by Nanny Vogel and had, at the time, enjoyed its tenderness. Later, however, Nanny Vogel had revealed her true purpose in giving him such a delicacy. It was so that she could tell him about the calves that gave their lives to produce such a treat, and how they were raised to keep their meat white and tender. Falconer had had nightmares, and had never tried veal again to this day; looking at the tutor's arms now reminded him of the white flesh of which he had once, and only once, partaken.

Seeing his gaze, she put both of her bony elbows on the table, and began to explain. 'I can see you admiring the milky whiteness of my skin, Inspector. It was seen as sinful, in the beliefs of the Strict and Particulars, for a woman to be coloured by the sun, like a man. They were expected to have enough to occupy them inside the home and with the children, and not go out to flaunt their skin in the heat of the summer unless it was covered.

'I can also see a question in your eyes about my slightness of build. That is nothing to do with metabolism, and more to do with control. Greed was considered one of the greatest of casual, everyday sins that may not even be detected, until the evidence showed on the frame of the sinner. I control my intake of nourishment, not only with the recipes of the denomination, but also with the careful monitoring of calories.

'Many of the Christians in this world are starving, and my carefully controlled, limited intake of nourishment is evidence of my one-ness with them. I empathise with them completely, and humble myself before them.'

What a load of old crap! thought Falconer, and tried not to let his emotion show in his face. Carmichael, he noticed, had ceased to take notes, and was standing, facing into the far corner of the room, away from the corridor. His head was bent, and his shoulders were very gently shaking. The man was laughing! How he would have like to join him, but he felt a very strange atmosphere around this woman, and he had to admit that he was unnerved by her.

Making the interview as short as possible, he finished by asking her where she had been at the time Roberts had been attacked. She had answered him simply and eerily. 'I was at prayer, Inspector. I was at prayer,' and he collected Carmichael and left the room with relief.

When they were back in the car, Carmichael had a question for Falconer. 'Why did they all keep fiddling with something at the top of their legs? You probably couldn't have seen it because it was under the table, but I could, and anytime you asked them something that unnerved them or was unexpected, they put a hand to their upper leg and made a sort of twisting motion.'

'I'll tell you when you're a big boy, Carmichael. I don't even want to go there, at the moment, but I think I know what they were doing, and it would explain why the women all wear long skirts, and the men, very baggy-cut jeans.'

'Tell me now, sir,' pleaded Carmichael.

'Not just yet because I think I'd be sick. I'll tell you, if it becomes relevant at any time, or at the end of the case, it if doesn't, but please don't mention it again, as I do actually feel rather nauseous.' Falconer had been more affected by this discovery, on top of meeting Jocasta Gray, than he had expected. It all seemed very warped and twisted to him, and he realised he hadn't quite understood the sort of people he was asking Roberts to go undercover to investigate.

Back in the office for a break from interviewing, he decided to give Philip Christmas a ring to see if there had been anything interesting discovered from the body of Monica's husband. He was put through by one of the other staff, and, after greeting the doctor, said, 'I was just calling to see if you had any news for me.'

'I'm sorry,' came the reply, 'but I'm afraid I'm up to the elbows in Quentin Raynor.'

'I know you have to write a report, but if you could just spare a minute away from your computer, I should be very grateful,' Falconer replied, a trifle pompously.

'I don't think you quite understood what I meant, Harry. I'm literally *up to the elbows* in Quentin Raynor. One of my assistants is holding the phone for me while I'm rummaging around in his body cavity, with my hands round his spleen.'

'Yuck!' Silence. 'I'm so sorry. I had no idea. When I asked to speak to you, no one told me that.' Falconer was appalled at the grisly vision his mind conjured up.

'Never mind! And while we're speaking, and don't worry, I can quite happily converse while I'm working, do you remember all those promises of a paperless office we were given, when the rise of the computer really got going? Now we've got the twin demons of having to record everything onto computer files, and still file paper printouts, with memos and e-mails, and all the other forms of modern communication to contend with. It takes three times as much time, and we still have the same volume of paper. And when you want something, can you find it? Can you heck as like! Three times as much work, for less than half the efficiency; that's my opinion. What say you, Harry, boy?'

'I think I'd like to end this conversation now, Philip. I'm actually feeling a bit nauseous just thinking about what you're doing while we're speaking. I'll tell you what: raise the subject again when you haven't got somebody else's blood on your hands, not to mention half-way up your arms.'

'I'll get back to you as soon as I can, and I'll give Forensics a nudge as well. That's two murders and one attempted murder we're dealing with, and I'm sure we both think alike, when I say I don't want my workload increased in the near future.'

'Agreed! Bye!' Falconer hung up as soon as he had the opportunity. What a bloody job that man did, with both senses of the adjective. The very thought of what Christmas was doing as they had spoken had left him feeling rather unnerved, and he wanted no mental pictures at all of what was going on at the other end of that phone call.

No sooner had he hung up than the phone rang, and he had to pull himself together with a jerk. He found Mike Welland, the landlord of the Ox and Plough, on the line, sounding a bit excited, but at the same time, there was a tinge of embarrassment in his voice.

'How can I be of assistance, Mr Welland?' asked Falconer, surprised to receive a call from this particular individual so soon after his visit to the pub.

'It's about my nephew,' Welland began. 'He's come to stay with me to get over a heavy bout of flu,' he explained, 'and arrived yesterday afternoon. I suppose he must have heard me talking to the wife, or someone in the bar with a bigger than normal gob, spouting off, but somehow he evidently overheard some stories that were not for his ears.

'When he woke up this morning – late, I'd like to state, which is unusual for him – he was very quiet, and, at first, I put it down to his energy levels being depleted by his illness, but later, the wife found him crying in his room, and managed to get out of him what had upset him.' Falconer held his peace, and let the man get on with his story. There was no point in rushing him. He must let him tell it in his own time.

'It seems he'd got wind of something going on at the chapel – that it was haunted, or something. Anyway, the little terror – he's nine, now – let himself out of the pub, just after I

133

checked him, which must have been just a bit before midnight. We like our early nights, the wife and I. We've never been ones for staying up late, even though we run a pub.

'Anyway, off he goes, all wrapped up against the cold, a torch and his mobile phone with him, in case he gets himself into bother. Apparently, he legged it down the Market Darley Road, keeping to the shadows, then crept into Tuppenny Lane, shaking with excitement at the adventure he was going to have, and the tales he'd have to tell the next day. Then, when he was approaching the chapel, he saw it – or rather, them.'

'Go on, Mr Welland. I'm listening, and taking notes,' Falconer couldn't help interrupting him at this dramatic juncture. 'What did he see?'

'Two figures in dark, loose cloak-y things with hoods, one of them sort of supporting the other one, as if he were drunk or something, making their way through the gravestones. He thought at first that they were ghosts, but when the drunken one groaned, it frightened the shit out of the poor little lad; pardon my French, Inspector.'

'What happened next?' asked Falconer, thinking what luck it was that the boy had decided to go out at night exploring. This would narrow things down nicely, as far as timing went.

'He took off like a bolt of lightning, back to the safety of the pub, in case *they* 'got' him, then he slunk off to bed without waking either of us, but my wife got it out of him this lunchtime. He was afraid that, as he'd seen them, they might come looking for him to drag him off to the graveyard or something daft like that. Great imagination, our Darren's got.'

'I'll be over this afternoon to speak to him, if that's all right with you, for I'll need one of you to be present as an appropriate adult when I talk to him.'

'No problem, Inspector Falconer. Thanks for your interest,' and the man was gone, no doubt to help out at the bar, but he'd be closed when they went over to speak to his nephew so there shouldn't be any clash of responsibilities by that time of day.

Immediately, his internal telephone rang, and he answered it to find Bob Bryant on the line. 'There was a call for you just now, but you were engaged, so it got diverted to me. You've got a message from a Mrs Littlemore of Steynham St Michael.'

'Oh, not again! And what exactly did she slur, this time?' asked Falconer facetiously.

'She sounded perfectly sober,' answered Bob Bryant, knowing what had been said about the woman at the station.

'Really?' Falconer questioned this statement.

'Well, almost. She said that there was one of them hooded buggers skulking around the chapel again, about two o'clock this morning, but that she'd heard chanting and stuff earlier than that. Those were her exact words, and when I asked her to expand a little bit, she said you'd know what she was talking about, and she'd wait for a visit from you.'

'Thanks a bleedin' bunch, Bob, but I've got to go out there anyway, a bit later. I'll just know to wear a gas mask now, to stop myself getting drunk on the fumes coming off her.'

'Way to go, Harry!' commented Bob, cheekily, before ringing off.

'What's going down in Gumshoe City, USA?' asked Carmichael, returning to the office after a short lunch break.

'We're off to Steynham St Michael again ... and I assume you're still watching those American cop shows on the television.' Falconer answered.

'Yes, sir. What are we going back for, this time?'

'Well, you knew we'd have to go back, but I've just had a call from the landlord of the Ox and Plough. Apparently his nephew, who's staying with him at the moment, took himself off on a little adventure late last night, and saw more than he bargained for, in the mysterious hooded figures department. And that Littlemore woman's phoned in to say she's had two more sightings, one about two this morning, and something about chanting earlier on.'

'Oh, great! All we want to do is bring a murderer to justice, and we've got to spend the afternoon with kids and drunks!' They must not have had enough chips in the canteen, for it was unusual for Carmichael to come back from a meal in a tetchy mood.

'Only one kid and one drunk, Sergeant,' Falconer clarified.

'That doesn't make it any better, does it?' Carmichael replied, and actually frowned.

'Whatever's the matter with you today? We didn't have much time for conversation this morning, but this afternoon you're like a bear with a sore head,' asked Falconer.

'I was just thinking about last night. My ma came round, and that made three sets of haywire hormones in the house, including the dog's. In the end I went for a walk, and let the two women discuss their aches and pains and past experiences in peace. I didn't want to hear any of it, and frankly, I felt left out. None of us fell out, but I like Kerry to myself in the evenings, when the boys have gone to bed. I don't want to sit around in my own home and hear about breech presentations, forceps, and episiotomies, thank you very much.'

'Well, please don't feel put out if I don't join you in your little snit. I phoned Doc Christmas just now, and halfway through the conversation he informed me that someone was holding the phone for him while he scrabbled around inside Quentin Raynor to remove his spleen.'

'Dear God!' exclaimed Carmichael, and suddenly smiled, and commented, 'It's nice to be on your own, when you get a bit of a fit of the heebie-jeebies. Thanks for that, sir. I feel a lot better now. Let's away!'

Darren was scrubbed up, his hair slicked down, and smartly dressed when they arrived at the pub, and he told his story fluently and coherently. He had evidently been reassured by his aunt and uncle that the police had everything under control. If only! Falconer asked him if he'd used his torch to see the figures better, but got the expected negative response. Darren hadn't dared, in case they'd traced the source of the beam of light to him.

'If they was zombies,' he said, with complete seriousness, 'they'd have eaten me, and my mum would've been awful cross. But I did take a picture with my phone,' he suddenly confessed. 'Then I got right into that hedge around the corner where that lady what drinks lives. It was right spiky, what with it being November, but I got myself tucked away, in case they'd noticed the flash. But everything was all right, so that's when I legged it back here, before they 'got' me and did unspeakable things.'

'You never said anything about no photo,' commented his aunt, scowling at him, with no worries whatsoever about what the boy considered to be 'unspeakable things'.

'Clever boy!' exclaimed his uncle, beaming his pride at the boy's ingenuity.

'Let me see?' asked Falconer, excited now.

'It's not very good,' said Darren, sadly, as he got his phone out of his trouser pocket. 'Here!'

Falconer looked at the small offering, but it was much better than he had expected it to be. 'Would you mind sending that photo to my phone, Darren? I'm sure the lab boys could work wonders with it.'

'Oh, boy! Am I going to be part of a murder investigation?' asked the lad, who evidently did a lot of eavesdropping.

Mrs Welland had obviously got tired of the proceedings, and left the room. She had a pub to open this evening, and she had a lot she wanted to get done before then. Having the little one to stay was all right, but he did cause quite a bit of extra work.

'This photo might possibly be used as evidence. It's timed and dated, and could prove very useful to us, Darren. Thank you very much,' Falconer added, as his phone indicated that it had received the photograph.

But the inspector was not to escape so lightly from this visit. There sounded a cry of, 'No, Jake!' from upstairs, and the unmistakable thunder of bounding paws down the staircase. Jake entered the room with a deep 'wuff' of welcome, and shot straight over to Falconer, who had been sitting rather uncomfortably in a wooden chair.

He was even more uncomfortable, when he found himself with his legs in the air, his body on the chair-back, which was now on the floor, while Jake licked his face as if it were the most delicious thing he'd ever tasted.

'Get orf 'im, Jakey boy!' yelled Welland, grabbing the dog

by its collar and heaving. Jake reluctantly left his new best friend, and whimpered pitifully as he was dragged out of the door, looking back over his shoulder appealingly.

Carmichael helped Falconer to his feet and handed him a cotton handkerchief, a clean one of which was issued to him every day by Kerry, with which to mop his sopping face.

'Are you OK, Inspector?' asked Welland, concerned about whether the man had hit his head on the floor on toppling backwards with the weight of the dog. He didn't fancy being sued over having an over-friendly dog.

'May I use your Gents, please?' Falconer asked, in a rather tight voice, and whispered to Carmichael as he went past him, determined to scrub his face as clean as he could, before leaving the pub, 'I feel sick. I hope I'm not going to chuck.' With a moue of distaste, he exited, scrubbing his face vigorously with the handkerchief, and discreetly spitting into it, leaving Carmichael wondering what the fatal attraction to the inspector was, for dogs. Whatever Falconer had got, he just wished he had it, too.

Amy Littlemore was more sober than usual, and told them that she had had to go out for a couple of little walks the night before. A bruise on both her upper arms suggested that this might have been due to some rather physical disagreements with Malcolm. It was lucky they kept the central heating so high, or he'd never have seen her without a cardigan at this time of year.

She said she'd gone out about eleven o'clock, and heard some weird sort of chanting in what she referred to as 'foreign', and had come in again, because she didn't like the sound of it, but it was definitely coming from either the chapel or its grounds.

At about 2 a.m., she'd gone out for longer – this must have been the culmination of the disagreement – and, on walking down Tuppenny Lane opposite the chapel, had seen a hooded figure disappearing inside its doors. That had been enough to scare her back home, but she'd remembered to report it this morning, because she knew it might be important.

As they sat in the car outside Forge Cottage, Carmichael commented, 'That's three confirmed sightings we've had for that period. Mrs Squiffy heard chanting round about ten, but didn't see anything. That lad, Darren, saw two figures about midnight, and Mrs Squiffy saw one at about two o'clock.'

'And we've got a photograph of sorts, although I don't know how much enhancement it'll take. We'll just have to wait and see what the lab boys can do with it. I know they can work wonders these days, so we might be lucky. At least it's not got its back turned towards the camera.'

'I say, sir?' asked Carmichael. 'What do you think we'd get, if we crossed Mr Spliffy with Mrs Squiffy?'

'A right royal hangover, Carmichael. Come on, let's get on with the rest of these interviews, before I lose my mind. And I can feel a headache coming on. That damned dog!'

Later that afternoon, Monica Raynor had begun sorting out Quentin's clothes for the charity shop, going through his pockets religiously. He was a terror for shoving money in them, because he couldn't be bothered to get his wallet out and put it away properly.

She'd already found about a hundred and fifty pounds in change and small notes, when she delved a hand into the right-hand pocket of a jacket he'd worn a lot recently and, grasping what she thought might be another fiver, pulled out a piece of paper about the same size as the expected banknote.

Its message was short and simple: 'Friday – midnight – chapel. J. x'. It wasn't signed, as such, but as Quentin's body had been found on Saturday morning, actually *in* the chapel, it was evidently of some importance, and she put it away safely, to take into Market Darley the next day for Inspector Falconer.

Chapter Thirteen

Tuesday 9th November

Falconer didn't realise it when he left home that morning, but it was going to be an eventful day; just the first, however, of more of the same. When he arrived at the station, he found Monica Raynor waiting for him, and he conducted her up to his office, mulling over what she could have come to see him about.

After they had exchanged greeting, and she had made herself comfortable in a chair opposite his, she scrabbled around in her handbag, eventually handing him a rather crumpled piece of paper.

'I found that in the pocket of one of Quentin's jackets,' she informed him, a woman coping admirably with a dreadful situation. 'It appears to be for an assignation on the night of his murder, so I thought I'd better bring it in to you. Maybe one of his little lovelies has struck back at him for using her, and this time he simply didn't survive the onslaught.

'I'm sure he was very good at telling women what an awful marriage he had, and how unhappy he was at home. For all I know, he promised goodness knows how many of them that he'd leave me, but he'd never have done that. He'd have lost half the business, for a start, not to mention half the marital home. Tell me, who'd want him when I'd finished with him, financially?'

Falconer was too embarrassed even to attempt to answer that question, and stared at the scrap of paper, working out whose name began with 'J' who was involved in the case, and the only answer he came up with was 'Jocasta Gray'. The note was handwritten, not printed, so he could get a specimen of her handwriting, and pass it over to the experts, but should he do

141

this surreptitiously, or overtly? He'd have to give that one some thought.

He was still mulling this over in his mind when the phone rang with the information that DC Roberts had regained consciousness during the night, and it would be permissible for him to receive a visit, so long as the inspector didn't stay for too long, or distress him in any way. He was still very weak, and trying to cope with the information about what had happened to him, as he remembered nothing of the beating, but he had expressed an urgent desire to speak to Falconer, so that's why they were calling him.

Grabbing Carmichael by the arm as soon as he entered the office door, and not even giving him time to take off his coat, he sped him back out through the building, and straight into his own car.

'What the heck's going on, sir?' asked Carmichael, puzzled by the inspector's urgency.

'Roberts is conscious, and wants to talk to us,' explained Falconer, skidding heart-stoppingly on a patch of black ice on his way out of the car park.

Chris was in a normal ward now, and they found him propped up on pillows, trying to turn the pages of a daily rag. 'You had us worried there, Roberts. It's seems that you might have penetrated deeper undercover than you realised,' Falconer greeted him.

'We thought you were a goner,' added Carmichael, lugubriously.

'So did I!' replied Chris, trying to sit further up in the bed, and wincing with pain. 'But I haven't lost a lot of memory, and I've been dying to talk to you guys.'

Falconer winced, not just at the casual use of the word 'dying', but at him and Carmichael being referred to you as 'you guys'. 'That's great news!' he retorted, trying not to show his disapproval of this mode of address, considering what Roberts had been through. 'Tell us everything you remember after you stopped making notes, and Carmichael here will get it all down.'

Carmichael took the one visitor's chair that sat by the bed and removed his notebook, ready for action. 'Cor! This .is just like being interrogated!' came from the bed. Chris may not be mended physically, but he certainly seemed very like his old facetious self. 'I di'n't do nuffink, Occifer! I'm bein' fitted up 'ere!' he said, and looked to see if Carmichael had taken this down, only to receive an old-fashioned look from the sergeant.

'I'm not that easily fooled,' said the latter, and, a distressing habit, licked the end of his pen, as if it were a pencil, ready to begin.

'Before we start,' said Falconer, 'I wonder if you recognise this handwriting?' he asked, and handed the note that Monica had given him, to Chris.

'Of course I do,' he replied, trying to raise an eyebrow, and failing, due to the presence of stitches on his forehead. 'That's the tutor's handwriting – Jocasta Gray. I've got notes in it written all over the only piece of work I handed in for marking. I'll let you have it, or you can go round to collect it from my rucksack from my mother's.'

'Excellent! Now I only want her fingerprints,' Falconer replied, smiling.

'You'll probably get those from it as well, as she had her hands all over it, annotating it and putting in cutting comments about my lack of understanding of the course.' This was said ruefully by the patient, but he did not try to express this feeling through his face, having just learnt that he was going to have to act as if he had had too much Botox, for a while, at least.

'And did I make a note that one of the students in the discussion group was the owner of a van? That's Daniel Burrows, doing philosophy. And his mate, Aaron Trussler – physical education, and built like a brick shit – sorry! – outhouse – had a bruised hand, and that was on my first day, when we were looking for whoever did for that workman.'

'Even better!' Falconer was very pleased about this, as it meant he didn't have to pursue the woman for either identification of the writing on the note, or Jocasta Gray's fingerprints, and he now had two male suspects. He had no desire to see the tutor's pale features, or her emaciated figure again, so soon after their first encounter, but he'd bulked out his list of people to watch. 'And now, I'll let you get on with your story, Roberts.'

'I had a coffee with that Elspeth girl,' Chris began, 'on that last day I remember. I even had the audacity to touch her hand, or maybe she touched mine – it's all a bit hazy – and then I schmoozed her like crazy – all the corny lines I could think of on the spur of the moment.'

'Crikey! You're dedicated, aren't you?' interrupted Carmichael. 'I've seen her and I wouldn't have the stomach for it. She's got a face like a pizza!'

'Carmichael!' Falconer chided him, but secretly agreed, and remembered his own thoughts about extra garlic bread when they had met the unfortunate-looking girl. It had taken a very brave officer to flirt with such a countenance as that of Elspeth Martin.

'It worked, though. She said I could come along to the meeting of the 'advanced' discussion group that evening, but that I'd have to go to her place first. That was because this 'advanced' group is the one that goes a-chanting and a-desecrating, in the old S&P Chapel in Steynham St Michael.

'She got me sorted out with this habit-thingy with a hood, and I followed her car. I must admit to feeling a little bit windy as I drove behind her as to what I was getting myself into, and so quickly. I thought it would take more than a few lascivious leers and a touch of her hand to gain access to this inner circle. I think she'd taken rather a shine to me.'

'So what happened when you got there?' Falconer nudged him, to keep the story flowing. He didn't want some busybody nurse coming along and expelling them from the ward because they were tiring the patient too much.

'We all parked up a disused farm track to the back of the chapel, so that our arrival wouldn't be noticed by anyone in the village, then we put on our robes – and very grateful I was, at the time, for its warmth. It was absolutely freezing – and we trekked across this fallow field, me hoping that we wouldn't run into any poachers who might take a pot-shot at us in surprise.

'Anyway, we reached the chapel, and Jocasta Gray had the key, but only the one to the front door – I think it's the north door – so we had to go round one-by-one, about a minute between each of us, to get in. I was second-to-last, so I was really grateful for the warmth of the habit by then.'

'What happened, when you got inside?' Falconer asked the question, because he could see that Carmichael needed a fractional break to catch up with his notes.

'I couldn't believe my eyes! That Jocasta Gray calmly produced what looked like, and turned out to be, joints, for everyone. It was really eerie, in just the moonlight that penetrated those little windows, seeing all these cloaked and hooded figures, calmly smoking grass.'

'Did you take one yourself?'

'I had to! I lit it when everyone else did, from a burning candle, but I managed to waste most of it, and when I did have to take a toke, I didn't inhale it: just kept the smoke in my mouth for a few seconds, then blew it out again, making appropriate noises of appreciation.'

'I wouldn't have thought of doing that,' commented Carmichael.

'No, I don't expect you would have,' replied Falconer, trying to envisage an occasion where he had to help his partner from the scene, Carmichael leaning heavily on his shoulder, with his build and weight …

And then he remembered what Darren had said – the little nephew of the Ox and Plough's landlord. He had seen someone being helped from the scene. At the time, he'd thought it may have been the near-comatose body of Chris, being steered towards a vehicle, but now he doubted that.

Chris had seen that the inspector was lost in introspection, and had waited for him to re-join them, mentally.

'Anyway, after all the joints were lit, they started some weird chanting: I think it must have been in Greek, because I couldn't understand a word of it, or identify the language. We only had the one candle to light us, and it made the hairs on the back of my neck stand on end. Then Jocasta announced that, as the Lord had seen fit to smite a sinner in pursuit of his sin, they would leave another message for the village.

'She got out this pot of paint – said she was sorry that it was black again, and then they all took it in turns to write – oh, what was it – something like, 'be sure your sins will find you out', because that was what had happened to the workman. He had sinned, and the Lord had smitten him – some daft religious babble or other, about sins and punishment, with the emphasis on punishment. It was all a bit scary, and it really put the wind up me. I didn't realise they were that zealous.

'I just wanted to get out of there: they were a bunch of crazies. At certain points in the chanting, they all agitated their left legs. I haven't the faintest idea why. I can tell you, I was on the point of doing a 'number two', and desecrating – more like defecating, I suppose – my nice new cloak, when suddenly it was all over.

'We all made our way out, leaving as we had come, back across the field, leaving behind us only the scent of skunk and wet paint. Then things get a bit hazy. Nobody put their car lights on to leave, to avoid calling attention to themselves.

'I was just hauling this hairy habit over my head, when I felt a tremendous blow to my right shoulder. I remember yelling, 'Ow! That's is going to leave a bruise, you know,' and then I got an enormous whack round the head, and I don't remember anything else until I woke up in here. I don't know who did it, because I don't remember who had gone and who was still there. I just know it was bloody painful and, apparently, I'm lucky to be alive.'

'Thanks, Roberts. You did a good job under enormous pressure, and in the face of real personal danger. You'll make a good undercover cop.'

'I don't think I like undercover, sir, with all respect. I don't think I want to do that again. Even a cat has only nine lives.'

Chapter Fourteen

Wednesday 10th November

The weather had turned slightly less bitter during the night, and there was a slight dusting of snow when Market Darley awoke the next morning, thus Falconer drove carefully to work, aware of how easily he could lose control of his beloved car in these conditions.

His journey took him through a light fall of tiny flakes, but he had high hopes of this ceasing shortly, as the sky was not threatening, or, in fact, the right colour, for there to be any serious snowfall that morning, but it did bode badly for the winter that was on its way.

Carmichael entered the office about five minutes after the inspector, and called out a cheery good morning, but the sound of his voice was swallowed by silence, like a tasty morsel in the maw of a gannet, and the smile of greeting slid from his face with the liquidity of shit down a cowshed wall.

Falconer was staring over his desk at the sergeant in disbelief. 'And who have you come as today, Sergeant? Nanook of the North? Quinn the Eskimo?'

Carmichael, against the weather, was wearing an antique fur coat (the kind worn by men in the early years of the twentieth century on the other side of the Pond), a sheepskin hat with ear-flaps, and fur boots.

Stopping halfway through removing his coat, he looked at Falconer and asked, 'Who the heck are those guys? Look, sir, it reverses to ordinary coat material,' and he demonstrated, by pulling one of the sleeves inside out.

'Thank God for small mercies,' answered Falconer, in response to this last. 'Nanook of the North was the titular part in a silent film made in 1922, and was also the master of bears in Inuit mythology, who was responsible for the success or otherwise of the hunters, deciding who should find and hunt their quarry, and punishing violations of taboos.'

Good grief! Here he was, back to infringement and punishment again. This case entered every corner of his life, and he would be glad to get it out of the way, so that he could get back to being a normal human being, and not one who analysed everything they did, to see if it was sinful or not. It was really getting to him, this cult.

'Quinn the Eskimo is the titular character of an old song called 'The Mighty Quinn', recorded by, I think, Manfred Mann, a very long time ago, now. Ask your grandmother about it. I bet she'd remember.'

Carmichael's curt reply was, 'What's 'titular' mean?'

'From the title,' answered Falconer, just as curtly. 'So, why are you dressed like that? Is it for a bet? Are you entering a fancy-dress competition? Or are you playing an extra in a film being made locally, that I simply don't know about?'

'I could smell snow when I put my head outside this morning,' was Carmichael's, again, short answer.

'I can't believe you actually managed to squeeze behind the wheel of your car dressed like that.'

'I didn't. I put the coat in the back, and took it out and put it on when I'd parked in the car park.'

'Well, don't go out with me looking like that. People will think there's a grizzly escaped from somewhere and running loose in Market Darley. Where the hell did you get it?'

'I found it in the attic in the house next door. It must have belonged to old Reg's wife. Everyone said she was a big woman,' Carmichael answered.

'I don't know about big: she must have been bleedin' enormous if she wore that thing.'

Falconer, not having been in the greatest of good moods that morning when he'd seen the weather conditions, decided he'd go for a stroll round the town to cheer himself up. It wasn't bitter, as it had been in the previous days, he could do with the exercise, and he'd rather like to sulk in peace.

'I'm off out,' he declared. 'I don't know when I'll be back. Take any messages while I'm gone, and I'll look at them when I get back.' And with that, he had grabbed his coat, and was out of the door without a backward glance at the rather bewildered sergeant.

His wanderings finally took him to a maze of narrow streets that used to serve as workmen's cottages. They fronted straight on to the narrow pavements that ran past them, and had only yards at the back. Some had been turned into workshops and the like and, as he walked along, thinking how different life used to be in the town, was suddenly startled out of his reverie by the appearance of an ice-cream van, which turned rather swiftly into one of these converted workshops, which now had wide wooden doors that opened inwards.

Falconer stopped in the doorway of a corner house that had become a small newsagent's, and watched for a while, but nothing else happened, so he went inside, bought himself a newspaper, and exited to lean against the wall, apparently absorbed in the news of the day.

It was not long before a white van turned up, and also entered the workshop, and he remembered that one of the students had a white van. It would be almost too much of a coincidence if it turned out to be the same one, but he had managed to memorise the number plate, and, taking a pen from his jacket pocket, wrote the number down on the edge of the top page of the newspaper.

A quick glance up and down the old street revealed that a couple of the houses had been knocked together on this side of the road, and a flat sign, not a hanging one, announced it as The Dew Drop Inn. He decided, immediately, that this may be the perfect place from which to conduct a covert surveillance – at least, as long as Carmichael didn't dress the way he had arrived at the office this morning.

After keeping covert observation for another fifteen minutes or so, the most he thought he could get away with before

149

someone challenged his motives for hanging around there, he set off back to the station, determined that he and his sergeant would spend their evening in the Dew Drop tonight, watching out to see if the ice-cream van returned here after its dubious rounds.

It had been spotted late at the college, and in fact, late in other locations, but none of the sightings had been after about half-past ten, so if they arrived about nine, then they could jolly well stay there till closing time, chancing their arm on discovering something. If that didn't work, he'd get Chivers to see what he could do about getting a couple of new faces in there, on 'obo'.

He was, therefore, in a much better mood when he arrived back at his desk, much to Carmichael's relief, and Falconer jumped straight into what he had seen, and his plan for their evening together. 'It's a bit rough down that way, sir,' observed Carmichael, a lifelong habitué of the town who had only recently relocated to Castle Farthing.

'I know; so no fancy clothes or coats. It's jeans and a leather jacket, or something similar for you, and I shall wear my 'old Harrys', and my oldest coat, which I wear for any gardening work in the winter. We're going temporarily undercover as a couple of layabouts with no interest in the area whatsoever, so we don't want to get blown wide open like Roberts, and get out heads bashed in, do we?'

'Not given the choice, sir, no.'

'And no turning that coat inside out and wearing that, tonight. Even with the less opulent side showing, with your build, you'll stick out like a sore thumb – a baddie from a Bond film in a backstreet pub.'

'No, sir. You had a message while you were out. Do you want me to read it?'

'Why didn't you say something as soon as I got in?' asked Falconer, crossly.

'Because I couldn't get a word in edgeways, with respect, sir.'

'My apologies, Sergeant. I was a little excited by my

150

discovery. Go on.'

'It says simply, 'Do you want to meet for coffee and discuss the case so far?' and it's from Dr Dubois. There's a telephone number here, too, if you want it.

Oh, he wanted it! The message was from Honey. Even thinking her name made his insides do a little flip, and he took the piece of paper very gingerly from Carmichael's reaching hand, as if it would self-destruct, if he didn't handle it carefully.

Clearing his throat with both embarrassment and anticipation, he gave Carmichael his orders for the rest of the morning, before going somewhere more private to call the good doctor. 'I want you to get over to Mrs Roberts' house – phone first to let her know you're on your way – and get DC Roberts' rucksack.

'I want that piece of work he said he'd had marked, and I want it fingerprinted and, just for good measure, I want all the prints we've got put through the system. I reckon that Jocasta Gray is in this up to her scrawny little neck, and I'm going to meet someone later who will be able to confirm my opinions. I'm not sure when I'll be back.

'Oh, and I've left the registration numbers of that white van and the ice-cream van to be run through as well. I've noted them down for you. I don't think we'll have any luck with Mr Spliffy's vehicle, but I need to know who the registered owner of that van is. That should make very interesting reading. With any luck, it will turn out to be Aaron Trussler from the college.'

'Yes, sir.'

As it happened, Dr Honey Dubois was free on the instant, so Falconer was left no time to rush home and change and generally spruce himself up, or to get himself worked up into too much of a tizzy. When he called her, she suggested that they meet in a local coffee house – the same one in which Chris had met with Elspeth, although he didn't know that – and said she'd be there in about half an hour.

He, of course, was first to arrive, and was already sitting with a half-drunk latte on the table in front of him when he saw her come through the door. Rising to his feet to greet her, he asked her what she would drink, and went to the counter to order for them both, as his first drink had gone cold. Musing as he went, he thought that he had none of the symptoms he had shown, with the exception of a slightly raised heart-rate, when he had met his last love, and from whom he had inherited Ruby and Tar Baby. Maybe that was a good sign.

He felt strangely comfortable and calm with Honey, as if he had known her a very long time. The raised heart-rate he identified correctly as lust. On his way back to the table, carrying a small round tray with their drinks and some individually wrapped biscuits, he had time to take a serious look at her.

She was very beautiful, her features reminding him of illustrations he had seen of Ancient Egyptian artwork, and he judged her to resemble the Nubians of ancient times. She held herself erect, her head up to look the world in the eye, and for this he fell for her even more. She was a tall woman, a member of an ethnic minority who neither felt out of place, nor inferior to any other person in any way. She looked proud to be who she was, and what she was.

His reverie was broken as, on his approach to the table, she said, 'I thought you'd gone to Costa Rica to pick the beans yourself.'

'Sorry,' he said, turning slightly pink. 'The service is always rotten in here, but at least the coffee's good.'

'That's why I suggested it as a meeting place. Good coffee and neutral territory. That's the best way to meet for the first time, professionally, don't you agree?'

Nodding his head in concurrence, he thought, 'And for the first time, personally.'

'Have you been kept up to date with developments?' he asked, fiddling with one of the wrapped biscuits to stop himself reaching across the table and taking her hand in his.

'Yes, thank you, and I have got some idea of the sort of person we're after. Look, shall I just tell you what my thoughts are, and we'll see if that tallies with who you think you're after?'

'Good idea! Go ahead!'

'Knowing what I do about what has happened, I'd say we're looking for a man, or maybe a very strong woman. A baseball bat's a hefty lump of wood and, given a sufficient swing, could do a great deal of harm in a determined enough woman's hands.

'I also think we're looking for somebody who needs to be in control. That's something that's very important in his or her life – control. They live by a set of rules – maybe not conventional ones – and if they, or anyone else, cross the line, then that must be dealt with.'

'That's transgression and punishment again!' Falconer exclaimed. 'That seems to come up all through this case.'

'Then maybe you're looking for the person who's meting out the punishment.'

'That's the conclusion I've come to, but what is the transgression, and who is the punisher? That's the nub of the whole thing.'

'I don't think you're looking for anyone in that village,' she said. 'I think you'll find your murderer in that strange little group from the college.'

'I know full well that the tutor's involved in this business, somehow, because of the Greek that was painted on the chapel wall: I just don't know how she's involved. And that DC of mine, who was beaten to a pulp, has regained consciousness, and told me about two of the male students in that group: one who actually owns a van, although I don't know the colour, and is on a car maintenance course, and another who said he'd hurt his hand changing a wheel on his car. Either of them would fit the bill very well.'

'Don't go jumping to any conclusions yet. It might seem that a lot has happened, but it's early days yet. I think there's a very tortured soul involved in this somehow. We just have to find out who it is, and I think everything else will just fall into place.' Honey sounded very confident as she said this, and Falconer was impressed. Here he was, going off on surveillance tonight, and she was telling him not to rush off and do anything rash.

He'd not change his mind on that one though, after the physical evidence he had witnessed himself that morning. You never knew what was going to come crawling out when you turned over a stone.

They finished their coffee in companionable conversation, and when he looked at his watch, it was much later than he had thought. As they parted, Honey said, 'We must do this again, sometime, and maybe not just because work dictates. What do you say?'

'Yes!' He managed to make this come out in a normal volume, and not as the shout that he had instinctively wanted to use. 'That would be lovely, er, Honey.'

'Goodbye then, for now, Harry,' she called, as she walked away, and disappeared amongst the other shoppers out in the street.

When Falconer got outside the coffee house he punched the air in celebration. She wanted to see him again! And for pleasure, not for work! This was, indeed, a red letter day for him.

When he returned to the office, it was to find Carmichael in a positive tizzy of excitement. 'Where've you been, sir? I've got the most unbelievable news for you!'

'Tell me, Carmichael. My luck seems to be in, all round, today.'

'I did what you told me, and got that essay – in fact, I took the whole rucksack – from Mrs Roberts, and I got the fingerprint boys to do a rush job for me. While they were doing that, I put through the vehicle registrations numbers you gave me. No luck with the ice-cream van, as per usual, but the computer came up with a name for the owner of the van.'

'Well, don't keep me in suspenders. Whose is it?'

'It belongs to an Aaron Trussler, originally from Hampshire, but I checked, and he's studying at the college. He's one of those we interviewed.'

'What about Jocasta Gray's fingerprints?' asked Falconer,

hoping he was going for gold.

'Jocasta Gray, my bum! That's what she calls herself now. I don't know how she got to be a tutor at that college – probably declaring qualifications she's not entitled to – but she's an ex-tom.'

'A tart!' exclaimed Falconer, completely floored.

'That's right, sir. She's got a list of arrests as long as your arm, but they're all up in London, and they stopped about five years ago. She was calling herself Tracey Smith back then, and there's not been a peep out of her since under either name, and we've got no other aliases on record for her.'

'Well, I'll be blowed! Have we had anything back on those fibres from Steven Warwick's clothes yet?'

'I don't think so, sir. They've identified some from the matting where he was killed, but there are still some still to be accounted for.'

'Then I think I'll just give them a little nudge. Are you still up for tonight's little adventure?'

'As long as it doesn't include being beaten up with a baseball bat, sir.' replied Carmichael, with a completely straight face.

'I don't think it will, but I'll get Bob Bryant to get some of the patrol cars to be on stand-by, in case we run into trouble and need to call for back-up.'

'Good idea, sir.'

'Dress inconspicuously, and I'll meet you in The Dew Drop Inn at half-past nine, I think. We don't want to be hanging around in there any longer than is necessary, and I don't suppose there'll be any action over at the workshop, until ten or half-past, or even later. I just hope the pub doesn't close before we've seen anything. It's not somewhere I'd like to be found loitering after dark.'

'Me neither, sir. I said it was pretty rough round there, and it's even worse after dark. You ask Merv Green about it. There's many a time he's been called out there to break up fights and rescue pub landlords from behind their bars when their pub's been busted up in a mob rumble.'

'I shall be sure to wear my tin hat,' retorted Falconer, and then got one of Carmichael's looks.

'You'd better take it seriously, sir. People get badly injured, if not killed round there.'

'Yes, Sergeant.'

Falconer arrived at their rendezvous a little early. He sported a heavy five-o'clock shadow on his chin, being a man who has to shave twice a day if he's going out in the evening, and this gave him a suitably seedy air when considered with the old clothes he was wearing.

Carmichael arrived a minute or two before the half hour, unspotted by Falconer, so inconspicuously had he dressed, and so sinister and large were some of the other pub's patrons. He greeted the sergeant informally, to tip him off about their mode of address this evening, calling, 'Evening, Davey. Glad you could make it. Thought the old trouble and strife would lock you in the house.'

Carmichael, recovering well after his initial startled expression, cottoned on, and replied, 'Evening there, yourself, Harry. What can I get you, s ...?' He just managed to suppress the 'sir' on the end of that question.

'I'll just have a half of best. I'm a bit bilious tonight. Must 'ave been the old lady's rotten cookin' again.'

Again, Carmichael was momentarily startled by the change in the inspector's accent, but coped well, and was soon returning to the table with a half-pint glass in each hand.

The pub was quite empty so early in the evening, so Falconer had been able to grab a table beside the small window from which he could easily see anything that was going on across the road.

They stuck doggedly to their table, stringing out their halves of bitter like a couple of old ladies on the breadline with their halves of milk stout, in the past. By a quarter-past ten, it was much busier, and neither of them dared to move to get another drink in case their chair was requisitioned.

Across the road, in the workshop, a light sprung up inside,

and the doors were opened to allow access. About five minutes later the ice-cream van drove in, followed, within a few minutes, by the white van, and Falconer was up and out of his seat before Carmichael realised what was going on.

Outside, the inspector concealed himself in the shadow of a neighbouring doorway and made a call on his mobile phone, keeping his voice as low as he could, but no one from opposite could have heard him. There was too much going on inside for anyone in there to be bothered with what was going on outside.

Carmichael approached him and was told that back-up had been requested. 'I've said we'll stay here until they arrive, unless anything starts to happen to let them get away. If it does, I've told them we'll go in and cause a ruckus to delay them, all right?'

'Thanks a bundle, sir. I guess I must be fonder of my face than you are of yours.' Carmichael was definitely rattled.

'We'll just pretend to be a couple of drunks who have wandered in. There's no need to go in there brandishing our warrant cards and yelling that we're police, is there?'

'I hadn't thought of that one, sir. Well done. *Look!* Someone's getting into the driver's seat of the van.'

'Come on, man, let's get across that entrance and make like we're off our faces!' ordered Falconer, who was first away from the starting blocks.

He shot across the road in the obscurity of shadow, then staggered across the access to the workshop, and pretended to lose his balance, rolling around on his back, and singing loudly and tunelessly. Carmichael followed, and made a fine job of not being able to lift him up, eventually joining him on the ground, laughing hysterically at the sort of nothing that drunks habitually laugh at. Maybe they'd learnt something from Amy Littlemore, after all.

There was a shout inside the workshop, and the person who had got into the van, got out again, and walked towards the two figures rolling around on the ground out on the pavement. Whoever was on the inside stayed put and left it for the driver of the van to deal with. There must be at least two other people inside, given that one person had opened the doors, and two others had driven in.

So concentrated was the driver on the laughing and singing coming from the two drunks, it wasn't until it was too late that he became aware of sirens and two patrol cars, one to the right, and one to the left of the doors, skidding to a halt. They had entered the road from opposite ends and, therefore, had both directions covered. Uniformed officers were out of them in a split-second and onto him, others running helter-skelter inside to apprehend whoever was in there too.

Three men were led from the scene in handcuffs, and Falconer was not surprised to see Daniel Burrows and the large, muscular figure of Aaron Trussler, amongst them. The other man, older than the students, managed to still his progress as he got to Falconer's side, and hissed, 'I'll come for *you* when you're sleeping. Don't expect to wake up! And your mate, over there!' indicating Carmichael, who was talking to one of the uniformed men.

Chapter Fifteen

Thursday 11th November

First thing the next morning a warrant was sworn for the arrest of Jocasta Gray, and PCs Merv Green and 'Twinkle' Starr were sent out to serve it, calling firstly at the college, and secondly on her home address, where she was apprehended and brought in for questioning.

When she arrived at the station, Falconer left her stewing in an interview room until he was good and ready to talk to her. 'I can't believe that she's behind this drugs thing: that *she's* actually Mr Spliffy,' he said to Carmichael, while he was consciously wasting time; making her wait until he was prepared to give her some of his.

'Neither can I, sir, but I suppose that's where she got the skunk for the group to smoke,' replied Carmichael.

'Yes; no doubt telling them that it would put them in touch with their spiritual selves, or some such guff!' Falconer was angry.

'Why are people so gullible when it comes to things religious?' the sergeant asked, genuinely perplexed.

'Because they desperately want to believe that 'this' isn't it. They need to know that, when they die, they're not going to simply cease to exist. They want there to be something else ahead of them, so if someone tells them there is, and it's put to them in a way that catches at their imagination, they'll go along with anything, not to have to believe that after death, that's it, forever,' Falconer explained.

He had not told Carmichael about what had been hissed in his ear the night before. It would probably give him nightmares, but there was no need for it to do the same to the unexpectedly sensitive Carmichael.

'But that's why you've got to make the best of what you've got, sir. Because this *is* it,' replied Carmichael.

'That's right, Sergeant, and anything else would be a bonus. Life is the performance, not just the dress rehearsal. Live every day as if it were your last, because one day you'll be right!'

'Blimey! That's a good one, sir.'

'And I know that you do – live every day as enthusiastically as you can – Carmichael. You've got the right idea.'

'Thank you, sir,' replied Carmichael, somewhat nonplussed by this unexpected praise.

'Now come on; we've got someone quite evil to interview, and I want her nailed for everything she's done, whatever it turns out to be. I don't care if we have to add 'not displaying a valid road tax disc' to her charge-sheet; I just want it to be as long as it possibly can be.'

'This isn't like you, sir.'

'She fooled with young minds, and that's unforgiveable. Those memories will be with those students forever. There's no way she can atone for the twisting she's done with their thoughts and beliefs.'

Jocasta Gray sat in the drab interview room with only a uniformed constable by the door across the room from her for company. Although the building had been newly refurbished to serve as a larger police station for Market Darley, rooms like this one had been painted in the same old depressing colours, for no one wanted a suspect to feel comfortable while being interviewed.

While she waited, she went over in her mind her transition from prostitute to spiritual guru. It had been good while it lasted, and would make a good story to relate to the police now that it seemed to be over.

The two policemen entered the room, duly set up the recording device, and the interview commenced. Some old biddy from a church had 'saved' her, when she was living rough, and had found her temporary accommodation and rehabilitation, and this she now related to Falconer and Carmichael, Carmichael taking notes even though the interview was being recorded, such a habit had it become.

She had instantly seen the prospects of using religion to cover more nefarious activities, and had gone along with all the help offered her, responding with the expected gratitude, and supposed change of ways.

She'd always indulged in a little dope, and made contact with her old dealer (Gary Stockman, the man who had been arrested alongside Trussler and Burrows) with a plan not just to get herself a little group of gullible people to hang on her every word (this was part of her character, she said, and nothing to do with dealing), but to 'suffer the little children', as it were: to sell drugs from an innocent vehicle like an ice-cream van. That was the way to make money. She didn't want to do the prostitution thing any more, lying on her back and thinking of a better life.

At this point in her life story Carmichael was so startled that he drew an unintentional line off the edge of the page of his notebook and right across his trouser leg, and a muffled 'oh heck!' was unintentionally recorded on the tape.

'I got into the Strict and Particular cult thing more or less by accident. It was part of my subject – such as it was – by then, having hustled myself into the college as a tutor, and the old members of it began to intrigue me. I could understand the way they controlled their lives and their families, having harsh rules, the breaking of which brought punishment down on their heads from within the chapel members.

'It was Elspeth who first drew me out on the subject, and she was immediately mesmerised by how they had lived, and suggested that we should revive it in some way, perhaps using the students at the college as a base. It was more her idea than mine, but I went along with it, because I had become a bit of a control freak, and liked the idea of – I don't know – perhaps the power, and a little adulation.

'Before I knew what was happening, she had got a few people together and we formed the discussion group. I had enough to do with working with my old dealer, and I could see that some of the recruits weren't exactly enthralled, so I approached the ones I thought might be useful for the other side of my business – that's where Aaron and Daniel came in – and got the inner circle going in the old chapel.

'As for the lads, Aaron knew a bit about vehicle maintenance, and could keep the old van running, and change the number plates, and Daniel was hungry to experience everything in life that he could. The fact that they felt like this was a bonus, because I was only really looking for someone to relieve my partner on the rounds, but they did all that, and went along to the drug handovers.

'Everything was going very smoothly, until, one night, we really got a bit too doped, and I put that writing on the wall of the chapel. Hubris! Arrogance! And the next thing I knew there was a dead body in there, and I began to get a little rattled.

'Of course, I told the inner circle that God had smitten him down because he was a sinner. I did the same when the man who turned out to be one of your lot got beaten so badly. By the way, I haven't the faintest idea who painted the second and third messages on the chapel wall, but I kept quiet about that, even apologising for having to use black paint when we had our last meeting.

'And then there was another death, and I began to think it might be time to move on, but the van was doing so well, and my savings were swelling like they never had done before, so I chickened out of disentangling myself, and just suggested that maybe the van ought to move on to pastures new.

'That was only a couple of days ago, and now it's too late, and I've got to do what I've been telling silly gullible kids to do; take my punishment. After all that control at being the pale, skinny leader, I began to lose weight because of fear of punishment. Will I get a long sentence?'

'Yes,' was Falconer's bleak reply. 'What about the murders and the attempted murder?'

'That was absolutely nothing to do with me. I'll put my hands up for defacing a chapel, but that was only the Greek, done in red paint, because that was the colour that Aaron happened to have with him in his van, but I had nothing to do with murdering or beating anybody. I know absolutely nothing about those incidents, and can only advise you that there may be a psychopath in my inner circle, and I haven't the faintest idea who it might be.'

'Interview suspended at 9.45 a.m.,' Falconer intoned for the recording, reached over to switch it off, then said, 'OK, we'll leave it for now. We'll speak to you again later, Ms Gray,' and swept out of the room, Carmichael in his wake, asking the officer who had been in the room with them to escort Ms Gray back to her cell.

Back in the office he sat down at his desk and put his head in his hands. 'What's up, sir?' asked Carmichael, taking his own seat. 'We've got Mr Spliffy locked up, only he turned out to be a girl, and her partners-in-crime too. And that's got to be a good thing, getting all those drugs off the streets. They were being sold on a daily basis, so that's a lot of drugs, when you add it all up.'

'I know, but it doesn't leave us any further forward with our other case, does it?'

'I think it does, sir. So it wasn't Ms Gray. She said herself that it was more than likely to be someone from her inner circle, and I believe she's right. Who else would have been able to get keys, and actually to know that anything was going on there? After all, who, apart from the people in the village, would have known about the writing on the chapel wall? It was hardly front page news, was it, sir?'

'You're right, Carmichael! It must be someone from within that group. I mean, this case involved, as you said, getting access to the keys and the cloaks, if any of our witnesses are to be believed. How could someone from outside the inner circle have accomplished that? We've got to look at the group members again: interview them until one of them squeals.

'We've got Trussler and Burrows in custody, so we might as well start with them, and get warrants for wherever they live. I don't think it's likely to be that Stockman – he's a menacing so-

163

and-so all right, but he's probably only interested where his *business* is concerned. That baseball bat's got to be somewhere, and if it's not in that workshop, then someone is hiding it, and that's not on. There will be evidence of blood on that weapon, and, no doubt fingerprints. Oh, yes, that baseball bat is a very incriminating item.'

Aaron Trussler was the first of the two students to be brought in for interview, and denied any knowledge whatsoever of a baseball bat. The only one he had ever seen in the flesh – or the wood, to be more precise – had belonged to a friend of his older brother, back home in Devon.

Not in the mood to give up so easily, Falconer asked him about his whereabouts, first on the late evening of Monday the first of November. This produced an initial reaction of, 'Obviously not where you think I was,' followed by a period of what passed for deep thought.

'Got it!' he finally yelled in triumph. I was over at a mates putting in a new clutch for him. That's one of the reasons I'm doing the car maintenance course, so I can earn a bit of money on the side, to help finance my time at college. How could I have forgotten that! He gave me a couple of beers afterwards, well, quite a few, really, and I crashed on his sofa, because I was over the limit. There you go, Mr Plod. That's strike one to me! What else have you got?'

Falconer looked at him, his fine physique, and his well-muscled frame. He was certainly a good candidate for wielding a baseball bat, or whatever had killed Steven Warwick. If his alibi could be proved, that was another suspect gone up in smoke.

'Where were you on the night of Wednesday the third of November, then?' Falconer asked, hoping to catch him out. Maybe he'd only cooked up one alibi, and he could catch him out with the other two dates.

'That's an easy one. We had a meeting – the inner circle, that is, but I expect you know about that already. I was there till late, and I have quite a few witnesses who will verify that.'

'Damn! Of course that had been the night of the inner circle meeting, because it was after that that DC Roberts had received his near-fatal beating.

'Who left first?' Maybe this was the way to trap him, and he could check what he said with the other members about the order of leaving.

'I had to go first. If you must know, I had to get to the workshop that night, to change the number plate on the van again. I was getting terribly fed up with that, but at least it paid, and getting through college isn't easy these days, you know, what with tuition fees and no grants.'

'You'll have plenty of time to study in prison, Mr Trussler,' Falconer informed him, and watched as his face fell, and he realised he would be tried and, no doubt, convicted for his part in distributing drugs via an ice-cream van, of all unlikely vehicles. That was probably why it had been chosen: because it reeked of innocence and children.

This though, could also be verified, unfortunately. Just for the hell of it, Falconer produced his third question. 'What about the night of Friday the fifth of November?' It was his last chance, before he moved on to Burrows, and he had little hope of anything incriminating.

His hopes were immediately dashed. 'I was at a mate's house. He had a firework party, and we started about eight o'clock. We had a bonfire and a load of fireworks, and then, because it was Saturday the next day, we made a bit of a night of it. I knew I had my course the next day, but if I didn't go overboard, and stayed over at his, I knew I'd be all right.'

'You've got an answer for everything, haven't you, Mr Trussler?' barked Falconer, his mood plummeting.

'I've got an *alibi* for everything, you mean. You'll have to do me for that other thing, but I had nothing to do with them three attacks. That's not my style. Violence to others, and the taking of human life, are the most damning of sins, and I wouldn't condemn my immortal soul for that.'

Golly, he may be a bit of a rogue, but Jocasta had certainly got to him, at some level.

Daniel Burrows proved to be a very different sort of suspect to interview, requesting at the very beginning to be asked questions that he need answer only with yes or no, but that didn't suit Falconer's bill at all, and he told him so, in no uncertain manner.

'Young man, you are already under arrest for being an active participant in a drug distribution gang in Market Darley. You will be tried for this, and will, no doubt, go to prison.

'At the moment, however, I have asked for you to be in this room so that I can ask you about your involvement in two murders, and a third attempted murder. We have all the evidence we need for the drugs charges. This is a much more serious matter, and carries a life sentence, should a judge see fit to award it.'

'I had nothing to do with those attacks,' Burrows answered, 'And you can't prove any different.' His smug self-assurance was already getting on Falconer's nerves, and he'd like to have had just one minute alone with him, but that wasn't going to happen, thank God, because it would be the end of his career.

'I want to know where you were on the nights of Monday the first, Wednesday the third, and Friday the fifth of November,' he almost shouted.

Burrows appeared to think for a long minute, then looked up with a cheerful smile, and informed him that he could account for the third, because he had been 'all-cowled up' as he put it, and smoking dope in the Strict and Particular Chapel in Steynham St Michael.

'Apart from that, I simply can't remember where I was on either the Monday or the Friday night. At a guess, the answer would be in my room studying, but whether that's accurate or not, I can't say. It would be of no use whatsoever, even if it were the truth, because there would have been no witnesses. I have the good fortune to have a single room, and the added benefit of privacy that that bestows on me.'

Falconer could feel his hands wanting to make throttling motions, and he ended the interview and dismissed Burrows back to the cells.

'Supercilious little git!' he spat at Carmichael, making the sergeant feel quite affronted.

'Him, not you, you fool,' the inspector said, in a somewhat strangled voice. 'If you could have read my mind during that little interlude, you'd have found it dwelling on rather old-fashioned policing procedures that definitely aren't in the handbook, and never really were.'

'I wanted to give him a good thump, too, if that's any consolation,' confessed Carmichael. 'He's so cock-sure of himself, and he knows we can't touch him without evidence.'

'And what we don't know,' replied Falconer, slightly calmer now, 'is whether there is any evidence. This case is driving me mad. There are too many suspects in it, and far too many weirdoes for my liking. I had to get rid of him before he started dipping into his philosophy course, to try to run rings round us and confound us with science, because I would have gone for him then, and I would also have kissed goodbye to my pension at the same time.'

By lunchtime they were no further forward with regard to the murders and the beating of DC Roberts, and Falconer's frustration was beginning to show.

'I don't think I've ever been so confounded in my entire life! I know it's one of that group: I just don't know which one, but my money was on the men, and now Trussler's come up with alibis for all the relevant times, and that Burrows is so relaxed I'm surprised he's conscious at all. Somebody's laughing up their sleeve at us, and I don't like that at all.'

'Isn't there someone you could talk to about it?' asked Carmichael, innocently.

'Of course! I can give Hon ... Dr Dubois a ring, and seek her opinion. We're supposed to be consulting, after all. Thanks Carmichael! Brilliant man! I'll telephone right away, and see if I can catch her.'

But his luck was out. Dr Dubois was not free until the next day, so he would just have to wait twenty-four hours, which situation, of course, dropped him right down into the pit of despair again. He spent the afternoon applying for search warrants, and mumping and moping about the station, thoroughly disheartened and demotivated. His mood wasn't helped when forensics said they had done all they could with the photograph, but couldn't bring out any facial features on the figure, because it was completely hidden by the hood of the garment it was wearing.

Falconer returned home that night in the dark of a November's evening, thoroughly depressed. Just when he thought he'd wrapped the whole thing up, and done a 'solve-one-get-one-free', he had been turned out of his throne, and left with only half of his kingdom intact, and he wanted that other half so badly, in the shape of the person who had taken two lives, and nearly ended a third.

He flounced into the house, uncharacteristically sulkily, threw down his briefcase, hurled his coat at the rack on the wall, and went straight to the kitchen, without stopping to greet the four cats who had rushed to greet him. Having decided to have beans on toast with lashings of brown sauce for his evening meal, his guilty secret, he was determined not to delay his enjoyment of this treat, in the hope that it would cheer him up a little.

He had only just got the tin of baked beans out of his kitchen cupboard, when the phone rang, and he swore under his breath, as he rushed to answer it.

It was Monica Raynor on the other end of the line. 'I hope you don't mind me calling on this number,' she opened the conversation from her end. 'I got it from Dimity. It's just that I haven't been entirely honest with you about my whereabouts during these awful events in the village.'

'What do you mean, you haven't been entirely honest?'

'That first body.'

'What about it?'

'Dimity wasn't the first to find it. I was!'

'You?'

'Yes. I had an … an assignation, I suppose you'd call it, with

Steve Warwick.'

'Did you?' Falconer was dumbfounded at this confession.

'We were having a bit of a fling,' she admitted. 'I was supposed to pretend to go out on a call, then meet him at the chapel. We'd been using the little vestry, you see. He'd got the key because he was supposed to be finishing up there, on his own.'

'Go on. I don't believe I'm hearing this. Why didn't you say something to me sooner?' he asked.

'Because of Quentin going missing. Then he came back. Then he went missing again. And then he was dead, and I was getting all the sympathy of a recently widowed woman. And by then, it seemed so tacky to admit to having an affair, when Quentin's body was barely cold.'

'I can understand that, but why didn't you have a discreet word with me? I could have suppressed the information while we worked out whether it had anything to do with the case. So, go on, tell me what happened when you got there.'

'The door was unlocked, as I expected it to be, so I went inside to see where he was, and I thought I saw him lying on the stone table they used for an altar, as a little 'come on'. I even thought, 'Yes, I wouldn't mind sacrificing you, even if it is only your morals that are at risk.' Then, when I got nearer, I could see there was something very wrong. He was lying sort of strangely. His position didn't look natural.

'Of course, when I got close up, I realised he was dead, then I heard someone outside, and belted up to the organ loft out of the way. I had no idea who it was, and I didn't want to be caught there by the murderer, did I?'

'And it was Dimity – Miss Pryor,' Falconer continued for her.

'No!' she exclaimed. 'No, it wasn't her. It was some girl that I'd never seen before. She had a pot of paint with her, and she did that graffiti on the wall – *vengeance is mine sayeth the Lord* – then she just calmly put the lid on her paint pot, and went out again. I couldn't believe my eyes.

'I just stayed where I was, so shocked, I couldn't move.

There was Steve, on the altar, dead, and there had been that girl, just painting on the wall, as if nothing was out of the ordinary. I stayed there for quite some time, literally paralysed with fear, then I realised I had to pull myself together, because I had to go back to the office, and I didn't want Quentin to see that there was anything wrong.

'That was when Dimity came in, followed by all the others, and I curled myself up into a little ball to try to make myself as inconspicuous as possible, because there was no way I was going to take the blame for any of this, and I didn't want Quentin to find out I'd been cheating on him. Again.' Her voice stuttered to an embarrassed halt, as she came to the end of her confession.

'Why on earth didn't you tell me sooner? I've been running round in circles trying to identify the person responsible for these crimes. I've had to question your fancy man's workmates, and his family and friends. I've been questioning people in the village, and I've interviewed a lot of people at the college as well.'

'I'm so sorry. I've been such a coward.'

'Well, why don't you make up for it now, and tell me what the girl looked like?'

'I don't know! I told you, I was so scared, I thought I was going to wet myself. I just screwed up my eyes tight shut until I heard her leave, once I'd seen her start her painting.'

'But you'd seen the woman,' Falconer countered. 'Do you think you'd recognise her again, if you saw her?'

'Oh, yes,' confirmed Monica. 'I could do that, all right, I just can't describe her. If I see her face again, though, I'll be sure.'

'But you must know what she looks like. Was she tall or short?'

'I don't know. I was looking at her from above.'

'Was she fat or thin?' asked Falconer, desperately trying for some sort of description.'

'Not thin. That I do know, though her figure was foreshortened by my view, and she wore baggy clothes.'

'Was her hair short or long? Fair or dark? Straight or curly?'

he continued, desperate to nail her down on some details.

'Don't know. Let me think! Don't rush me! It wasn't dark, it was sort of fair. It wasn't curly either. I think she must have had a ponytail or a plait, or something like that, because I know it wasn't short, but it wasn't flying around over her shoulders, or anything like that, but that's all I can tell you. I simply don't remember any more.'

'Well, thank you for coming clean in the end, Mrs Raynor, and for scouring your memory about the girl's description.'

'I'm actually quite grateful to Quentin, for going this way,' she added, somewhat cold-heartedly, in Falconer's opinion. 'Instead of being rivals for his, in my case, doubtful affections, Roma Kerr and I have become firm friends. I haven't had a proper female friend since I was in my late teens, and it feels like I've got a lot of catching up to do. I mean, Tilly and I were always friendly – you remember Tilly Gifford – but she's such an insatiable gossip that I could never confide in her, and know my secrets would be safe. It's different with Roma.'

'How very nice for you,' said Falconer, muttering under his breath, 'Bully for you!' as he ended the call.

Apart from that rather bizarre verbal post script that was along the lines that he had been thinking along himself. It must be one of the girls from the inner circle, as Monica's call had just drawn a line through Jamie Huntley, and he, Falconer, had been following a path to nowhere with Trussler and Burrows.

No wonder they'd been so confident he would find nothing incriminating. There was nothing to find. What a fool he'd been, being led from the straight-and-narrow like that, just because they'd been involved with Mr Spliffy, or *Ms* Spliffy, as they were obliged now to think of the character.

That left Elspeth Martin, Antonia Knightly, and Amelia Harrison. Maybe he'd give Carmichael a call when he'd had something to eat, and they could make a surprise call on all three, this evening: take them by surprise, before they have time to appreciate the seriousness of the arrests of Trussler, Burrows, and Jocasta Gray.

A quick call to the sergeant confirmed that he'd drive over to

Falconer's, and they'd set off at about eight o'clock.

Carmichael arrived dead on time, and they eventually set out in Falconer's car, Carmichael's parked a little further round the end of the cul-de-sac, after Falconer had asked him in, while he finished turning off lights, generally fussing around, and finally donning warm clothes, for the weather had turned bitter again. 'So, where are we going first?' asked Carmichael, having had the bones of Monica Raynor's phone call explained to him over the telephone.

'We'll pick up that Elspeth Martin first, then go on for the other two. Martin will be easy, as she's in the Halls. I've got home addresses for the other two,' Falconer replied. 'We'll need to bring in all three of them for questioning then, if we get lucky, get search warrants. I want whoever did this put away, because they're damned dangerous.'

'I couldn't agree more, sir, and I bet Chris Roberts does too. Any idea what's happening with him?'

He's going to be signed off sick for at least a couple of months, while his broken bones mend, then, I suppose it'll depend on how his mother is. If she's recovered sufficiently to cope after her stroke, then he'll go back off to Manchester. After the time he's had here, I bet he'll be glad of the peace and quiet up there.'

'He's not had an easy time down here, has he, sir?' asked Carmichael, reflecting on the many and various injuries that the DC had sustained during his short service in Market Darley.

A bit of luck meant that they actually found Amelia Harrison at Antonia Knightly's house, as they were spending the evening together, discussing the arrest of their tutor and two of their group members, so it was a double arrest that took place at the Knightly household; something of a shock for Antonia's parents, who agreed meekly to let the Harrisons know of their daughter's arrest.

These two were driven to the station, where Carmichael duly booked them in, then joined the inspector, for their trip to the halls of residence.

By now it was nine-thirty, because of the paperwork involved in booking them in, but they were sure they would catch their third quarry unawares. Into the Halls they went, checked her room number, then started climbing the stairs to the second floor.

Her room was the third door down on the left but when they knocked there was no answer, and no light showed at the base of the door from inside. 'Hell and damnation!' swore Falconer. 'She's got wind that we were on the way!' he exclaimed angrily.

'Either that or she's just gone out, sir. There could be a quite innocent explanation,' Carmichael suggested.

'I suppose you could be right,' the inspector had to admit, and they trailed downstairs again, all adrenalin evaporated, all excitement gone. Falconer had hoped for a hat-trick of arrests tonight, and he had been cheated of his final quarry.

The drive home was almost in silence, except for a grumble from Carmichael, who began another complaint against the newest inhabitant of Castle Farthing. 'That bloke has been getting on Kerry's nerves, now, sir,' he started, without preamble.

'What bloke, Carmichael?'

'That one I told you about, who thought he was a great wit, and was always shoving his nose into other people's business. You remember? The one who made fun of me and the dogs.'

'Right, so I do. What's he been doing to upset Kerry, then?'

'Well, now that's she's quite big, what with being pregnant, every time he sees her he calls out, 'Have you seen my football, love? Oh, you've eaten it, have you?' and it's really getting on her nerves. She knows how big she's getting, and doesn't need a daft old beggar like him to keep drawing attention to it.'

'You'll just have to tell her to ignore him, and maybe he'll get bored, and pick on someone else,' Falconer advised him.

'I've already done that, but this chap doesn't ever seem to get bored by saying the same thing, over and over again.'

'Give him time. I should think, remembering what he was like, that the Brigadier will be the first one to crack and give

173

him a four-penny one.'

'I hope so, sir, because I don't want it to be me.'

'You keep your hands to yourself, Sergeant. I can't have my partner up on a charge of assault. I need you by my side, so be warned.'

'Yes, sir.'

To try to lighten the mood, and to sweeten the bitterly disappointing end to the evening, Falconer asked if Carmichael would like to come in for a cup of tea.

'I'd love to, sir, but there's something I've got to do first,' he replied.

'What's that?'

'Kerry gave me a letter to post on my way out, and I've already forgotten to put it in the village post box. I noticed you had one at the end of the close, so I'll just take the car down there, pop it in the box, then I won't have to think about it again,' Carmichael explained. 'I'll never remember to do it if I leave it till I get back to Castle Farthing.'

'Fair enough! I'll get the kettle on, then, and leave the door on the latch for you.'

As Carmichael drove off, Falconer let himself into his house, and went straight through to the kitchen to do as he had promised, setting out cups and saucers on a tray, and putting the teapot, milk jug, and sugar basin (full) next to them. He filled the kettle, then bent to stroke the cats who were, all four of them, round his legs, meowing like mad.

'Whatever's up with you lot, then?' he asked, bending down to stroke them, and his answer was just another chorus of urgent mewing. Noticing that the back door was unlocked, he put this down to his unexpected decision to go back out that night, and turned the key. He must have left it open when he took the rubbish out, before he ate.

His next goal was to get his work shoes off and his slippers on, so he headed straight for the sofa and bent down to unlace his footwear, when he was aware of several things happening simultaneously.

The chorus of cats had moved, with him, into the sitting

room, and had grown louder. One of its singers had changed its call to an angry hiss; he noticed a shadow he had not been aware of before, from behind; and as his instincts thrust him forward, and out of his seat, a heavy object cracked him a hard knock on the arm.

There was a yell from the front of the house, a chorus of hissing and spitting from behind where he had been sitting, and a baseball bat crashed down where he had just sat, the second swing already in motion when he had barely escaped the first.

He grabbed his arm as pain flooded up it, there was a squealing noise from his attacker, who had been attacked at a low level by the defending cats, and then a figure flew through the air, and both it and his attacker disappeared down behind the sofa. But his pain was agonising, and he had thoughts only for that at the moment, tears pouring out of his eyes in reaction.

Gritting his teeth, and following the noise behind his furniture, he laid eyes on a furious Carmichael pinning Elspeth Martin to the ground, a discarded baseball bat about a foot from her hands, and his four pets sitting round them booing enthusiastically. The young woman struggled like a man as he dialled 999 and called for back-up, and it was all Carmichael could do to hold her. His superior weight won in the end, though, and when a patrol car arrived he had her firmly pinned down and sat securely on her chest to make sure she didn't get up again before assistance arrived.

The officers from the patrol car cuffed her and read her her rights, and Falconer then explained who she was, and that he had been about to arrest her himself earlier this evening. That changed the complexion of things, and they took her back to the station to be booked in like her fellow group members for questioning in the morning. The baseball bat was wrapped up and covered, one each end, by evidence bags, and put lovingly into the boot of the patrol car. Forensics would be able to extract a story from that, and what a story it would be.

As the uniformed officers led a hand-cuffed Elspeth Martin off the premises, Falconer thanked Carmichael for forgetting to post his letter, then, at Carmichael's imbecilic expression, explained that if he hadn't gone out to post it he could not have come in time to save him, Falconer.

'But she might have got us both, sir,' replied Carmichael, looking a little shaken after his encounter with such a violent young woman.

'I doubt it, big, strong chap that you are.'

'She was so strong, though. Chris described her as chubby, but there wasn't an ounce of fat on her. She was solid muscle, and she knew how to use it.'

'Well, come on in, now, for that cup of tea. I could do with a bit of company for the next half hour or so,' Falconer urged him.

'Not until you've had that arm x-rayed, sir. It could easily be broken, the strength of that one.'

'OK, but you'll have to drive me. It's too painful to use, so I suppose we'd better get on down to the hospital.'

'She could've killed you, sir, if I hadn't come back.' Carmichael spoke in a chilled voice.

'I know, and I wouldn't have been the first, either.' replied Falconer, beginning to shiver, not just because of the temperature, but because of the shock.

Chapter Sixteen

Friday 12th November

Falconer didn't leave the hospital until a little after one in the morning, with his arm heavily bandaged and splinted, but not plastered. He was told it would probably give him considerable pain for the next week or so, but that it wasn't broken, just badly bruised, bone as well as flesh. During that time he wouldn't be able to drive or to operate machinery, and he should be careful not to put too much strain on it.

Carmichael drove him home and promised to pick him up in the morning, but not too early as he needed his rest after a shock like that. Those girls could just stew in their own juices until his inspector was rested enough to question them, as far as the sergeant was concerned, and, for once, Falconer didn't disagree with him.

When Carmichael came to collect him the next morning he was still in pain and woozy from the painkillers. They only dulled the sensation of injury in his arm, and he was glad not to have to drive. He'd had to have a strip-wash because he'd been told to keep the bandages on his arm dry, and although this was no problem usually – he'd had to do it countless times in the army – he was used to being able to use his right arm to get to all those secret little nooks and crannies, and his left hand just wasn't up to the job.

On the lavatory he'd had a minuscule moment of envy for Arabs, who were supposedly proficient with their left hand at this sort of thing. He had never before realised how very necessary and difficult it was to wash just one hand really thoroughly. And getting dressed had been sheer torture, especially getting his injured arm into a shirt and jacket, with the hard plastic and metal splint under the bandages making it an even harder job.

The cats had had to make do with a perfunctory scattering of dried food in their bowls, and a rather lackadaisically poured stream of water into their bowls, and were sulking at the lack of attention.

Breakfast was out of the question, and he had already decided that he'd get something from the canteen when he got to the station. Maybe Carmichael would be kind enough to cut up his food for him so that he could get away with using just a fork.

He wasn't looking forward to interviewing Elspeth Martin – she of the twin personalities: one, mild and gentle, and careful not to sin; the other a wild beast that slew fellow human beings without an ounce of guilt. Weirdly, he began to work out how many grams there were in an ounce, then realised this bizarre train of thought was probably a side-effect of the painkillers, and tried to distract his mind with other thoughts. Elspeth Martin behind bars – now there was something to think about!

And the Christmas decorations! They seemed to have sprung up in every shop in every street, and it was still November. It seemed like only a few days ago that all the shops had been stuffed with Hallowe'en goodies, and now here was Christmas, ready to be rolled out like a magic commercial carpet. Slade blared from some outdoor loudspeakers as they rounded the market cross, and he felt as if he had been cheated out of the last bit of his year before all that nonsense started again.

In the station canteen he decided that, if Carmichael were to be 'mother' with his breakfast, he might as well treat himself to a full English. By God, he'd earned it! And he had the bandages to prove it!

They sat in silence, as Carmichael gravely cut his bacon, egg, sausage, and fried bread into bite-sized pieces, and Falconer looked on fascinated. No one had done this for him since he had been a young child, and it made his feel quite nostalgic for the lack of responsibility that being in the nursery meant – except for the duration of Nanny Vogel's reign, that is.

As he was thus wrapped in nostalgic thoughts, he became aware of Carmichael speaking to him. 'What was that?' he asked, guiltily, wondering just how long his reverie had lasted.

'I just wondered if you'd like me to feed you, sir,' repeated Carmichael, holding up a forkful of bacon which dripped egg yolk. 'Open wide, sir.'

'Shut up and give me that fork, Carmichael. Someone might see! For goodness' sake, I'm not totally incapable. I just can't use my right arm and hand at the moment.'

Completely unoffended, Carmichael confessed that he couldn't do anything with his left hand; it was just another tool for holding things. As far as eating went, if he tried it, he knew he'd shove the food up his nose, or somewhere else inappropriate.

'That's as may be, Sergeant, but I'm perfectly capable of feeding myself, left-handed or not. But thank you for the offer, anyway,' he added, in a quieter voice. The man's heart was in the right place, even if his brain worked a little differently from the norm.

'Are we going to interview that Martin woman after you've eaten?' asked Carmichael, after he'd gone back to the counter and come back with three bacon rolls for himself.

'I thought you'd had breakfast at home,' commented Falconer, inspecting Carmichael's loaded plate.

'I did, sir, but you know how it is. I'll need the fuel, so I might as well fill the tank while I've got the opportunity. And what about this Martin?'

'We'll get straight on to her. She's got a lot of questions to answer, and it's obvious we've got our killer after what happened last night.'

'She's built like a weight-lifter, sir. I don't know what Chris was on about when he said she was chubby. I mean, I know she wears baggy clothes, and all that, but there's not a scrap of fat on her, and she can certainly fight her own corner. At one point I thought she was going to get the better of me.'

'Well, I'm glad you're going to be in that room beside me. I don't fancy my chances against her at all. She'd make mincemeat of me in just a couple of minutes.'

'Yes, sir.'

'You're not supposed to agree with me, Carmichael. You could at least say I had a slight chance.'

'Yes, sir.' Carmichael was keeping out of this one, and sat happily on the fence, eating his bacon rolls.

'Oh, and by the way, let me explain to you what those cult members wore around the tops of their legs,' said Falconer, loading his fork with a tidy pile of baked beans.

Carmichael was still shocked if far better acquainted with the usage of the cilice when they left the canteen and went off to carry out the interrogation of their number-one suspect.

When they got to the interview room Martin was already there, PC Starr just inside the door on guard, although what use she'd have been against this mauling monster, Falconer had no idea. Then he remembered how many self-defence courses Starr had been on, and he had to admit that she'd have also had the advantage of being light and quick.

The tape was started and the interview began. Martin sat at the other side of the table, no solicitor present, and no desire to have one there. 'I'm accountable only to God for my sins, whatever you say,' she had stated, for the tape, and had left Falconer a little flustered at the confident tone in which she'd said this.

'I want you to tell me what you were doing on the night of Monday the first of November,' he said, wondering how she would respond to direct questioning.

'I did a number of things. Which of them would you like me to tell you about?' Boy! She was cool!

'Did you see a Mr Steven Warwick, who had been working at the Strict and Particular Chapel in Steynham St Michael?' he asked.

'Only briefly. When I killed him,' she answered, still unruffled.

'So you admit that you killed him?'

'Of course I do. Lying is a sin.' It all sounded madly logical, when looked at from her point of view.

'And murder isn't?' Falconer was aghast.

'Not when you're the Lord's instrument, and are smiting a sinner,' was her reply.

'But ... how did you know you were the Lord's instrument?'

'He told me, when I prayed to him for an answer.'

'An answer to what?'

'To what should be done about Mr Warwick. He was a married man, and he was committing adultery with a married woman.'

'So, why didn't you kill her as well?' This interview was lurching into the realms of fantasy.

'Because it's always the man's fault. And anyway, I could get round to her any time I wanted. But I had other fish to fry, shortly after that.'

How had fish got themselves into the questioning? Was it the symbol of Christianity she was going on about? For a moment, Falconer's head swam as the painkillers gave him another psychedelic jolt, but he managed to say, 'So, tell me about it,' in a reasonably normal voice.

'I knew what had been going on in the chapel, because I overheard them one evening, arranging another one of their little meetings as they were leaving the chapel. It was obvious what they'd been up to. And I knew he'd be there that day, finishing off, and God had told me to smite him, so I went there with the Lord's work to do.'

'So what exactly happened? Did he just stand there while you took a swing at him? And what was it you hit him with? It certainly wasn't the baseball bat.'

'I took in a tyre iron from the boot of my car.' So that might explain the oil stains on his clothing, thought Falconer. 'I had a loose cape on, so it was easy to hold it beneath the folds of that. I simply told him that I had a message for him from a woman in the village. I said she'd told me to tell him she'd left him a note to change the time of a meeting: very vague I was, so that he'd think I didn't know what they were up to. I said she'd told me she'd hidden it in the pages of one of the hymn books, on the top shelf of that bookcase that held hymn and service books.

'Of course, as soon as he started looking for it he ignored me, and I got out the tyre iron and gave an almighty swing at his head, and that was that. Down he went, like a sack of coal. My old gran used to burn coal, and she said that was what they'd use in Hell because it burnt so hot.'

Ignoring this last aside, Falconer continued his questioning, which had definitely developed an air of unreality which complemented the semi-detached mood the tablets had created for him. 'Where did you get the table cloth you covered him with?'

'That was on top of a cupboard in the tiny vestry. I just shook the dust out of it before throwing it over him.'

'And you didn't have any difficulty moving him?'

'I didn't expect to, because I work out, you know. I like to be in control of my body, and keep it in as good a shape as I can, so that I'm fit to do the Lord's work when he calls me to it. But he was a really big man for me to lift up on to that altar, and the first time I tried it I dropped him face first on to the front corner of the left-hand side. Caught him right in the eye, that did, as I found out when I turned him over. What a butterfingers I felt. Not enough upper body strength!'

'So how did you find out that Chris Roberts was an undercover policeman?' That was the thing that Falconer wanted to get to the bottom of. He'd sent Roberts undercover, and he wanted to know how that cover had been blown.

'Easy as ABC,' she answered. 'I gave him a lift, and he wanted to be dropped off at that big roundabout just outside the town. It was a doddle keeping him in sight until he finally reached where he lived. I parked at the end of the road, feeling quite excited, as I'd gone to school with a girl who lived opposite.'

'But you're in the halls of residence,' interrupted Falconer, puzzled that she wasn't still living at home.

'My parents and I don't see eye to eye about my beliefs, and they 'encouraged' me to leave by paying my rent for the room. And I didn't give a fig. I knew I made them feel uncomfortable, but that cut both ways. I didn't approve of the way they ate too much and drank too much alcohol. My mother was also a terrible gossip, and I found that sinful as well. So I went.

'But there wasn't anything to stop me calling in on an old friend and asking a few questions, now was there? As it happened, she was out, but her mother asked me in for a cup of tea, and I told her all about this chap at college that my best mate fancied, and said I thought I'd seen him go into the house opposite.'

'"Oh, that'll be Mrs Roberts' son, Chris,"' she said, with no idea of the consequences of what she was about to tell me. "Mrs Roberts had a stroke, you know," she rambled on, "but luckily her son, Chris, is in the police force, so he was able to get transferred down here to look after her for a while."'

'Well, that was it, as far as I was concerned. We had a traitor in our midst, and he must be removed. I prayed about that. The baseball bat was a gift from a relative when they'd gone on holiday to the States, and the good Lord suggested that I might like to try it out.'

My arse, he did! thought Falconer. 'But you didn't put him in the chapel. Why not?'

'Because I didn't want what had happened being tied up with our group, and this was more personal. If you remember, I told you once before that I like Chris, but you didn't take any notice of the use of the past tense. I had liked him, until I found out what I did about him: him being a police spy and all that. Anyway, I just loaded him into the car and drove him somewhere out of the way. How did I know that doctor was going to come along and find him?'

'So you left him for dead?'

'Of course I did. If I start a job, I like to finish it.'

'So, how did you distract Chris enough to whack him into that state?'

'I said I had to get something out of the boot, so would he be good enough to shove the habits on the back seat. I left mine on top of the car, so it'd take him just that tiny bit longer. By the time he'd got them both through the car door, I'd got the bat out of the boot, and just swung like fury, and the Lord must have been in me, because I caught him hard enough for him to be slightly out of it. The rest of the beating was easy.

'I was horrified when you thought you were breaking the fact that he was in hospital to me, when I thought you were going to tell me he was dead. That was why I was so upset. I hadn't done the Lord's work efficiently enough.'

This was all said in such a matter-of-fact voice that Falconer's blood was chilled, and while on that topic, he wondered at her amazing *sang froid*, to have done all that she had done, and not turn a hair.

'What about Quentin Raynor? You weren't punishing him just for being the husband of an adulteress, were you?'

'Absolutely not! He'd met Jocasta somewhere; I don't know where, but I knew that he had been seeing her on the quiet. In fact I'd overheard them in a coffee house in the town, arranging to meet in the chapel. Of course, that wasn't what they actually said, but I knew very well what they were up to. She didn't give any details, because there were other people around, but she slipped him a piece of paper under the table, and just whispered, "Midnight. Read the note." Luckily I can lip-read. I've got a deaf cousin, so I learned all about it.'

'So how on earth did you stop Jocasta from being there to meet him?'

'Something cropped up, or I don't know quite how I'd have managed it. She got a phone call at the end of the day, when we were finishing up the coursework for the week, and she asked me to stay behind after the others had left.

'She told me she had to go and collect something that evening, straight after the inner circle gathering – there was something about there being no one else available to do it, and that she'd have to fill in. Her problem was that she'd arranged to meet someone, and she couldn't just phone or text him now, because he thought his wife was on to him, and he couldn't get a pay-as-you-go mobile until after the weekend, because he was too busy.

'Perhaps I could get a message to him, letting him know that she'd have to rearrange, and for me not to worry about anything, because she was hoping he would be another convert to the inner circle, and would give us access to another generation through him.

'Well, that was a load of twaddle, but it suited me perfectly. Here was an unrepeatable chance to get him on his own. He was an adulterer, and he'd sullied our leader; our lovely Jocasta. Of course, she'd have to accept her own punishment for it when she was faced with it, and confessed her sins; but for now, I'd settle for him.'

'It was easy enough to be the last to leave. Everyone else had smoked a bit of dope, but I'd not inhaled, to keep a clear head.'

'Some of you were seen that night. There were witnesses to your presence there,' Falconer interrupted her.

'Trespass is a civil offence,' she answered coolly, and carried on with her story. 'I used the same pretext as before. When he turned up, I told him that Jocasta couldn't make it, but had left him a note in one of the hymn books on the top shelf, only this time I'd had the chance to go back to my car, under the pretext of leaving, and come back with my bat, which was concealed under my robe. The rest, as they say, is history: a direct repeat of it, in fact, but without the tablecloth this time.

'Oh, if you see Chris, would you tell him I really liked him, and I'm sorry he was a sinner, or at least hoping to be – with me.' She blushed a dark red at this point, and looked almost coy, except that, with her acne, which had worsened considerably in the last few days, she looked more like one of the more evil models from Madame Tussauds.

'Interview terminated at …' Falconer had to get out of that room before he was sick. The piety of the woman in the face of what she'd done had turned his stomach, and he had to get some fresh air before he lost that lovely breakfast that Carmichael had so carefully cut up for him.

Once back in his own office, Bob Bryant rang to say that when Elspeth's room had been searched, the tyre iron had been found on the top of her wardrobe, beneath a pile of clean bed linen and towels. Her car had revealed the presence of a blood-stained robe, and a spare.

That only left the other fibres from Steve Warwick's clothing, and a brief call to the forensic department came up with a result on those, but a perfectly innocent one. It was believed that, just before he finished his work in there, Steven Warwick had lain on the threadbare rug that sat in the choir stalls, to touch up the wall there. The fibres were a perfect match, although the joker on the other end of the line suggested that the fibres on Warwick's clothes probably represented more than were left in the rug by now. That was all, apart from the few fibres from the other threadbare specimen, where Doc Christmas said the man had been felled, but that was only to be expected.

When Carmichael came back into the office he took one look at Falconer and told him to go home. 'If you don't take a couple of days off on sick leave, I'm going to report you to Chivers for not being fit for work. I can finish up here for you. You get off out of it. You could do with a complete break, and at least your arm's not actually broken. Go home and do nothing for a couple of days, until you've finished those painkillers.

It made sense, and so he did.

Epilogue

Friday 19th November

Falconer was feeling a good deal better by now, and found that he could drive again. He had, therefore, decided that he would go back to work the following day, a Saturday, so there wouldn't be too many people around, he hoped. But before he did that, he wanted to pay a last visit to Steynham St Michael, and speak to Dimity Pryor. He knew she'd like to hear the real story, and he was also sure that, if the story came from him, she would feel better about the chapel.

The weather was bitter and windy that morning when he set out, and dirty-grey clouds were beginning to scud across the sky. Falconer, not being a countryman, had no idea what that indicated, but just hoped that it kept itself at bay until he had completed his visit and returned home.

He located Dimity in the charity shop that she managed in the High Street, and she immediately closed up for a while so that they could go back to her cottage to converse in private.

As she put on the kettle she called through a question to him. 'Would you mind if I invited Vernon and Charles along? They were here with me when all this was starting, and we were thrown so much together after what happened earlier this year, that I think it's only right that they should hear everything from the horse's mouth – not that I'm calling you a horse, or anything rude like that.'

'No problem,' he called back. A few days off had not only helped his arm, but his general mood, and he was feeling magnanimous today, sitting in this cosy little cottage in front of a log fire which Dimity had set a match to when he had arrived.

Within ten minutes there were two more 'be back soon'

187

signs on shop doors in the High Street, and Vernon Warlock and Charles Rainbird had arrived, blowing on their hands and stamping their feet to keep them warm as they entered.

Dimity distributed cups of steaming hot tea and passed round a plate of chocolate digestives, and Falconer got stuck into his narrative, to many 'ohs' and 'ahs', and managing to omit the bits which involved Monica Raynor and, at the end, there was a short silence as his audience struggled to break the narrative spell.

'Such wickedness!' commented Dimity, at last.

'Such cunning!' added Charles.

'And all done by a girl, of no age at all,' finished Vernon.

'I'm surprised you haven't had Tilly Gifford round sniffing for titbits. She's the village gossip-hound, isn't she?' asked Falconer, helping himself to another biscuit.

'Oh!' exclaimed Dimity, 'I forgot! She'll be back today.'

'Back from where?' Falconer enquired.

'She's been away on a three-week winter break to the Canaries,' Charles Rainbird informed him, then burst out laughing. 'She's going to be furious that she missed all the action.'

'Remember what she was like last time?' asked Vernon with a little snicker, then sobered, as they all did, as they thought back to what had actually happened in that dark time of their lives.

'Well, there's nobody local hurt this time,' Dimity announced, and then looked horror-stricken. 'Oh, no! I totally forgot about poor Quentin. I suppose what I really meant was nobody from our little circle.'

'Don't worry about it,' Falconer advised her. 'It's all finished with now, bar the shouting, and I don't think we'll have any trouble at all with a conviction, although she'll probably go to an establishment for the criminally insane, because as far as I'm concerned, she's completely lost the plot – gone gaga – lost her marbles – however you want to put it.

'And you know, when I stood in the chapel the day Quentin's body was found, I read that quotation on the wall, and I knew I'd seen it somewhere before recently, and I've just remembered where.'

'Be sure your sins will find you out,' murmured Dimity. 'It was in the anonymous letter that led to my cousin Gabriel's suicide.'

'That's right, Miss Pryor. This village does seem to have deep religious roots.'

'And until this year, I thought all that was in the past. Still, old sins cast long shadows, although that doesn't seem to have been so in this case,' she added.

'Unless you count the shadows cast by the Strict and Particular's unusual take on punishment,' Falconer replied.

'I suppose you could be right at that, Inspector. I suppose we'll just have to wait for the sun to go in, as far as that's concerned.'

'Oh, by the way, your keys,' Falconer suddenly remembered.

'I'd forgotten all about those, with all the trouble that's we've had,' exclaimed Dimity, shocked at how remiss she had been.

'The set the builders had was found in Mr Warwick's pocket, and I'll get those back to you as soon as I can. The key the cult used was an old one that just happened to fit. Apparently Ms Gray used to collect such things for decorative purposes, then realised they might be a bit more valuable if she put them to a more practical use. That will also be returned to you in due course, but at the moment, it's a piece of evidence, and must remain with the police until after the trial.'

'Don't give it another thought, Inspector. It was very astute of you to remember them at all, but I shall sleep more soundly in my bed knowing that they are all accounted for.'

Carmichael called round on his way home that evening to see for himself whether the inspector was well enough to return to work the next day.

Satisfied with what he found, he began to fill Falconer in on what he'd missed in his absence. 'We seem to have acquired a little cat,' he began, crouching down to make a fuss of Falconer's four furry housemates.

'How's that?' Falconer enquired, busy making a pot of tea for his visitor. That was easy enough, with one arm still a little unreliable.

'She just turned up out of the blue a couple of weeks ago, and she's been round every day. A few days ago she started coming into the house – the cold, I expect – so I took her to the vet to see if she had a chip, but nothing.

'The vet said she was a pedigree – an Abyssinian, I think he called her – and we're allowed to keep her; unless she wanders off again, I suppose. Oh, but she's a fantastic cat, sir. She's so clever, you wouldn't credit it.'

'So you know the sex of this pet, then,' Falconer cut in sarcastically.

'The vet told me,' replied Carmichael, trying to retain his dignity. 'He also said she'd been spayed.'

'Have you got a name for her, yet?'

'She's so into everything, we've decided she's a right little monkey, so that's what we've called her – Monkey. You'll meet her when you come round for Christmas. Now, don't look at me like that. You promised ages ago that you'd come this year, and I'm going to hold you to that. Kerry and the boys would be devastated if you changed your mind just over a month from the actual day.'

'OK! I surrender, Carmichael. I'll come, as promised.'

'And that Dr Dubois's a lovely lady, isn't she, sir?' asked Carmichael, just tossing in the question lightly, not recognising that he'd just lobbed a bomb into Falconer's life.

'Has she been at the station?' the inspector asked, his face not knowing whether to go pale with shock or redden in embarrassment, and ending up rather mottled.

'She came in on Monday and spent most of the day there interviewing Miss Martin and making phone calls. And she was in again on Tuesday and today. She's done a full assessment on Miss Martin, and is arranging for her to go to a secure psychological unit until her trial comes up. She says it would be inhuman just to shove her in a prison on remand, but I told her it was inhuman what she'd done to three people, leaving two of them dead and one of them badly beaten. In the end we agreed to disagree, but she's a cracking looker, isn't she, sir?'

'I suppose she is,' replied Falconer, now mourning, that he had not returned to work after the weekend, but then had a vision of himself acting strangely from the effects of the painkillers, and perhaps making a fool of himself in front of her, and decided that it may have been for the best. He wouldn't have wanted her to see him like that.

'Oh, and she asked me to give you this, sir,' said Carmichael, extracting an envelope from his pocket.

It was a get well card, signed, 'from Honey, affectionately, x'.

Falconer fell into the armchair behind him with a *whump*, and told Carmichael that he'd see him tomorrow. Tomorrow was another day, after all, as Scarlett O'Hara had once said.

Driven To It

A Falconer Files Brief Case: #5

Andrea Frazer

Chapter One

Mrs Abigail Wentworth capped her lipstick, fluffed up her tinted beige curls, and looked at herself in the mirror. Sadly, it was still her mother's face that looked back at her, but as there is no escape from that cruel beast, Anno Domini, she merely picked up her perfume atomiser and sprayed herself generously with a fine flower-scented mist. She was as ready as she could be for lunch with her old schoolfriend, Alison Fairweather, who would be visiting Market Darley that day for their annual luncheon in the town.

Although they didn't live very far apart geographically, their lives were so different that this meeting was one of only two that took place each year, the other being in a hotel or restaurant in the vicinity of Alison's home. Thus they hadn't seen each other for six months, and Abigail wanted to look her absolute best, to show that she wasn't ageing as fast as her friend. It was a matter of pride to her that she appeared just that little bit more youthful than Alison.

Scrutinising herself in the full-length mirror on the wardrobe door, she thought how well she had retained her figure over the years, whereas Alison had allowed her body first to swell, then to sag, as the years took their toll. Well, there was nothing about Abigail's body that a well-made corset couldn't set to rights, and she had one of these on for today's luncheon. Although it wouldn't allow her to eat much, it did ensure that she could get into a dress a size smaller than she wore on a day-to-day basis, and this pleased her enormously.

Having not grown much heavier with the years, it meant she was also still able to walk in relatively high heels, and this, of course, would emphasize the difference in their builds. Alison always wore trainers these days, something that Abigail wouldn't be seen dead in. At least *she* hadn't let herself go over the years and still tried to retain a little grace and elegance, particularly when she was to see her old friend.

She particularly looked forward to these six-monthly lunch meetings with Alison, as it always brought news of other old school chums. They had all started on a level playing field at St Hilda's, but the winds of life had scattered them in completely different directions, and Abigail revelled in the fact that so many of them had failed to reach their true potential.

Sally Carter had screwed up big-time, producing five illegitimate children one after the other, and all with different fathers. At school, she had been the romantic, and fell in love at the drop of a hat. As far as Abigail had been informed, she now lived in some sort of hippie commune, amongst all the other dross of the late sixties that had never adapted to the conventions and responsibilities of adult life. Alison said that, even at her advancing years, she still wore flowing kaftans and numerous strings of beads, and plaited her hair in the hope that what sparse growth there was left would turn into dreadlocks if she waited long enough. Alison reckoned that the whole lot would fall out before that happened.

Suzie Beeton had gone to the other extreme, marrying a man of the cloth, and lived an impoverished life in a house rented from the Church of England, now that her husband had retired, forever waiting for the odd occasion when he was asked to undertake locum work, to bring in a small addition to their meagre income.

Mary Dibley had had ambitions to be a career woman, but without a chance of even sighting the glass ceiling above her. Always a slow, almost bovine, character, she had worked her way to level two in administration at a large company, and there she had stayed, doggedly working away, year after year, always hoping for but not quite achieving promotion.

And finally there was Lesley Lovelace, an impatient girl who had never wanted to wait for anything, and who couldn't stick to one subject for more than twenty minutes before she started to fidget and generally cause havoc in whichever classroom her lesson was taking place.

Over the years Abigail had listened avidly as Alison had told her of Lesley's five marriages and four divorces, and she was eager to hear whether Lesley was still with the last partner she had heard about, or had moved on to number six yet. She had also had, to Abigail's knowledge, two face-lifts, and this was another subject on which she yearned for information. Had number two sagged yet, or had she gone for number three, and ended up looking like some sort of over-stretched monster?

In Abigail's opinion, she herself was the only one of the old crowd who had prospered and lived a respectable life, taking care of her social position, and dealing with the ravages of time with dignity. Who would have thought that it would have been her, Abigail Thorogood, as she was known back then, who would have the delightful detached house, the sleek Mercedes, and the membership of the country club – with a holiday home in Brittany too?

Oh, how she loved these reunion lunches with Alison!

Alison, as usual, was waiting in the bar for her, as parking in Market Darley was getting to be a nightmare these days, and the hotel car park had been full, forcing Abigail to seek on-street parking, making her arrival a little tardy. But nothing could dampen her good mood today, and she made her entrance to the bar, trailing clouds of Chanel 19 in her wake, a smile of welcome on her face, and a great ball of *Schadenfreude* in her heart, waiting to be satisfied.

Lunch was its usual avalanche of news, Alison doing most of the talking, Abigail making suitably smug comments.

'She hasn't! Not a third one! She must look almost oriental with everything stretched so much.' 'Like a wild cat? How appropriate! Lesley always was the catty one at school.'

'Twenty grandchildren? Where on earth does she put them when they visit? It's just as well she lives in a commune, otherwise she'd need a mansion.'

'Oh, they all get slotted in somewhere. They don't think anything of it, being brought up as they were,' explained Alison.

'What a complete whirlwind it must be with their parents visiting a well. Poor old Sally!'

'Suzie, shopping at jumble sales? I thought they'd be better off when her husband retired, but you say the pension is small, and they haven't got any savings? What a shame. She always dressed so fashionably at school. It must be such a disappointment for her to have to acquire her clothes that way.

'Still hoping for promotion? At her age? Mary must live in a different world to everyone else – one filled with false hopes and impossible ambitions. She'll be retiring soon. How can she go on chasing promotion when she's headed for her pension?'

On and on it went, Abigail's self-satisfied comments coming faster and faster. Alison thanked her lucky stars that it had been an all girls' school. Having to provide progress reports on a crowd of boys too, would have been too much. Sometimes she thought that Abigail enjoyed the misfortunes of her old friends just a little too much for comfort, and knew that she thoroughly disapproved of the way she herself dressed.

Being who she was, though, Alison didn't care a fig. She dressed comfortably, and was at peace with her life. If she hadn't been, she would never have continued these lunches for so long, knowing that Abigail merely used them to make herself feel superior.

There was only one interruption to the flow of their conversation, and that was when Abigail stared beady-eyed across the room, over Alison's shoulder, and said, very quietly, 'I'm sure I know that face.'

'Who's that?' asked Alison, who had been interrupted mid-news bulletin.

'Nobody,' replied Abigail. 'I just thought I saw someone I recognised, but it doesn't matter. Carry on with what you were saying. What did she do next?'

At Market Darley Police Station, Detective Inspector Harry Falconer and Detective Sergeant 'Davey' Carmichael were deep in conversation on a very important subject, considering what next month would bring.

'For a start, your height and build would give you away instantly,' Falconer said. 'Who else could you be, but yourself? Neither of them would fall for that one. Just take them into the bedroom, like Kerry's always done before, and hope they don't wake up. If they do, at least you have the excuse that they were left downstairs, and you were just being helpful in bringing them up to their room.'

'But I so want to wear one, and it's the only opportunity I'll get in a whole year. I think I'd look great!' Carmichael almost whined, in his desire to fulfil his dream scenario.

'I think you'd look terrifying. Like the Incredible Hulk does paedophilia.'

'Sir!' The sergeant was most indignant.

'Well, how would you feel if you woke up and found a great red giant in your bedroom? And you're sure to trip over something or knock something over. You're not exactly graceful, you know.' retorted Falconer. 'It would be bad enough to find the Jolly Green Giant, without introducing a scarlet one into the mix. Anyway, do they even make them in your size? You are a bit on the huge side.'

DS Carmichael was nearly six and a half feet tall, and built like a battleship. Considering this last question, he sighed, and admitted that he would probably not be able to buy a Father Christmas outfit to fit him, and that he'd better leave it to his wife Kerry to drop the filled pillowcases into the boys' room on Christmas Eve.

'It's just not fair. Maybe I can get Kerry to run me up one. You know how good she is at making costumes,' he suggested, wistfully.

'Your wife is due to give birth to your first child in less than two months. Not only has she two boys to look after while you're at work, but she's got those two dogs of yours, one of them pregnant, and that stray cat you adopted. Don't you think she has enough to cope with for the moment? And when would she get the time to just "run something up"? The boys would be sure to catch her at it, and ask her what she was making, and then your cover would be blown before you'd even had the chance to try it out.'

'OK, OK! I get the point! But it's still not fair,' replied Carmichael, his face set glumly.

'Whoever said life was fair, Carmichael, was lying. Some things we just have to live with. Anyway, didn't you have enough of dressing-up when you had that pantomime-themed wedding last New Year?'

'That just gave me a taste for it, sir.'

'Well, it looks like it's Tough Shit City for you then, Sergeant. Come on, let's get on, or we'll never finish this paperwork today.'

Chapter Two

Abigail left the hotel with the usual smug smile she wore after what she called one of her 'catch-ups', but the smugness was tempered with a slight feeling of unease, and she decided to take the long way home through the back streets to allow her thoughts to settle. She had a lot to think about.

Pulling out of her parking space, she turned into Abattoir Road, one of the old and narrow streets that comprised the old market heart of the town and suddenly jammed her foot on the accelerator. There was a thud as she hit a pedestrian who had appeared in front of her, and then a sickening thud, as the unfortunate man hit the road surface several feet in front of her vehicle which, as she had been so late to apply the brake, was still in motion. When the car reached the body, it did a double bump, as both front and back wheels rolled over it, and by the time Abigail managed to halt the vehicle, she was several yards in front of where her victim lay, mangled and obviously dead.

She sat for what seemed like for ever, drenched in a cold sweat at what had just happened, her heart pounding, her breath coming in short little gasps. She could hear other pedestrians calling out for an ambulance to be summoned, and for the police to be called, and finally made a shaky exit from the driving seat. What had she done?

It was a quiet time of day, just after lunchtime, and there were only three people present, at the moment, clustered around the body to see if there was any help to be given to the poor victim. 'I can't find a pulse,' said an elderly woman, who had been a first-aider in her working days.

'He's definitely not breathing,' commented a younger woman, who had a pushchair with a child in it, which she had left on the pavement in her haste to come to the victim's aid.

'No chance. He's a goner. Look at his injuries,' added a middle-aged man who had been on his way back to his office, a little late back from lunch today.

Abigail leaned against her car and tried to take deep breaths, hoping that she wasn't going to pass out. What on earth had happened back there? What had really happened? It had been all so quick, though, when she thought about it now, it happened in slow motion in her mind, making it all the more horrific. She'd killed a man. What to do? What to do, now?

Within a couple of minutes a police patrol car drew up and a man and a woman got out of it. PC Merv Green and PC 'Twinkle' Starr had been on patrol in the vicinity, and had answered the call for assistance at an RTA immediately.

They instantly took over the scene, PC Green instructed the middle-aged man to stop traffic at the end of the road – luckily it was a one-way-street, and spoke into his personal radio to ask how long they would have to wait for an ambulance. PC Starr headed straight for Abigail Wentworth, to see if she was in need of any treatment for shock, or would be capable of making a statement in the not too distant future.

The ambulance arrived in less than five minutes, loading into the vehicle what they knew would be categorised as a DOA, the state of extinction of life and the time of death determined by the doctor who received the body at the hospital.

As the ambulance team left with their grizzly cargo, PC Green gathered together the three witnesses and took down their names and addresses, asking them if they could make their way to Market Darley Police Station to make formal statements, and offering a lift to as many as they could get in the patrol car. Only the man who had been stopping traffic entering the road claimed that he really ought to pop into his office first, but promised to present himself for interview within half an hour.

PC Green had transferred his attention to Abigail, whose skin looked grey under her make-up, and every day of its fifty-eight years, immediately after the ambulance had arrived. Within the space of a few seconds, she had gone from a well-preserved, attractive and elegant woman-of-a-certain-age, to a shocked and frightened elderly lady. She was still leaning against her car, and he bent down to speak to her quietly.

'I think I ought to get you back to the station and have a doctor look at you, before we go any further with this matter, but before that, you need a nice cup of hot sweet tea. I can call another car, so that you don't have to travel to the station in the same vehicle as the witnesses to the accident. That'll be the best thing all round, don't you agree?' he asked, a frown of puzzlement making small creases on his brow. Something here didn't add up, but he had no idea what.

At the station, PC Starr had placed her witnesses in separate interview rooms and arranged for tea to be brought to all of them. The elderly woman had given her name as Madge Moth, and an address only a few streets away. The younger woman, pushchair and child still in tow, had said she lived on the other side of town, but had been visiting her mother, and was going to do some shopping before she got the bus home, when the accident had happened. The middle-aged man arrived only a quarter of an hour after the patrol car, and gave his name as Arthur Black, a deputy manager at one of Market Darley's banks.

PC Green would not be back until he had a second car in which to transport Abigail, and had summoned a SOCO team to record any evidence of the accident left on the road surface. Someone would also have to erect a 'road closed' barrier at the end of the road, and arrange to have the vehicle towed away.

PC Starr started with Mrs Moth, who was fairly calm, having seen her fair share of mishaps in her role as first aider over the years, and who had a fairly high tolerance to shocks. She was in good shape, and just wished she had more to tell than she did. She had been the only one headed in the same direction as the car and, therefore, hadn't seen its approach.

The first thing she had been aware of was the thud, as the car hit the pedestrian, then a squeal of brakes, as the car had tried to stop. She had not witnessed the actual accident, merely been present, but was facing in the wrong direction, when it happened.

The policewoman waited patiently as the woman signed her statement, and then asked her if she would like a lift home, to which she received the reply that Mrs Moth was perfectly all right, thank you very much, and knew her way home, without the necessity of suffering a police car depositing her on her own doorstep.

Next, she spoke to Arthur Black, the man who worked at the bank, to find that he had been walking towards the town on his way back to work. He had not particularly noticed the car when it turned in to the street, but had noticed that it had suddenly accelerated after it turned.

He'd thought, at the time, that maybe the driver was late for an appointment, but then the car had immediately hit a pedestrian, and he was aware, at the time, that it seemed to take longer than he thought would have been necessary, for the brakes to be applied. Events had rather overtaken thought at that point, and he had ceased to think again until after the poor man's body had been taken away from the scene of the accident.

He did admit to being rather shaken by the way that the car had not only hit the pedestrian, but had then continued on, running over the body with both sets of wheels, before coming to a halt. 'Women drivers!' he commented, with a sour look. 'And elderly drivers!' he added. 'God preserve me from both of them. They're a positive menace on the roads! It shouldn't be allowed!'

Katy Cribb, the young mother with her child, had professed to have missed the actual accident, because she was picking up a soft toy which her daughter had thrown out of the pushchair, but she had heard the screech of brakes, and had then heard noises that she didn't want to think about, but which she feared would haunt her dreams for a good while to come. Yes, she might have heard the car accelerate, but on the other hand, she might not have. She really couldn't be sure, because everything had happened so fast.

PC Starr sighed, and wondered at the all-enveloping state of motherhood. The young mother seemed more concerned lest her daughter Cassandra had seen what had happened, and whether this would scar her tiny mind for the rest of her life. Starr sighed again, and hoped that when ... if ... she and Merv made a go of things, and eventually had children, she wouldn't descend into this morass of maternal fog that blinkered her to the rest of the world and its doings.

PC Merv Green, meanwhile, had also returned to the station, with Abigail Wentworth in his custody. After the administration of tea and sympathy, he attempted to extract a simple statement from her, but found that she was more concerned with what this tragic accident would do to her social standing, than with the fact that she had killed a man.

'Whatever are people going to think of me? I've always had a spotless reputation, and now they're going to think that I'm a cold-blooded killer,' she moaned. 'I promise you that I can't remember a thing from when I left the hotel, to the moment that my car drew to a halt after ... what happened.

'It's all just a blank, and as for the man, I've never set eyes on him in my life before,' she stated, her voice a little firmer.

'How do you know, if you don't remember anything?' asked Green, logically.

'I must have glimpsed his face, and it was only that that lodged itself in my memory,' she retorted, a little acidity leaking into her voice as she made this statement. 'Who knows the mystery of how the brain works?' she asked, a challenging expression on her face.

Green took down her statement as best he could, considering the number of times she fled off on a tangent about what this would do to her social standing, took the name and address and contact numbers of the friend with whom she'd eaten lunch – 'Just so that I can confirm your mood in the hotel restaurant,' he reassured her – then got a patrol car to take her home. He had something on his mind, and he wouldn't feel at peace until he'd unburdened himself. He just needed a few other bits and pieces of information before he could do so.

Falconer and Carmichael, having not long finished a rather tricky case, were in an unusually informal mood, and Green found them throwing paper balls at each other, both convulsed with laughter. Carmichael had done wonders in relaxing Falconer's previously stern manner in the time they'd spent as partners.

After peeking round the door, Green cautiously closed it again, then knocked and waited to be invited to enter. By the time this happened, all was sober and industrious in the office, and he was glad he'd withdrawn his head before either of them had seen him. It had obviously been a private moment of celebration and triumph that he had almost walked in on a few seconds before.

It had, in fact, been nothing of the sort; merely a silly piece of horseplay when Falconer had thrown a paper ball at Carmichael, who had said something unusually crass, even for him, and Carmichael had responded with a volley of hastily rolled balls of his own making. The sergeant had, for over a year now, been trying to release the inner child in the inspector, whereas Falconer had decided that he didn't have one. In fact, as a child, he was convinced that he had an inner adult, but Carmichael had just proved him wrong.

The only sign of their recent childish behaviour was a slight grin that still hovered around both their mouths, as Falconer asked Green what he could do for him.

'RTA. It's a case of a woman running down a pedestrian earlier today, sir,' he began, not sure exactly how he could express his misgivings.

'Dead?' asked Falconer.

'As a doornail, sir.'

'And have you got the driver?'

'Yes, sir.'

'And she admits guilt?'

'Yes, sir.'

'So what is it that's bugging you?' asked the inspector, in the dark for the moment.

'One of the witnesses – we've got three – says she definitely accelerated just before she hit him, another thinks she might have heard it. The driver not only hit the victim once, but the car carried on down the road and ran both sets of wheels over him before it came to a halt.'

'Nasty! Do you have confirmation from either of the other two witnesses?'

'From all three of them, sir.'

'There must be something else, Green: something you haven't told me yet.'

'There is, sir. The driver denied point-blank that she had ever set eyes on the victim before, but I'm pretty sure she'd never taken a proper look at him. She claims not to remember the accident itself, and she didn't come back down the road to see him lying in the road, but stayed leaning against her car until our patrol car arrived, so how on earth did she know she'd never seen him before?'

'Come on, man. Spit it out. There's more, isn't there?'

'Yes. I stayed with her while the paramedics examined the body, and I could see her face reflected in one of the windows of her car. When one of the ambulance men said, 'He's a goner,' she smiled, sir. She looked as pleased as the cat that's got the cream, and I think we ought to know why that was, if he was a complete stranger.'

'Well spotted, Green. I think we'd better take a look

into this one, Carmichael. There's obviously more to it than meets the eye. Have you got all the relevant information – victim's details, witnesses' contact numbers and anything else we might need to know?'

'Right here, sir. I typed up a report before I came to see you, so that there wouldn't be any delay.'

'Come on, Sergeant. We're on!' called the inspector, grabbing the printed sheet from Green's hand, and heading out of the office. 'You can read that to me *en route*.'

Chapter Three

Green's report identified the victim as a Mr James Carling, and a wage slip had been found in one of his pockets indicating that he worked at the Swan Hotel and Restaurant. That was to become Falconer and Carmichael's first port of call, to see what sort of man James Carling had been, and whether Mrs Wentworth ate there frequently.

The receptionist, a Miss Susan Chester, had worked at the hotel for five years, and knew Abigail by sight, explaining that she ate there quite often with her various groups of women friends, but also had this one particular meal, once a year, that she ate with an old friend from her schooldays, and that she looked forward to this meal avidly.

She also told them that James Carling had only worked there for a matter of weeks, and that she knew little about him, except that he was a harmless old thing who never put a foot wrong, and went out of his way to be polite and helpful. He had seemed to settle in well, and was on good terms with the other members of staff with whom he came into contact, and there had definitely been no complaints about his service.

The manager, Ronald Wild, could not really give them any further information, except for the fact that James Carling, known by everyone as 'Jimmy', had moved up from Brighton about three months ago and had secured his position at the hotel a few weeks after that. Mr Wild knew none of the details of Jimmy's private life, and he didn't think any of the other staff would be able to help with that either.

Jimmy Carling, although always cheerful and happy, had played his cards rather close to his chest regarding his personal life, both current and before he had moved to Market Darley. Wild surmised that there might be an ex-wife or two in the past, as the man was obviously gregarious, despite his age, which was near that of retirement.

After checking the victim's address, Falconer decided that they should go and pay Mrs Abigail Wentworth a call, just to confirm what Green had written in his report, and to, sort of, scout her out on her home turf.

The house they pulled up in front of was large and detached, the garden meticulously cared for, the paintwork in pristine condition. It was an expensive property, and its owner was probably justly proud of it. The garden path too, although created from crazy-paving, sprouted no weeds between its pieces of varied-colour slabs, and the brass door furniture which greeted them in the porch shone like gold.

Abigail answered the door to them wearing a frilly, but suitably modest, housecoat, and apologised about her apparel. She had had a long hot bath when she got back from the police station, to try to soak her tensions and shock away, and had then consumed a large gin and tonic, deciding that she wouldn't be getting dressed again until the next day. She could stay as she was for the rest of today, as she wasn't expecting any visitors.

Falconer apologised, in his turn, for appearing on her doorstep on such a distressing day, but explained to her that the sooner the whole matter was sorted out, the sooner she would be able to put it all behind her and get on with her life.

She accepted this as a perfectly reasonable explanation for their presence, and ushered them into an expensively furnished, but nevertheless welcoming, sitting room, which Falconer was convinced she always referred to as her 'drawing room'. As soon as they were seated, she offered them coffee, and disappeared off to the kitchen to make it, while they sat looking around to see if the room might give them any clues to the lady's personality.

There were silver-framed photographs everywhere. Some must have been of her children and, as she had explained to Green, her late husband, as she was a widow of twenty years' standing. The loss of her husband must have caused her a great jolt, but she must have had great fortitude and courage to have survived this, and carried on to build a busy life of her own.

In solitary state, on a side-table, stood a wedding photograph, in black and white, of the couple on their wedding day, both smiling happily into the camera lens. Falconer always found such photographs sad, when encountered during the course of his investigations. His presence alone indicated that something cataclysmic had happened, either to one of the couple, or someone close to them, and he wondered at the effortless optimism on their faces, when life had as much tragedy to offer as it had joy. There was no sign that one of them would eventually be left to cope on their own, only the ecstasy that they were at last married, and their lives could now be lived together as one.

There were as many photographs of her late husband as there were of her children, and she must have worked hard to keep his memory fresh, as if he were only somewhere else in the house, perhaps in another room. Some people removed all photographs after losing a partner, as they found it too upsetting to be reminded of what had been expunged from their life for ever, but not so Mrs Wentworth.

Carmichael had settled himself down on a chair just out of view of anyone sitting on the sofa, where he had assumed that Mrs Wentworth would sit to hand out the coffee, and just awaited her return, his notebook out and open on one knee.

She re-entered the room just as Falconer had finished his consideration of her family pictures. She put a tray down on the coffee table and poured a stream of steaming liquid into three tiny porcelain coffee cups. 'Milk and sugar?' she asked, looking directly at Falconer.

'Just as it comes, please,' he replied, taking the tiny saucer from her hand, which betrayed only the tiniest indication of a tremble as she handed it to him.

'Milk and sugar?' she enquired again, this time spearing Carmichael with her eye.

'Yes, please,' he replied. 'And, oh, it's quite a small cup, so about four sugars should do it.'

'And how many do you normally take?' she asked, genuinely interested.

'Six,' he informed her, and waited for his thimbleful of coffee to be handed over.

Niceties over with, Falconer began his questioning, but could not shake her from anything she had said to Green when she had made her statement earlier. 'And you're absolutely certain that you didn't know this man before the accident?' he asked, finally.

'I have never laid eyes on that man in my life, before today,' she stated categorically.

They thanked her for the coffee, and allowed her to

show them out. They might not have learned anything new from her, but Falconer felt he had her measure. She was a strong, controlled woman who wouldn't let anything slip, unless she wanted you to know it.

Back at the office, Falconer consulted Green's notes again, and dialled the number of the friend with whom Abigail Wentworth had eaten lunch earlier that day. She should have had enough time to get home by now, and, if not, he had her mobile number too. No doubt Mrs Wentworth had already been on the phone, telling her the tragic events that had occurred in the aftermath of their meal together.

He finally got her on her mobile, as she had gone on from Market Darley to visit one of her children, where she planned to stay overnight. When pressed, she admitted that she hadn't heard from Abigail, as she had only just turned on her phone, but had noticed that there were six messages which had come in during the afternoon. Falconer thanked God that his timing had been so lucky. If this woman did have anything to tell, it might have been suppressed if Abigail could have got to her first.

'I feel I need to ask you if Mrs Wentworth had a happy marriage,' he said, having had a brainwave just before he made the call. What if Jimmy Carling had been an old flame of Abigail's – or, even more damning, an old lover. Maybe all those photographs had just been a smokescreen. The fact that he had turned up in Market Darley would have given her a hell of a jolt, considering how she valued the way her peers perceived her.

'I need you to tell me if there were any affairs, or any point in the marriage where it seemed they might break up,' he said, keeping his fingers crossed under the desk.

'Not that I really know of,' replied Alison Fairweather, then added, 'There was a bit of a kerfuffle round about the same time that they found out Robert – that was her husband's name – had cancer, but I never did get to the bottom of it.

'You have to understand that Abigail and I only met twice a year – our school reunion lunches, we dubbed them – and that a lot went on in her life that I never got to hear about.'

'Was there anything during lunch today that was different about her? Anything she did, anything she said?' he tried, once more crossing his fingers.

'She seemed just as usual. We talked about our old school chums – well, I did. She just listened and passed judgement on them all, which was the way it always is when we get together. I'm a bit like '*The Old School Times*', for her, as I keep in much closer touch with old friends. I'm the one with the 'gen'; she's the one with the black cap, to condemn the guilty.'

'Are you sure there was absolutely nothing. Not even a word, a phrase, or a glance?' he continued, not wanting to give up on this thread of his investigation.

'Well, there was one thing, but I don't see how it can have anything to do with anything.'

'What?' Falconer almost spat into the phone in his eagerness to be in possession of whatever information she was about to give him.

'We were just about to start dessert, when she suddenly looked up, stared across the restaurant and said, 'I'm sure I know that face,' but she never followed it up, and I had no idea who she was looking at, so I didn't pursue it. If I had, she could have had me skewered there for hours, telling me some story in which I had no interest whatsoever.'

'You don't really like Mrs Wentworth, do you?' asked Falconer, chancing his arm just a bit, but he'd got the feeling that there was a certain amount of suppressed impatience in the woman on the other end of the phone, as she talked about someone she had known for most of her life.

'Not really,' admitted Alison Fairweather. 'She does so love to hear the negative things about people, or what she considers to be negative. It makes her feel superior, and I'm afraid she's been like that ever since we were at school. If any of our crowd decided to live a life different from the pattern that Abigail had chosen for hers, she thought it was disgraceful behaviour, and pitied them.

'The people I tell her about are all very happy with the way their lives have turned out, but Abigail can't see that, so she hugs information to herself, and feels sorry for the others. I only keep up the luncheons because I actually feel sorry for *her*.'

'Thank you very much for your time, Mrs Fairweather. You've been very helpful,' he concluded, and ended the call.

'Come on, Carmichael,' he said, 'Time we went home. We've stayed late enough for one day. I want us to set out bright and early tomorrow, though. I've got the keys to Jimmy Carling's flat, and I want to take a little look round there. I've a feeling that our Mrs Wentworth had a bit of a fling with that particular gentleman.

'It would have been just about the time her husband was diagnosed with cancer, and I think, instead of leaving him, she stayed to nurse him through his last illness. I just have a bit of a hunch that our Mr Carling may have been her secret lover about twenty years ago, and she recognised him today, and thought that if he saw her he might tarnish the bright and shiny reputation of which she is so proud.'

'I'm still going to have a look to see if they do one in extra-extra-extra large,' mumbled Carmichael, still continuing a discussion they had had that morning, worrying at it, like a terrier with a bone.

After Carmichael had left, Falconer picked up all the paper balls they left scattered across the office floor after their horse-play earlier, and put them in his briefcase for the amusement of his cats when he got home. They loved nothing better than a plethora of paper balls to stalk and catch and throw in the air, and it did save him having to clear up blood from the carpet in the morning, if he wore them out thusly, and discouraged them from massacring the local wildlife.

Chapter Four

It was only a few minutes past eight-thirty when Falconer turned the key and they entered Jimmy Carling's flat, which was in one of the old houses that had been split into two separate dwellings in Abattoir Road.

'Cor! He'd have been a real bit of rough for Mrs Wentworth, wouldn't he, sir?' exclaimed Carmichael as he looked around the sad little flat. The furniture was a mixture of old and battered, and newer and tawdry. The bed in the bedroom was unmade, and was badly in need of its sheets changing. In the kitchenette area, the sink was stacked with unwashed pots, and the breakfast dishes from the previous day were still on the tiny breakfast bar.

'Not exactly up to Lady Muck's standards, is it, Sergeant?' Falconer replied, swivelling his eyes round to see where they might search for evidence of an old, but not forgotten, relationship. 'I'll go through the bedside cabinet, and you have a look through that old sideboard over there, and we'll see if we strike it lucky.'

Both pieces of furniture seemed to be stuffed with old envelopes and papers, and Falconer could only consider that Jimmy Carling had wasted no time on having a clear-out before he had moved here, but just stuffed everything he could into the furniture to be moved, with probably a pie-crust promise to himself that he'd go through everything when he was settled. And then hadn't!

There were plenty of papers to sort, but most of them were of the junk mail type, virtually nothing being personal. Falconer did think he'd struck gold when he found a couple of small envelopes addressed in an old-fashioned female hand, but these had turned out to be letters from the old man's mother, and he must have kept them in memory of her.

At one point, Carmichael gave a yell but this, too, was a false alarm, and produced only a couple of epistles from the man's sister, keeping him up to date on family news. After an hour they had to call it a day, and left the flat as they had found it, returning to the office glum and defeated.

Back at their desks, Falconer voiced his resolution to have another go at Abigail Wentworth, and face her with the suggestion that she and Carling had been old lovers. After all, they had nothing to lose, and, maybe, everything to gain.

Although still a little pale when they arrived, Abigail was in full make-up, and fashionably dressed, when she opened the door to them, at about ten-thirty. She looked surprised to see them again so soon after their call of the day before, but her manners were set in stone, and she asked them in with no demur, showing them once more into the room with the comfy seats, and retreating again to the kitchen, to make tea this time. Carmichael couldn't face another run-in with such a tiny cup, and had high hopes of a mug this morning, and Falconer couldn't grudge him his attempt to get his hands on a larger drinking vessel.

Sadly, the sergeant had misjudged Abigail's refinement, and the tray she bore in for them today had beautifully painted, but small, teacups on it, however, at least they were bigger than the ones in which she had served coffee yesterday.

Falconer asked for his with just a tiny splash of milk, but she looked hard at Carmichael when she enquired whether he wanted milk and sugar. 'Yes, please,' he gulped, evidently intimidated by this strong woman.

'And how much sugar would you like today, Sergeant?' she asked, her eyes daring him to give her an outrageous answer.

'Six,' replied the sergeant, who had been avoiding eye contact, and had not noticed her steely look, but he wasn't deaf, and he heard her whispered opinion. 'Ridiculous!'

When she was settled, Falconer declared that he was going to ask her a very personal question, and promptly did so. 'Did you, in your youth, or at any time during your marriage, have an affair with a Mr James Carling?'

Abigail was so startled that she sprayed tea down the front of her pretty mint green frock, and sat with her mouth open in apparent amazement. 'If you're referring to that unfortunate man that I ran over yesterday, I have already told you that I had never set eyes on him before yesterday, and I am not one to tell lies. I'd never met him before, and I told you that yesterday. Now, I'd be grateful if you'd finish your tea, then leave my house immediately. I can't think what put that idea into your head, but I am scandalised that you actually asked me that question.'

Back in the car once more, Falconer and Carmichael looked at each other, shrugged simultaneously, then burst out laughing. 'Lord, I put my foot in it that time, didn't I?'

'Big time, sir, and in size twelve uniform boots!' confirmed Carmichael.

They returned to the office, Falconer knowing he was on the right track, but somehow, he had things slightly out of kilter. Somehow, he'd muffed it. 'We'll collect those witness statements and call on the three other people who were actually at the scene of the accident. Maybe they'll have remembered something else,' decided the inspector, determined that Merv Green's hunch, and the reflection he had seen of Abigail's face in the car window, meant something important. That had been no accident, and he knew it.

As Carmichael gathered the necessary paperwork together, a thought struck him and he asked, 'Is that chap still upsetting Kerry – the one in Castle Farthing that you said is getting up everyone's nose?'

Carmichael stopped scrabbling at his desk and slumped down in his chair. 'Technically, no, sir. Kerry's Auntie Marian – you know, Marian Warren-Browne, who used to run the post office? Her godmother. Well, she, apparently 'had a word' with him, about upsetting Kerry in her advanced state of pregnancy, but it only seems to have made things worse.'

'How could it?'

'Well, now, when he sees Kerry, he does a fake start of surprise, puts a finger to his lips, then turns around and tiptoes away in the most hammy manner imaginable, which just upsets her even more.'

'The man obviously has no idea what effect he has on her. Why don't you have a word with him?'

'I thought of that,' said Carmichael, 'but I can't imagine what I'd say. "Stop tiptoeing off when you see my wife?" It sounds so daft. And the most distressing thing is, he seems to think it's all a huge joke. I'll be glad when this baby's born, and Kerry's hormones return to normal. Maybe she won't be quite so sensitive, then. I've had just about enough of him, I can tell you, sir.'

'It won't be long now, Carmichael. Just hang on in there. Maybe he'll get bored.'

'I certainly hope so. I don't want to have to take him round the back of the pub and give him a punch up the bracket.'

'What quaint phraseology you use. But that course of action is not recommended for your career prospects, Sergeant. Now, let's get off and speak to these witnesses.'

Madge Moth lived just around the corner from Jimmy Carling's flat, in a terraced house that was slightly larger than the ones in Abattoir Street, and she lived in the whole building, not just part of it.

She was an elderly woman whose hands were gnarled with arthritis. She had a deceptively sweet, high-pitched voice; but she pulled no punches, and the sweetness of her tone belied her nature.

'You can come in if you like, but I've got nothing else to add to what I said yesterday. I think there's tea in the pot, and I've got a few biscuits left. Go through that door to your right and sit down, and I'll be through in a minute. But don't expect any revelations.'

Through that door to the right was a parlour almost as grim, but not as grubby, as Jimmy Carling's living quarters. The furniture was heavy Victorian, the carpet hectically coloured in dull orange and brown swirls. The curtains were only partly pulled open, and little natural light penetrated through the window, which faced north.

Mrs Moth joined them almost immediately, her grip on the tray unsteady, as she wrestled with her damaged hands, and Falconer got up to take the tray from her. 'I can manage perfectly well, young man,' she trilled at him. 'What do you think I do when you're not in the house to help me?'

Embarrassed, Falconer retook his seat, and accepted a cup of tea and a biscuit. Carmichael, too, was intimidated by this fierce, fragile woman, and even refused sugar in his tea – a first since Falconer had known him. It was probably a good move on his part though, as the tea was only lukewarm, and would never have dissolved the six spoonfuls of sugar that Carmichael regularly enjoyed (how?) in his beverages.

The biscuits proved to be stale, and, after an initial nibble, they both placed the soggy discs in their saucers and decided to get this over with. 'I wonder if you would be so kind as to read through the statement that you made yesterday and tell us, having had time to sleep on it, if you have remembered anything else that may prove relevant, Mrs Moth,' Falconer began.

'I shan't, you know,' she replied with such haste that he only just managed to finish his sentence.

'Nevertheless, I should be grateful if you would humour me. A man is dead, and I want to know why.'

'Because he was run over by a car. Surely that's self-evident. No one would be feeling very chipper after what happened to him.'

'Please,' Falconer almost pleaded, still holding out the statement, waiting for her to take it.

'Oh, all right. If it'll get you two out of my hair and out of my house, give it here.'

She read her statement through thoroughly, then handed it back, commenting, 'Nothing new,' almost with relish.

'Another witness mentioned that she might have heard the car accelerating. Have you any memory of that?' asked the inspector, desperate for any crumb that might come his way.

'My statement stands as it is. I have nothing to add to it,' she declared, and stood, as a signal that they should leave.

222

Katy Cribb's house, on the other side of Market Darley, proved to be on a new development of houses, so recently built that the roads hadn't even been made up. Hers was a smart but small semi-detached house right near the beginning of the estate. She was in, a fact that became obvious as they reached the front door and heard the cries of her child issuing from inside, and she opened the door to them with an armful of squealing baby.

'Sorry about this,' she said, her head inclining towards her daughter. 'She had a bad night, and I'm just going to put her down for a nap. She's worn out, poor little darling. Come on in, and I'll be with you in just a minute. It's about that accident yesterday, isn't it?'

With that, she rushed up the stairs to deposit little Cassandra in her cot, where her wails would not be so intrusive. When she re-joined them, she read through her statement of the day before, and said that she'd been thinking about it and, although she'd been absorbed in retrieving Cassandra's cuddly bunny-wunny, she thought she really had heard the whine of an engine, as in increasing its revs.

Excellent! That was a tiny step closer to proving that Jimmy Carling was not the victim of an accident, but had been targeted on purpose. Of this, Falconer was absolutely convinced, and nothing would sway him from his belief.

They went straight to the bank because, even though it was a Saturday morning, they suspected that they would find Arthur Black in his office, and they were right. Banks had had to expand their hours over the years, and now offered a limited service at the weekend.

Black was absolutely sure that Abigail Wentworth's car had speeded up just before it hit Mr Carling. He had not only seen it increase its speed, but had heard the revving of the engine, and wondered why the driver had done this, and then had been so tardy in applying the brakes.

'Every little helps,' Falconer commented, as he announced that they were going to return to Abattoir road and have a final search of the victim's flat. This time they'd search the other way round. Carmichael could do the bedroom, while Falconer rummaged through the living room. Fresh eyes might see something that hadn't been spotted before, but, before that, he suggested that they take a short break for lunch, as working on an empty stomach with low blood sugar wouldn't see them performing at their best.

Chapter Five

After lunch in the staff canteen – a chicken salad for Falconer and double fish and chips for Carmichael, with six slices of bread and butter and lashings of ketchup – they set off for the sad little flat in a much more up-beat mood. It was amazing what food could do to the way one felt.

Once inside, Carmichael headed for the small squalid bedroom and Falconer started on the sideboard, filled with fresh hope. If there was anything to be found, it would be in this seedy little flat, and, what's more, they were going to find it today. Mrs Wentworth wasn't going to get away with what he was now convinced was cold-blooded murder.

He looked at every scrap of paper he could find, and even came across a few dog-eared black-and-white photos, that he presumed were of Carling and his family, but nothing connected to the case came to light, and he was wondering how Carmichael was getting on in the bedroom, when he heard his voice exclaim, 'Coo! There's an awful lot of colourful clothes in here!'

'What's that?' he called back.

'In this wardrobe,' replied Carmichael, with respect in his voice, for he loved to dress flamboyantly, although he'd never admit it. 'Come and have a look, sir!'

How could he resist such a tempting invitation? The

inspector dropped the handful of papers that he was meticulously sorting through and joined Carmichael in the bedroom. The doors of the old walnut wardrobe, which had been held closed with an old sock the day before, now stood wide open, a positive rainbow of shirts and jumpers glowing from its inside. How had he managed to ignore the wardrobe?

Ignoring Carmichael's fascinated inspection of the clothes within, one word chimed, over and over again, in Falconer's mind: pockets! He had to look in the pockets! Here was a whole new world of possibilities.

Pushing Carmichael aside in his new-found enthusiasm, he started first with the trousers, slipping a hand into each opening, in search of the treasure that would make an arrest for murder a certainty. He didn't believe that there could possibly have been nothing between victim and murderess.

Finally, he was rewarded, and pulled out an old, battered wallet which, on being opened, proved to contain a photograph of Carling, with what looked like a very close friend. He whistled with amazement, and called Carmichael over to see what he had discovered. The sergeant's reaction was equally nonplussed. 'Wow! What a turn-up for the books.'

The jacket pockets yielded nothing more. Falconer stared round the little room, hoping for just one more piece of the jigsaw to fit into the picture. His eyes were drawn to the bedside table which he had searched so diligently the day before. On top of it lay an old book, well-thumbed, and evidently much loved, and his heart rate rose. Maybe, just maybe, the last little piece of damning evidence was within its covers.

Taking it in his hands almost reverentially, he held it by its spine and shook it. A very thin, yellowing piece of paper fluttered to the ground. Slowly, oh so slowly, he bent down to pick it up, and unfolded and held it where both of them could read it. After exclaiming, 'Well, I'll be jiggered!' he placed both items into evidence bags and gave Carmichael a smug smile.

'Got her!' declared Falconer triumphantly. 'Come on! Let's go and arrest her.'

Abigail was flabbergasted when she opened her front door to find the two policemen from the day before on her doorstep yet again. 'What do you want now?' she snapped at them, a look of distaste on her face.

'We need another word with you, Mrs Wentworth,' explained Falconer politely. No need to feed her hostility at this early stage.

'I suppose you'd better come in then, but I've offered you all the refreshments you're going to get from me.'

Back in her expensively furnished sitting room once more, Falconer asked her if she had anything more to add to her statement about the 'incident' that had occurred the day before. He purposely didn't use the word 'accident', because he knew that this was not appropriate now.

'Absolutely nothing. I told you I couldn't remember the actual event, and nothing's come back to me since. Maybe I just shoved my foot down on the wrong pedal.'

In silence, the inspector removed the evidence bag containing the photograph of Jimmy Carling and her husband, arms round each other, and just watched her face as she looked at it. 'That is your husband with the victim, isn't it? I saw several photographs of him on display in this very room just yesterday.'

Abigail's face drained of colour, and a look of horror slowly developed across her features. Improvising as if her very life depended on it, she replied, 'Robert made a good many friends through his work whom I never met. This is obviously one of them.'

'They seem rather intimate to be just friends, don't you think?' he asked, referring to the arms-entwined pose.

'He probably did it for a joke. He did have a sense of humour, you know.' She was on more of an even keel now, her mind working nineteen-to-the-dozen so that she shouldn't be caught out like that again, but she didn't know what else Falconer had found.

Removing another evidence bag from his pocket, he handed the letter across to her, and just waited for her comments. The letter that had been so carefully preserved between the pages of the book for all these years was a 'dear John', ending the affair between Abigail's late husband Robert and James Carling, citing the diagnosis of his cancer, and his very limited time left, as the reason they could not set up home together as they'd planned.

Alison Fairweather, in her phone conversation, had certainly mentioned a bit of a kerfuffle at about the time that Robert's illness had been diagnosed, and it looked like this was what they had inadvertently stumbled upon. It also gave them a twenty-four-carat motive for murder.

Abigail had managed to suppress this scandalous affair all these years, in a bid to preserve her respectability. Now it would become public property when she was prosecuted for the murder of Jimmy Carling.

There was a sudden change of mood in Abigail as her face turned purple with rage, and she leaned forward and began to thump the coffee table with her fists to punctuate what she was saying. 'After' (thump) 'all' (thump) 'these' (thump) 'years' (thump) 'of keeping' (thump) 'this' (thump) 'quiet' (thump) 'and you' (thump) 'have to' (thump) 'come' (thump) 'along' (thump) 'and ruin' (thump) 'everything' (thump).

Falconer felt his sphincter contract with trepidation, and wracked his brains to try to remember whether there was such an offence as 'scaring the pants off a police officer'. Out of the corner of his eye, he noticed that Carmichael was so rattled that he had reverted to sucking his thumb.

'Didn't you know your husband was bisexual?' he asked, knowing that he risked having his face ripped off by this furious, screeching banshee. Carmichael was silent. His mouth was full of thumb, and he'd been brought up never to talk with his mouth full.

'He wasn't bisexual!' she yelled. 'He was homosexual, and he only married me for the sake of respectability. When he told me he was going to leave me I was devastated, but that was nothing to what I felt when he said he was leaving me for another *man*. How could he do that to me and the children?

'Then he was diagnosed, the very same day, with cancer, and I said I'd nurse him at home, if only he wouldn't leave me. He didn't have much time. It was cancer of the liver, and had spread throughout his body. So he stayed, and I've kept it quiet all these years, and then I saw that miserable little queen actually working in Market Darley – I'd found other photographs, when Robert was ill – which I of course destroyed – so I knew what he looked like.

'I had no idea what I was going to do about it, but I wasn't going to have the lid blown off this whole sordid thing, after so much time had gone by. I recognised him in the road, and my temper just snapped. How dare he turn up where I lived and just get on with his life as if nothing had happened? I made a split-second decision to get rid of him once and for all. Why should I have my reputation ruined after all this time?

'I'd already lost my husband twice. Once, when he told

me he was leaving me, and the second time when he died. Why should this predatory old scrote be allowed to live his life as if nothing had ever happened?'

Carmichael winced at her terminology, while Falconer realised that it was time he took charge of the situation, and got the woman cautioned, arrested, and delivered to the station where he could question her at greater length, and on tape. There was no way out of it now. He had incontrovertible proof that she had run down Jimmy Carling with malice aforethought, and she had finally admitted it.

When they had done all that they could for that day, the two detectives returned to the office to collect their coats, for it was bitingly cold out. 'Crikey!' exclaimed Carmichael. 'She was one scary lady. I nearly shat myself at her house, if you'll pardon my French, sir.'

'You're not the only one,' agreed Falconer. 'It's the first time since we started working together that I've been really worried about wearing beige trousers,' he added, diplomatically not mentioning that he had seen Carmichael sucking his thumb. 'You should've got her to have a word with that chap that's always worrying Kerry.'

'You should've suggested that before we locked her up, sir. But what bad luck, Carling turning up like that, after all those years.'

'Fatally bad luck for him, and catastrophic for her, too. I suppose if he had recognised her, it would probably have been all round the hotel like wildfire soon enough, and then done the rounds of the whole town.'

'She must have nearly choked on her pudding when she recognised him in the restaurant. And then the opportunity to get rid of him just presented itself to her when she was on her way home.'

'Yes,' agreed Falconer. 'You could almost say she was *driven to it*,' and he chuckled quietly to himself at his own wit, as Carmichael stared at him in bemusement.

THE END

The Falconer Files

by

Andrea Frazer

For more information about **Andrea Frazer**
and other **Accent Press** titles
please visit

www.accentpress.co.uk